Sage among the Pines

~ A NOVEL ~

Mark R. Anderson

First Edition

Fulton Books
Meadville, PA

Published by Fulton Books 2024

ISBN 979-8-88982-974-4 (paperback)
ISBN 979-8-88982-975-1 (digital)

Printed in the United States of America

Disclaimer

This book is a work of fiction. All dialogues, events, and characters are products of the author's imagination, with the exception of characterizations and locations in the village of Pinehurst, Pinehurst Country Club, Southern Pines, Vass, and Union Pines High School, North Carolina. Any resemblance to real persons, living or dead, events, or activities is coincidental.

*****

This does not constitute an official release of US government information. All statements of fact, opinion, or analysis expressed are those of the author and do not reflect the official positions or views of the US government. Nothing in the contents should be construed as asserting or implying US government authentication of information or endorsement of the author's views.

Advance Praise

Very entertaining and philosophical masterpiece…should be required reading by every teenager and young parent in America.

—Lt. Gen. Marv Covault, retired US Army
Author of *Vision to Execution* and *Fix the Systems, Transform America*

Grieving

Rand was motionless. His stoicism concealed the hollow feeling in the pit of his stomach and the disillusionment in his head. It seemed like things were happening independent of time and space. He was physically present, but his senses were unsynchronized with his surroundings. He was keenly annoyed by the loud ticking of his watch and surprised that nobody else was bothered by it. His depth perception was off, and his hearing was muffled. That is, until he heard the word *death* in the chaplain's eulogy, and then he snapped back into the moment with uncomfortable clarity.

His mind drifted to his daughter. What might she be thinking at this moment? No one could truly know or imagine. Out of kindness or compassion, people would say they knew how you felt, or they understood. But they didn't—they couldn't—until it happened to them. He wondered anyway, but it was only happening to him indirectly, so how could he know? All he could assume was that she needed him.

Rand Templeton thought of himself as the head of the family, the port in a storm, solid as a rock. He wanted to be the one whom his family leaned on for security, leadership, and love. Even if the reality was that his wife, Linda, was the head of the family, like most households, the family still let Rand keep his illusion about being the king of his castle.

Linda glanced at Rand sitting next to her and knew right away that his stoicism was an act, and she knew why. Rand's father raised his sons to believe that men were not supposed to show emotion, because it displayed weakness and instability. His father and his father's father were taught the same thing—boys did not cry. Linda was not stoic; she was visibly emotional. However, unlike Rand, her display of emotion was real and true, and it did not matter to her what anyone else thought. She did not have to appear to be strong; she just was.

Rand figured that the one thing his daughter and granddaughter needed now more than anything was a feeling of safety and stability, not the sight of someone falling apart. Linda was wise enough and strong enough to know that raw emotions at a time like this were completely normal, and whatever her daughter and granddaughter needed would be revealed soon enough. Rand and Linda, each in their own way, wanted to be whatever Cynthia and Lexi needed.

Colonel Randall "Rand" Templeton and his wife, Linda, sat at the graveside service, so close that their bodies were touching. It was a simple thing that instinctively comforted each other at this sad time. On the other side of Linda, their grief-stricken forty-year-old daughter, Cynthia, listened to the Marine Corps major who had knelt down in front of her.

"On behalf of the president of the United States, the commandant of the United States Marine Corps, and a grateful nation, please accept this flag as a symbol of our appreciation of your husband's service to country and corps."

Cynthia's trembling hands reluctantly accepted the neatly trifolded flag that had been draped over her husband's casket only a few moments ago.

Cynthia's only child, fourteen-year-old Lexi, was sitting beside her, staring at the casket. Lexi knew that this was the last time she would ever see her father, and the realization paralyzed her with grief. She did not want to move or so much as take a breath, because doing so would mean that time did not stop. And if time did not stop, they were going to lower him into the ground forever.

The Marine Corps major moved smartly to the head of the casket, where he drew a slow, perfect salute. All military members and veterans came to attention and rendered their final salute to Master Gunnery Sergeant Thomas Forester of the United States Marine Corps. Rand stood and saluted.

The silence of the final salute lasted fifteen seconds until it was broken by the crisp report of seven pristine M1 rifles firing as one, three volleys in perfect unison. The deafening sound of the 21-gun salute amplified the silence after. Then a marine bugler delivered a mournful rendition of "Taps." The slow, sorrowful notes once more summoned the dead in Arlington to come and collect their newest brother-in-arms.

It was these notes that brought Cynthia to her knees. Linda reacted, and with Rand's help, they caught their daughter. They had suspected she might break down during the service. Cynthia Forester could no longer hold herself up as the ceremony gave way to the reality that she would never again feel the safety of her husband's arms or the tenderness of his kisses. She would never again be captivated by the loving gaze of his steel-blue eyes.

Rand had attended more than his share of military funerals in his military career. He understood that as much as the ceremony was a tribute to the fallen, it also was intended to mark the beginning of life for the survivors without the deceased. As impossible as it seemed to them at this moment, Cynthia and Lexi would have to say goodbye to the past and start the long climb out of anguish and despair. Rand and Linda were prepared to adjust their retirement lifestyle in North Carolina to a more hands-on presence in Virginia, if Cynthia and Lexi needed them.

The funeral attendees mingled momentarily when the service ended, offering their final condolences. The Templetons and Foresters got into limousines to go to the Forester home in Occoquan, Virginia, forty minutes south of Arlington National Cemetery and twenty minutes from Quantico Marine Base, Tom's last duty station.

As soon as they arrived home, Linda went into her daughter's kitchen to put on a pot of coffee and lay out the trays of food that neighbors and friends had brought over. Cynthia and Lexi went upstairs to their bedrooms for some alone time before having to face anyone else. Linda suspected that it might take thirty minutes or so before her daughter and granddaughter reemerged. They would need time to get through that invisible threshold that separated the surreal from the real.

Jerry and Leah Forester would be coming over from the hotel after they changed clothes. Rand had discussed with the Marine

Corps Honor Guard about obtaining another trifolded flag for Jerry and Leah in their son's honor. He planned to give it to them when an opportunity presented itself this afternoon.

While Linda was in the kitchen and Cynthia and Lexi were upstairs, Rand found himself idling toward Tom's den in search of a quiet place to wrestle with his feelings. He grieved for the loss of his son-in-law and fellow soldier. Tom was a good man and good provider.

Rand looked at Tom's honor wall, adorned with plaques, medals, and photos. He had seen it at least a dozen times before, but never had it meant so much as today. He was proud of Tom's service as a highly decorated marine, with seven combat deployments to Iraq and Afghanistan. He thought it unjust that Tom had served so bravely in combat, only to die in a training accident at his home base.

The newspaper article about the accident was on the desk. It did not go into specific details about the mechanical malfunction that caused the crash of the CH-53 helicopter, only that it went down, and five brave marines lost their lives that day.

Tom was aboard the helicopter to observe his men from the air, where he could have the best view of the overall training exercise. The helicopter was doing heavy-lift resupply operations as part of the training. The CH-53 was a workhorse known for its power and reliability, but something went wrong, plunging the helicopter to the ground. Whatever the cause, it changed the lives of many people forever.

Rand scanned the newspaper article one more time, shaking his head ruefully.

A Secret Revealed

As proud as Rand was of Tom and as much as he mourned him, Rand wrestled between the love and the disappointment in his heart. It was not long ago that he learned about Tom's infidelity.

Rand mulled it over for a long while before passing judgment. He remembered when he was in army command positions and having to devote too much time counseling his troops about infidelity, especially during overseas deployments. It was well-known that military deployments put added strains on a marriage, especially with male and female soldiers together in combat. Deadly, stressful situations had a way of forging emotional bonds that sometimes morphed into relationships. Despite the military's best efforts, it happened, and Rand had to council his troops about ending it or dealing with the aftermath.

His experience in counseling soldiers about the peaks and valleys of marriage made him less concerned whenever he sensed minor disturbances in his own daughter's marriage. He dismissed it as normal friction in a household with a teenager and a husband that deployed.

One of Rand's philosophies was that even if Cynthia and Tom did have marital problems, he would never have interfered, believing that it was not his place unless one of them asked for advice. He further believed that there were only two people who knew all the little secrets shared between a couple, and each one of them had their own secrets as well. Rand wondered if outside intervention in a couple's affairs would be of any use unless the intervenor knew those secrets.

On the other hand, Linda was not inclined to hold back an opinion when it came to her daughter's well-being. They had the kind of mother-daughter relationship that had them talking on the phone two or three times a week about everything, from the most insignificant to the most personal. One day, Rand heard Linda crying after talking on the phone with Cynthia. He asked her about it, and that was when she told him about Tom's affair.

*****

Cynthia discovered her husband's affair by opening a message on his phone. After Tom came home late from work one night in an unusually surly mood, Cynthia asked what was wrong. As he undressed and threw his clothes, wallet, keys, and phone on the bed, he replied that it was a stressful day at work. He went right into the shower. Moments later, Cynthia heard a message pop up on his phone. Thinking it might be urgent from work, she opened it. It read, "I do not want to end it. Can we talk tomorrow?" It was from Lance Corporal Lutz.

Cynthia felt like she had been struck by lightning. She stared at the message for five minutes and then looked for more. Unable to rationalize it, she threw the cell phone on the bed, went into Lexi's bathroom, and locked the door. Luckily, Lexi was studying at a friend's house. Cynthia sat in front of the mirror, in disbelief, as she tried to wrap her mind around what she had just read. One minute she was concerned about her husband's difficult day, and then the next minute she was hyperventilating, engulfed by a tidal wave of confusion, panic, disbelief, and nausea.

Tom finished showering and walked into the bedroom wrapped in a towel. He saw the open phone on the bed and read the message. Cynthia must have seen it. Panic shot through him. He had to explain. He called out to her without an answer and then went into Lexi's room. He saw light under the closed bathroom door, and he tapped softly.

In a quiet, trembling voice, he pleaded, "Cynthia, honey, please open the door."

He stood patiently waiting for a response.

"Cynthia, please!"

Three minutes later, he heard movement, and then the bathroom door flung open. Cynthia's eyes were bloodshot and puffy from crying.

Tom was too ashamed to look her in the eye, but he uttered, "Honey, I love you with all my heart. You must believe me. Please let me explain."

She wanted to slap his face with all her might but could only stare at him with hurt and hatred in her eyes. She wanted to be mistaken, but he was about to confirm her worst fears. After an awkward silence, she found strength from deep within to confront her husband.

In an ice-cold tone, she asked, "What, Tom? What would you like to explain? Do you want to tell me what you were doing with Lance Corporal Lutz that she does not want to end? Do you want to explain how you were with another woman while I was home, raising your teenage daughter, who worships you? What exactly does the lance corporal not want to end?

"Do you want to use this opportune time to assure me that you were faithful during your deployments too while I was keeping together the house, the finances, the carpool, and our marriage after my eight-hour workday? Do you want to explain how you forgot your marriage vows when you left the house every day to be with the lance corporal? Or do you want to explain how you so easily forgot that I gave you the best years of my life?"

She stared at him with tears in her eyes, waiting for an answer. Tom was stunned and speechless.

She went on.

"I tell you what, I can see that your small man-brain has a lot to process. Why don't you go stay at the barracks on the base and then think about what I just asked you? Leave your key on the table. I'll let you know when I am ready for your answers."

Cynthia stormed past him to her bedroom and slammed the door.

This was it. This was the moment he feared ever since he started walking through the minefield of his own making. Each step he took with Lance Corporal Kelly Lutz could have exploded under him. He knew he was tickling a sleeping dragon's tail. The dragon had to wake up eventually.

Tom was officially at the lowest point in his life, and the dragon was wide awake.

Military Affair

The relationship between Tom and Kelly started not long after she transferred into his battalion as an administrative aide. Master Gunnery Sergeant (MGySgt) Forester and the other noncommissioned officers (NCO) were impressed by Lutz's job ability and work ethic.

During her first week on the job, she predicted some of the battalion's requirements and had files and forms ready even before they were requested. All her assignments were completed flawlessly and on time. Although MGySgt Forester was three levels up in her chain of command, he would see her working late sometimes and compliment her dedication. She liked being noticed and complimented by the top NCO in her organization.

Kelly Lutz enlisted in the US Marine Corps two years after high school with the goal of being one of the few and the proud. She had the personality and drive to succeed, but her money ran out in her second year of community college. She learned that the military would give her training and college tuition, so she enlisted in the corps and became an excellent marine with a strong military bearing. When she transferred to Quantico, her performance ratings were outstanding, her initiative was better than most, and her physical fitness scores were A1.

She was aware that being a healthy, physically fit, attractive single woman could be distracting to the disproportionate number of male marines, but she strived to not let a male-dominated workplace hinder her work performance. So far, Kelly had not had to deal with any harassment problems, but military rules and discipline could not completely corral human nature. She kept her guard up against any unwanted attention, especially during required physical training (PT) in the GI-issued shorts and T-shirts.

MGySgt Forester usually did his PT at the base gym during lunchtime. Lance Corporal Lutz coincidentally did her PT at the same time, because it was the least crowded time at the gym. At first, she felt a little uncomfortable around the MGySgt, because he was at the top of her chain of command, but she figured it would be okay since there was rarely any talk in the weight room. Additionally, she felt safe around him because he was married, he was older, he barely noticed her, and he was a supervisor.

Over time, though, she couldn't help but notice his impressive physical fitness. At least once a week, the two of them would spot each other on the bench press or squat machine. The first time this happened, Tom thought that it had the potential to be misconstrued as inappropriate, but he rationalized it as mandatory Marine Corps PT safety measures.

Although Tom was at the peak of his career, he did not feel like he was on top. Instead, he was troubled. He was feeling past his prime, he was approaching his last reenlistment, his intimacy with Cynthia was infrequent and routine, he had to work twice as hard to keep the same level of physical fitness as five years ago, and his daughter was growing up too fast.

He looked in the mirror and wondered how he got so old. Without knowing it, he was careening into a midlife crisis. It was the reason he liked working out and keeping up with younger, fit marines. The fact that an attractive young woman like Kelly Lutz worked out with him stroked his ego too. Conversely, she thought that doing PT with the top-enlisted marine of the battalion might enhance her performance evaluations.

Eventually, they started running together too. One day, while running, Tom asked her about her life outside of work. It was unprofessional and inappropriate of him, but she took his curiosity as an opportunity to be more casual with him. She answered him with unspecific, routine details about being a single female marine who was more career-oriented at this time in her life.

After the personal information line had been crossed, it became easier for them to talk about other personal topics. Each time they exercised together, when no one was listening, the discussions became more personal. It did not take long before a mutual attraction developed. Kelly denied it to herself at first and was torn about her feelings. However, against her better judgment, one day, she put out a feeler by mentioning to him her preference for more experienced men. The train wreck was put in motion, and no one could stop it.

Their first sexual encounter happened one cold February late afternoon when Tom was leaving work. Kelly was at her desk, on the phone with her mechanic. Tom passed by her office and overheard her arguing about the car not being ready as promised. He waited to ask if she needed a ride. Her car was not ready, so she gladly accepted his offer, especially since it was snowing.

When they arrived at her apartment, she invited him in to warm up. In every relationship, there was a moment, and this was it. Tom knew it was wrong, but the feeling of being desired was too addictive. His primal thoughts and hormones took over, pushing out any consideration of the consequences. They had a drink, and then they had each other. It was mutual and satisfying. Afterward, Tom raced home in the snow, abandoning caution because he was racked with guilt.

The following week, Tom and Kelly avoided each other at work because of guilt, emotional uncertainty, and shame—until Friday. In an accidental, awkward encounter in the hall, they both whispered that it should never happen again. But their encounters at work kept happening and were less awkward each time until suppressed desires finally overcame them, and they went to Kelly's apartment for lunch. Lunch turned into lovemaking.

The rendezvous that should never happen again happened several times over the next month. Their relationship was becoming very physical. Despite his intense sexual pleasure with Kelly, Tom felt ugly and self-loathed afterward. He wanted to stop, but his enjoyment of being desired trumped his reason. Still, in his gut, he knew he had dug a hole he could not escape.

Three months into the affair, Tom's guilt was too much for him. He hated himself and was becoming paranoid, suspecting that people in the office were talking about him and Kelly. One day, Kelly accidentally called him by his first name in the office. The breach of protocol was noticed by her immediate supervisor, and she was given a verbal reprimand later that day in private.

She later told Tom about the reprimand. It sent him into a fear spiral, and he reminded her of the consequences if their affair was discovered. She was too junior to appreciate the gravity of the situation in the same way he did, but she did not think this was a forever thing anyway.

Finally, he texted her on his way home.

"We must end this. I think you should consider a transfer."

After careful thought, she texted him back.

"I do not want to end it. Can we talk tomorrow?"

Tom was well-versed in the military's position on marital infidelity, conduct unbecoming in the chain of command, and fraternization. He could quote Article 134 of the Uniform Code of Military Justice: "Marital infidelity and adultery between military personnel will not be tolerated, and is punishable by fines, jail time, or discharge from the service if proven in a court. The most serious offenses involved chain of command and public disclosures that discredited the military and reflected negatively on the soldier's record."

By the time Tom decided to end the affair, it was too late. Some marines in the battalion had seen signs of a relationship. Those signs evolved into gossip that made its way up the chain of command. After formal discussions among Tom's and Kelly's superiors, an inquiry board decided that the affair was a clear conflict of interest in the chain of command and a fraternization violation. The board concluded that the incident did not warrant a formal complaint or investigation since it was consensual. Also, they wanted to avoid negative attention upon the Marine Corps.

It was ruled that Lance Corporal Lutz, a junior enlisted marine with an excellent rating, was a victim of the influence and patronage of a senior-ranking NCO. She was transferred, without prejudice, to a new assignment at a marine base on the West Coast. Her personnel record did not reflect any wrongdoing, although her performance rating upon transfer was slightly lower than other past ratings. It would not affect her career.

Tom's career, however, because of his seniority, suffered more severe repercussions. The adultery became a report in his personnel folder, and he was indirectly ordered to retire within the year. Tom's poor judgment and lack of control cost him his pride and reputation and his last four years in the corps. He did not yet know the extent of the damage to his marriage.

The Wife

Cynthia Forester was so much more than Tom's wife and Lexi's mother. She was a confident woman with a degree in pharmacology and a career, having worked for three different pharmaceutical companies. When she married Tom, she accepted the reality that a military life could affect her career growth in any one company if she had to relocate every few years.

Tom's career took them to California, Florida, North Carolina, and Virginia. Cynthia accepted the career sacrifices of longevity and promotability because it meant she got to be a stay-at-home mom during her daughter's formative infant and toddler years.

Cynthia did not care how the affair affected Tom's career. It did not matter how the military judged him. The worst thing for her was how his infidelity made an impact on her confidence in herself, in her husband, and in her marriage. Her self-confidence was shaken, because she secretly wondered if she had done or not done something to make her husband seek attention elsewhere. Her confidence in Tom was destroyed because he lied and could no longer be trusted, and her confidence in her marriage was shattered because she mistakenly thought they were happy. She asked herself over and over in her mind, *How could I have been so wrong about so many things?*

When she first discovered the affair, she was consumed by confusion, betrayal, and crippling sorrow. Her first reaction, born of disbelief, was to ask if she was mistaken. Maybe she misunderstood the phone text. When she confronted him and he confirmed the affair, anger gripped her, and she told him to get out of her house. It was no longer his sanctuary. She wanted to hurt him and for him to get out of her sight.

The anger and hurt, however, were juxtaposed to the selfless part of her that loved him in sickness and health, good times and bad, and did not want him to leave. Her feelings were all over the place and irreconcilable. Deep down, she wanted him to reassure her how much he loved her and that he was sorry. She wanted him to convince her that their marriage was safe and timeless. She wanted to not feel uncertainty and insecurity.

Unfortunately, Tom was too proud, too ashamed, and too speechless to own up to all the things she needed to know that night. She needed time alone to think. He was leaving for a little while, and for her, it was better that way.

Tom relived over and over in his head their confrontation outside of Lexi's bathroom. He was stupefied by Cynthia's sharp and precise response in the heat of the moment and under stress. He had never seen her this way before. They both learned something that night; Cynthia was so much stronger than he ever gave her credit for, and she was frighteningly calm under pressure.

When Cynthia's rage finally subsided, she began to consider how this would affect Lexi. True to her selfless nature, she decided not to reveal the affair to Lexi so it would not poison her feelings toward her father. Cynthia wanted to punish Tom, not Lexi.

Since before Lexi could walk, she was a daddy's girl. She often rode on his shoulders as a toddler. She lit up whenever he walked into the room. By her fifth birthday, he coached her T-ball and soccer teams. He attended or assisted every team she ever played on. He made time for his daughter every moment he was home. He taught her how to fish, swim, ride a bicycle, and exercise. If she needed to be picked up at school, Tom was there. Cynthia could have been there any of those times, but she enjoyed seeing the father-daughter relationship develop.

Cynthia and Lexi shared lots of mother-daughter time too when Tom was deployed or the activity played more to Mom's interests and parenting strengths. He rarely attended theater events, and he stayed as far away from the shopping malls as he could. Those were special times between Lexi and her mother. Still, Lexi and her dad had a great relationship, and Cynthia was not going to allow her husband's infidelity to break Lexi's heart.

After Cynthia kicked Tom out of the house, she explained it to Lexi by telling her that he was away on temporary duty (TDY). Going away on TDY was a routine thing in the military, so it would not arouse Lexi's suspicion. Tom understood that it meant he would not be able to see his daughter for a while even though he was only minutes away in a barrack on the base.

Within two weeks, Cynthia sought out a marriage counselor. She talked with Dr. Sylva twice a week about her marriage, the affair, and making Tom leave the house. After four sessions, Dr. Sylva asked if it was time for Cynthia to hear what Tom had to say. Cynthia thought it over and then texted Tom: "There are things I need to know. Come to the house this Friday at 7:30 p.m."

When Friday arrived, Cynthia asked if Lexi wanted to do a sleepover at Jennifer's house. Jennifer was Lexi's best friend up the street, so Lexi agreed without hesitation.

Tom received his wife's text and had time to think about what Cynthia needed to know. He was not sure how would he answer. Tom thought that the thing that held him back from trying to explain was the futility of it. Cynthia had caught him in a lie, so why would she believe anything he had to say? He didn't love Kelly, nor did he want a commitment to her. But Cynthia would not believe that, nor would she understand it.

If he was honest, all he could say was that there was a desire in him, driven by testosterone, which clouded his moral judgment just long enough for him to take sexual pleasure with a willing recipient. It was pure and simple. He took advantage of an opportunity at a time when he was feeling that the best years of his life were over. That was all it was. It was like what a friend had told him years ago: "In a nutshell, men are pigs, just slightly more polished than cavemen."

Cynthia would never understand it or believe it. How could she understand it? Tom believed that the only thing that separated men from animals was a thin veneer of institutionalized monogamy and sometimes wafer-thin morality, and he had abandoned his morality for brief pleasure.

He thought, *If I tried to explain my truth to her or if she could get into my head for one minute, she would be repulsed.*

In the final analysis, he reasoned that he was better off not saying very much.

He arrived at his house precisely at 7:29 p.m. He was anxious and mentally prepared to take a beating, even being nervous about what to wear. The corps did not issue instructions on the proper uniform for a confession and bloodletting. Tom took a deep breath and rang the doorbell. Cynthia let him wait and sweat one minute before she stiffened her back, took a deep breath, and answered the door.

Their eyes met, and Tom offered a smile.

"I figured I should ring the bell."

Cynthia dismissed his annoyingly weak attempt to diffuse the situation with inane humor. She turned away and went straight to the formal dining room. Her choice of location in the home set a formal tone for their discussion. They rarely used this room. It felt sterile and formal. She sat at the head of the table, again sending a message. Tom concealed his annoyance at having to endure her belittling. Still, he remained contrite. She had complete control, and he felt awkwardly vulnerable, fidgeting while waiting for her to speak.

Finally, she said, "I am seeing a marriage counselor. Dr. Sylva suggested that you and I talk so that I can have answers before I make any life-altering decisions."

Tom swallowed hard when she said it. Then he butted in.

"I know, Cyn. You deserve answers—"

She cut him off.

"I am not finished."

He was shocked and unaccustomed to her scolding him.

She continued.

"So I invited you into my house to hear what you have to say for yourself."

Even her word choices were sharp and tactical.

He thought, *Since when did I have to be invited? How is it her house?*

Tom had no legs to stand on, so he kept quiet and nodded, waiting for his turn. He cleared his throat.

"It is not my nature to get on my knees and beg forgiveness for my stupidity, but that is exactly what I am doing. I'm here so you can see my sincerity. Cynthia, I love you with all my heart. I always have. I love you, I love Lexi, and I love the life we have built together. I was stupid, I did a stupid thing, and I will do whatever it takes to fix this. Please tell me how to fix this."

Cynthia said softly and painfully, "Some things can't be fixed, Tom. Once a thing is done, it can never be undone."

He hung his head in his hands, trying to keep it together.

She had known this man half her life and could see he was hurting emotionally. It touched her heart. It was what she had hoped for. His reaction and repentance stirred her compassion. She eased her anger a tiny bit and offered a dash of hope.

"Things can never be undone, but if you work really hard, it might—and I stress *might*—be possible to work through them."

Tom lifted his head. But just as quickly as she offered hope, she resumed her detached demeanor.

"Do you know what you did to me, to our marriage?"

Tom nodded his head apologetically.

"Honey, I was too selfish and blind to think about anything except myself."

She tensed up upon hearing this and then questioned him angrily, "Selfish and blind? That's why you did it? What blinded you? Her body? Her age? Her intellect? The prom?"

Cynthia's sarcasm was like a scalpel. He paused, searching for answers. Hubris and humility were at war in Tom's brain. He was a proud man, a United States marine, a physically fit, trained warrior who was familiar with being in positions of dominance. But he was also a man of loyalty and wisdom who knew he had to take ownership of his mistakes. He was ready to resign and own it—almost.

But despite Tom's absolute remorse, he could not completely abandon his masculine pride. His spine stiffened, and he went on the offensive.

"It wasn't anything like that. You know what it was? It felt really good to be with someone who wanted me with enthusiasm. And you know what else? She was never too tired to show me how much. She never had that look on her face that said, 'Okay, let's get this over with, because my sleep is more important.'"

Cynthia was taken aback by his brutal honesty.

She yelled back, "So you fucked a woman half your age because she made you feel wanted? What about me wanting you every day of our marriage? Why wasn't that enough? Was it because I didn't show I wanted you by wearing lingerie and having stolen moments? Or because some nights I was too tired to feel sexy?

"Tom, you are an idiot. You were too busy or too blind to see that my desire for you was so much deeper. I not only wanted you. I needed you. I built a life with you! The security and trust I felt with you allowed me to rise above lingerie and simple gestures. It allowed me to create a home for us, build a life, and bear a child that we created together.

"Our trust and commitment gave me peace of mind so that I could focus on all the things that life demanded, like cleaning, cooking, errands, raising a child, being a mother and a father while you were out saving the world. The sense of security allowed me to resume a career, which, by the way, I initially put on hold for you.

"And yes, on the rare occasions when I had time to attend to myself, I was intimate with you even though I was dead tired. I just don't understand how you could be so unbelievably selfish and stupid!"

She surprised herself by expressing her thoughts with pinpoint precision. Tom heard every word even if he was struggling with comprehension. He was countering each of her points in his head, but she would move on to the next point until he was overwhelmed.

Before he could respond, she threw out one last question.

"Did you ever think that I wanted to feel desired too or, at the very least, appreciated?"

She covered her face and sobbed. If there was ever a time for Tom to salvage anything, this was it.

He thought for a moment and said, "Cyn, I love our life. You have always been so good to me. I know that! I guess I never told you how much I appreciate all the things that you do. That's on me."

"Tom, I'm not fishing for compliments. I just never ever imagined you would change teams in the middle of the game."

Tom, always the marine, was assessing his tactical situation. Cynthia was explaining things to him, but he had no idea where he stood. He assessed that she might want to salvage their marriage but also that she might toss him to the curb.

"Honey, I have not changed teams! Please believe me. I am here now, and I want to be here tomorrow too. I made a terrible, terrible mistake. It was a horrible error in judgment. Please let me spend the rest of my life making it up to you."

She heard him say the right things, but her heart still had a tourniquet on it to stem the bleeding. She knew his tactics too well, and he wanted to get past this quickly. He was not willing to explain himself in the level of detail that she wanted. She wondered if he even knew how.

She simply did not understand how he could have sex with someone but claim to have no emotional attachment. It had been a long time since she was a young single woman having sex without being in love, but even then, the two things were not very far apart. For her, there was always a hope that sex was leading to a deeper relationship. Tom was talking about sex as if it had no connection to love.

Is that how it is for men? she wondered.

Or was she just learning something new about her husband? Still, Cynthia needed specific answers.

"Is the affair over?"

Tom pleaded, "Yes! It was never really anything, but yes, it is over."

"Well, if it was never really anything, then we would not be having this conversation!" she said sarcastically, then continued her interrogation. "Is it over because I found out about it?"

He protested, "No. You only saw the text message because I ended it. I felt like shit the whole time, so I ended it."

"Tom, you are contradicting yourself. First, you said it felt good to be desired, but now you say it felt like shit?"

Cynthia could not help herself from being surgical in her attack.

"Do you love her?"

Tom burst out, "No!"

"Then why did you do it?" she yelled.

At that moment, the image of Tom making love to another woman came into her mind, and she screamed in disgust.

"Ugh!" She demanded, "How many times?"

"Cyn, let's not do this. It doesn't matter."

"It matters to me! Was she ever in my bed?"

"No! It was only a couple of times, it was never in this house, and it is over! It was never about love, commitment, or a life together. It was me taking advantage of an opportunity for sex. Is that what you need to hear? The details?"

His voice trembled. He did not dare tell her all the things he was thinking. It was an offer from a young woman, like stories he read about in men's magazines. He never imagined himself getting that kind of opportunity, so when it happened, he took it. No, he could never tell that to Cynthia. No wife would ever understand or accept that explanation.

She answered him.

"I don't know what I need to hear. This is all new to me. I've never had my marriage shredded before. I didn't know until now that when we made love, it was just a physical release for you. Everything I believed in was a lie. I never had to figure out if I'll ever be able to trust you again or if I can ever forgive you. I've never had to think about how to tell our teenage daughter that we are not enough for you."

Tom began to tear up.

"Please don't say that! It's not true! You can send me away, but I will always love you and Lexi. Everything we have is the truth. Are you really going to let one mistake cancel out the thousands of other things I have been honest about? You said that once a thing is done it can never be undone. Well, our life and love happened, and it can never be undone. We made a child, and she can never be undone. We have a lifetime of memories, and those can never be undone."

Cynthia interrupted him.

"I wish you had thought about those things months ago. You should go. Either I or my attorney will contact you."

Tom tried to embrace her when they stood up. She turned away. His voice was as emotional as she had ever heard. Her big, strong, cocky marine seemed very small at this moment.

He softly said to her, "Cynthia, I love you so much. Please don't throw away everything we have."

Their eyes locked.

"I didn't throw away anything. You did!" she said, closing the door on him.

Cynthia turned off all the lights and went upstairs. Her emotion-letting was exhausting. She took a shower and got into bed. She flipped through the book on her nightstand, hoping it would take her mind off the pain and anger. The words on the pages might as well have been in a foreign language.

She couldn't concentrate on anything other than her meeting with Tom. It played over and over in her mind. There were things that resonated well with her. It mattered to her that Tom ended the affair before she found out. Maybe he didn't want to destroy his marriage. His regret seemed genuine rather than contrived because he got caught.

Cynthia began to think about how they might make it work. What would their rebuilding relationship look like? The mental debate lulled her into an agitated sleep. She woke up on Saturday morning resolved to discuss it with Dr. Sylva.

Terms of Surrender

After her appointment with Dr. Sylva, Cynthia texted Tom that she was willing to let him come home on a trial basis. They agreed to meet at a local restaurant to discuss her terms.

When the time came, Tom was waiting in a back booth. As soon as she sat down, he told her how much he loved her and thanked her for giving him another chance. She squashed his enthusiasm right away by warning him that she was only following the advice of her marriage counselor rather than her instincts. His joy retreated.

Tom tried again.

"Cynthia, I want to come home. I'll do whatever it takes."

She withheld any sign of optimism, only offering to him, "This is a good first step, but we have a long way to go. Honestly, Tom, I don't know if I'll ever be able to trust you again. If I can't, I don't know if this is going to work, but I am willing to try. If you want this, you must agree to my terms."

He nodded and locked eyes with her, waiting anxiously for her demands.

She started.

"First, you must go with me to marriage counseling. We have so many huge issues to work through."

Tom nodded. She continued.

"Next, I don't know how we will tell Lexi what is going on, but I am not ready to have you back in my bed. Obviously, she will see you using the guest room. We will have to come up with a reason. Thirdly, I already got tested for STDs. If you ever expect to get back into my bed, you will get tested, and I must see the test results."

He recalled in his mind that Kelly always had condoms in her nightstand, but he knew enough to not offer that little nugget. He just nodded to Cynthia in agreement.

"Finally," she said, "I don't know what you need to arrange at work, but I don't want you anywhere near that woman ever again. Understand?"

Tom said, "I agree to everything, 100 percent, if you promise that you will really try to open your heart and let me back in."

He was trying to show sincerity.

She responded, annoyed, "Tom, you are not in any position to make demands or jokes. I told you, I don't know if this is going to work. A part of me wants to salvage what we have, but there is another part that is so hurt. I just hope I can let you in."

A week later, Cynthia let Lexi know that her father was due home from his TDY. When Lexi heard the garage door opening, she ran to the door in the kitchen to greet her dad as he walked through the door. Lexi was five foot six and almost fifteen years old, but he still lifted her off her feet, telling her how much he missed her.

His hug was tighter than usual, which made her wonder if he had been on a dangerous assignment and was thankful to be home. It didn't matter; he was home! She was excited and anxious to tell him about school and softball.

Tom walked around the kitchen counter to greet Cynthia. She offered her cheek as he tried to kiss her. Lexi didn't notice the snub.

Cynthia kept the affair to herself for a month, except for telling Dr. Sylva. Eventually, though, she needed to share with someone else just to validate her emotions. It came out one night while she was on the phone with her mother. She did not want to disparage her husband to her mom, but she was relieved that her mother finally knew.

Cynthia would never say anything to Tom's mother. She was not the kind of woman who would ever believe that her son was imperfect. The Foresters might have already detected that something in their son's marriage was off by Cynthia's apathetic answers to her mother-in-law's questions about Tom. Thankfully, Leah never probed further.

When Cynthia told her mother about the affair, Linda asked if Lexi knew. Cynthia was adamant that she did not want Lexi to know. Unbeknownst to Cynthia, Lexi had sensed a change in the house immediately after her mom discovered the affair. The tension between her parents in the house was so thick, she could have cut it with a knife. Something bad had happened between them. It was the kind of bad that made her mom cling to her anger like Velcro, even after Tom had to go on TDY the next day.

Three weeks later, Lexi discovered that her mom was going to marriage counseling. She saw a message on her mom's iPad from the Marriage Counseling Center of Northern Virginia, which explained her mother's mysterious weekly appointments. After her dad returned, Lexi saw her mother being cold and distant toward him even though he was being especially agreeable and accommodating. He would say things to her, and she would ignore him or not look at him at all.

When she did talk to him, her answers were terse and unengaged. When she looked at him, her eyes were cold and angry. Lexi was surprised too that her dad suddenly developed a snoring problem so bad that he had to sleep in the guest bedroom. She also noticed that every time he wanted to take her mom out to dinner, she was not hungry.

Lexi began worrying over why her mom was going to counseling. She wondered if her dad was going too. After seeing the contrasting way each parent was acting toward each other, she could only conclude that her mom was the root of the problem. Lexi had never paid attention to her parents' relationship before, but she was tuned in now.

Lexi noticed that when the three of them sat down for dinner, the conversation always revolved around her and what she was doing at school or at softball. When Tom asked Cynthia about her day, she would barely acknowledge him. She usually responded without looking up, saying only that her day was like every other.

Strangely, though, in private, Lexi would overhear them saying things like "When you do that, it makes me feel sad and unappreciated" or "That makes me feel like you need too much appreciation." Lexi thought it sounded like they were rehearsing lines in a play.

Over time, it was clear to Lexi that her dad was being much more loving than her mom. She did not know what was going on between them, but her mom's coldheartedness was making her angry.

Lexi could only assume her parents must have had a terrible fight. They gave each other the silent treatment in the past after fights, but this seemed much worse. Lexi hated being in the middle of it, because discussions only revolved around her life, or there was silence. One parent would emphasize a conversation with Lexi only to show that they were not talking to the other parent. Lexi thought it was so childish. They had fought before, but her father had never been exiled to the spare bedroom.

Another thing Lexi noticed was that her mom would peek in on her at bedtime to say good night, but she didn't stop by the spare bedroom to say good night to her dad. Her parents were not even kissing each other. This fight was dragging on too long, and Lexi hated it.

After Tom had been home from TDY for three weeks, Cynthia slowly resumed talking to him. The talking led to going out together and doing activities as a family. They went to a restaurant, a school meeting, grocery shopping once, and softball games. Lexi picked up on how her dad was trying to be more involved in her mother's activities too. He would never go shopping before. She was relieved to see things heading back to normal—most things anyway.

Cynthia was trying to soften her anger by doing things together as a family, but Lexi still sensed her mom's lack of affection toward her dad. His tone was gentle, and his words were loving, but her mom still seemed detached. One night, Lexi overheard her parents arguing about her dad retiring. Was that the cause of her mom's constant irritation? she wondered.

Lexi shared her worry with Jennifer. The two girls shared most things with each other. Jennifer told Lexi that her aunt and uncle split up after he retired. Someone said it was a midlife crisis. Neither girl knew much about midlife crises, so they googled it. They read the definition and explanation, but it made no sense how something as simple as retirement could cause so many changes in two people.

She did not understand how such an easily avoided adult issue could cause so much tension.

Cynthia's fear was coming true. She was struggling to get past Tom's indiscretion. She needed help figuring out why. She appreciated Tom's sincere participation in marriage counseling and how hard he was trying to make amends. He was using the tools and techniques that Dr. Sylva had taught them. They devoted a specific amount of time each day to describe their day to each other and how it made them feel. They had conversations about behaviors and emotional impact. They even scheduled date nights.

However, even though Tom was doing all the right things, Cynthia's trust and affection were not coming back. She confided in Dr. Sylva that her heart might never recover. Dr. Sylva assured her that it was a long process, and she needed to give it time. She had hoped that Cynthia would try harder to let go of her anger, but she knew that every person had different thresholds for dealing with emotional pain.

A big issue was that Cynthia was unable to let herself be physically close with Tom again. Every time she thought about intimacy, she would picture Tom with Kelly, which killed her mood. Tom was becoming impatient, because he wanted to make love to his wife. He wanted to show how much he loved her and wanted her. He accepted his exile in his own house, but his frustration was growing.

Military Exercise

In mid-March, Tom let Cynthia and Lexi know that he might be busy the next few weeks with a Marine Corps exercise at the base. His battalion was taking part, and it would be the last big military event for him before his retirement.

Every day of the first week, the exercise lasted past dinnertime. Tom was coming home after 8:00 p.m., and he missed one of Lexi's softball games. He apologized, assuring her that next week would be better, because he would be watching the exercise from the air, and he would be home by 4:00 p.m. each day. He had to work over the weekend, but he came home early Sunday and played catch with Lexi.

On Tuesday morning, Lexi woke up and found a note on her desk.

> Hey Boo Bear,
>
> After this week, we will have a lifetime to play catch. I'm so proud of you! Today is a helicopter day. Just look up in the sky and I'll be there.
>
> Love you forever,
> Dad!

That afternoon, in the middle of Lexi's softball game, the school principal rushed over to talk to the coach. The coach called Lexi in from the field and told her to go with Jennifer and her mom.

"Why?" she asked in a panic. "What's wrong?"

The only thing Mrs. Johnson said was that Cynthia asked her to pick up the girls right away and bring them home. Lexi knew something was terribly wrong, because this had never happened before, and Mrs. Johnson had been crying.

Lexi's heart was pounding. They arrived at Lexi's house. Two Marine Corps staff cars were parked out front. Lexi ran into the house.

"Mom?" Lexi called out, fearfully running to her mother.

Cynthia pulled Lexi tightly to her chest.

"Where's Dad?" she yelled out.

She saw a Marine Corps chaplain and a colonel sitting in the living room.

She screamed again, "Where's Dad?"

Cynthia burst into tears. Lexi collapsed in her mother's arms, bawling and screaming nearly unintelligibly.

"No, no! Dad is coming home. He is coming ho…"

Her voice gave out, and all she had left was tears.

The rest of the afternoon and evening was a blur. The colonel explained about the helicopter crash and that there were no survivors. News about the disaster spread quickly. Neighbors and close friends began showing up to comfort and support Cynthia and Lexi. Jennifer and her mom stayed with them through the evening. Cynthia heard someone asking her if there were family members she needed to contact. She was still in shock, but the question prompted her to call her mom and then Tom's parents.

After the Funeral

The immediate family members arrived back at the Forester house, and then neighbors came to offer condolences. Jerry and Leah arrived shortly after. They slouched under the weight of their grief and appeared to have aged ten years overnight.

Leah went into the kitchen to help Linda so as not to dwell on the loss of her son. She asked Linda how Cynthia was holding up. Linda did not know how to answer. The question, however, stirred her out of a mindless trance and prompted her to go upstairs to check on them.

Jerry, barely holding it together himself, found Rand in the study and handed him one of the two ice-filled tumblers in his hands. The men helped themselves to Tom's bourbon on the shelf and raised their glasses to the service and devotion Tom gave to his country. Both men were silent, but their faces hung with sadness.

Rand and Jerry had gotten along well with each other since they first met after Tom and Cynthia's engagement. As the two men studied Tom's medals in a frame on the shelf, Rand wondered if Jerry or Leah knew about the affair. They must have been curious about his sudden decision to retire. Normally, Rand was comfortable and casual with Jerry, but he felt like he had to tiptoe around the conversation, careful not to tarnish Jerry's memory of his son.

Upstairs, Linda gently tapped on Cynthia's bedroom door before going in. Cynthia was still in her funeral clothes, lying on the bed, clutching one of Tom's T-shirts to her face. She whispered through tears that she could still smell him. Linda got on the bed and nestled next to her daughter. She told Cynthia that she would stay with her for as long as necessary, but it might be rude to the visitors milling about downstairs.

Cynthia did not acknowledge her mother's words. Linda then whispered that a brokenhearted fourteen-year-old girl, whose world had just been lowered into a grave, was in the next room and needed her mother now more than ever. Still no response. Linda had tried to coax Cynthia, to no avail, so she returned to the kitchen. She understood that grief came in all forms and stayed for as long as it must.

Cynthia lay there, lost in her memories of her husband and her guilt over how she treated him these past few weeks, until her mind returned to the moment, and she processed what her mother had said. She slowly eased off the bed and went into the closet, avoiding the side where her husband's uniforms and clothes hung neatly, as marines were trained to do. She unzipped her funeral dress, let it fall to the floor, and put on a comfortable outfit in which to greet her guests. She went into the bathroom out of habit to see if she looked presentable, but she didn't even look in the mirror. Under the circumstances, her appearance seemed trivial.

Everything seemed like a bad dream. She had to think about each thing she was doing. Her body was in motion, but she didn't know why. Then she thought to check on Lexi. Cynthia went to Lexi's room to comfort her, but Lexi lay on her bed, unresponsive to her mother's voice or touch. Cynthia started to walk out of the room.

As Cynthia was closing the door, Lexi said in a callous tone, "Mom, the last thing I got from Dad was a note. At least when you kissed him goodbye that morning before he left for work, you got the chance to tell him how much you love him."

Lexi's remark plunged into Cynthia's heart like a blunt axe. Cynthia quickly exited the room, remembering that she had not kissed Tom that morning or any morning lately. Did her daughter mean exactly what she said, implying that fate gave Cynthia one final blessing, or did Lexi know she didn't kiss Tom, and it was meant as a toxic, sarcastic dart thrown to cut her? Did Lexi know that Cynthia was not kissing her husband goodbye or good night? She stood motionless in the hallway, trying to recover from Lexi's remark. After a few deep breaths, she forced herself to go downstairs.

Rand and Jerry were quietly talking with guests when they saw Linda coming downstairs. Rand excused himself and asked Linda if everything was all right upstairs. She told him that Cynthia was doing as well as could be expected and that she would be down soon. Rand told her what every parent felt when their child was suffering—that they would do whatever it took to try and ease her pain. In this case, it would take time, patience, and unconditional support to ease Cynthia's and Lexi's emptiness.

Cynthia finally came downstairs to mingle and receive the condolences from friends. Lexi came down shortly after. Cynthia's brothers, Clay, and Randy hugged Cynthia at the bottom of the stairs. They offered to help in any way they could. Clay said that they would stay longer if she needed them. They knew that no words or gestures would lessen their sister's grief. Randy hugged her and whispered that they would always be there for their baby sister. She forced a smile and thanked them and their wives for coming.

What Linda had said upstairs about how Lexi was feeling stuck in Cynthia's mind. Her mother was right. She needed to get over her sadness and be an everything parent to Lexi, who was lost in grief. Lexi needed a mother, a father, a pillar of strength, and a security provider, not a sullen, grieving widow. She had to become a stronger version of herself for her daughter.

Summoning an inner strength, Cynthia pretended not to be lost in grief until she wasn't, which helped her be able to mingle with her guests. She accepted their condolences and fought off the feeling of hopelessness. Lexi, on the other hand, sat in a trance in a corner of the room. She found it impossible to respond to people who tried to console her, instead watching how everyone interacted with one another. She was especially confused and angered by her mother's social interaction as if this was a party. Lexi was finding it difficult to do the most basic things, like breathing, and her mom was checking to see if anyone needed their coffee freshened up.

Lexi thought, *What the hell?*

Lexi was a young woman physically, but at fourteen, her emotional maturity was still developing. Losing her dad was the worst thing that had ever happened to her. In her grief, she was incapable of worrying about anyone else's feelings. Lexi believed she was alone in the world, and no one else could possibly know how she felt. She was void of any spark of life or hope. In contrast, everyone else was just sad. Her life was changed forever; their lives would be normal tomorrow.

Did they know that every breath she took was exhausting? Did they understand that the anchor in her life was gone? Could they possibly understand that everyone around her right now seemed like bad actors in a bad dream? She was completely alone. It would have helped if her mom understood, but how could her mom feel the same way? She had been so cold to Lexi's father these past few months. Lexi did not know why her mother was that way, but her anger toward her mom was soul deep and festering.

She continued watching her mom interact with visitors as if losing her husband was merely sad and inconvenient. Lexi believed that if her mother felt as much loss as her, she could not possibly be so composed and interactive.

What a phony! she thought as hatred hardened in her heart.

Lexi got up and meandered about, listening to strangers offer sympathy. She didn't know what to do with their sympathy; she didn't want it. What she wanted was to not feel so empty. She wanted to know that her dad would come through the door again. Could they offer those things? Could they? Instead, she said nothing and looked through them.

She kept wondering, *What will they be doing tomorrow? How could they possibly help, and how could they even begin to understand?*

After it all became too much and the room started spinning, she returned to her corner seat and closed her eyes.

Starting Over

By midafternoon, the guests had left, and family members cleaned up. It was time to begin the long, painful journey toward their new reality. Few words were spoken during the cleanup; fewer were needed. The emotional exhaustion had taken its toll, and everyone moved at a slow pace.

This family reunion was not a happy one, unlike so many others. Over the years, both Cynthia's and Tom's parents had visited many times. Rand, Linda, Jerry, and Leah were familiar and comfortable in their children's home. So they did not need help finding things. They knew where things were in the house and how to work electronics and appliances.

Rand and Linda stayed at the house in the guest bedroom while Jerry and Leah stayed at a nearby hotel. They all had planned to visit for at least a week after the funeral and then see how Cynthia and Lexi were holding up. Rand and Linda came from North Carolina by car, so they had greater flexibility with their schedule than Jerry and Leah, who flew in from Texas.

For the next week, all conversations were mindfully subdued, except for things like meals, weather, and errands. There was no need for a discussion about moving forward, and they were careful not to say anything to remind Cynthia and Lexi about Tom. They were surrounded by his absence enough without being reminded. It was too soon to discuss the future, and no decisions had been made anyway.

All four grandparents were there to provide emotional support, to help with routines and duties, and to fill the house with the sound of life rather than the silence of death. They were wise enough to know they were there to temporarily fill the void even if Cynthia and

Lexi found it inconvenient or distracting. It was supposed to be distracting, at least for a while, to ease the sting of bereavement.

When the time came, Jerry and Leah decided to keep their original flight arrangements and go home. They had to pay bills, get the dogs out of the kennel, go to medical appointments, and return to their busy lives. Also, they wanted private time to grieve. Everyone at the funeral and in the house was so focused on Cynthia and Lexi that few people considered Jerry and Leah's emotions about losing their son.

When the time came for them to say goodbye and walk away from the house that held their son's life story, they hesitated. It felt like their final moment with him. Rand and Linda saw their reaction and understood what was happening. They said their goodbyes quickly and headed inside to allow Jerry and Leah their privacy.

Tom's parents hugged Cynthia and Lexi tightly, not wanting to let go. Lexi realized then that her grandparents had suffered the same loss. Before this moment, she hadn't given it much thought. They had a tearful goodbye, punctuated by the sound of the car door closing. Cynthia and Lexi walked slowly back to the house, each with their selfishness and guilt.

Out of the Depths

The next day brought clear skies, warm temperatures, and bright sunshine. Rand sat on the overstuffed love seat in Tom's study, reading a book and appreciating how the sunshine radiating through the blinds lifted his spirits. The women were moving about the house—cleaning up after brunch, reading a newspaper, checking social media, and without realizing it, beginning their new life.

Cynthia laid out folders and paperwork on the dining room table so carefully and precisely that one would have thought they would break if handled too roughly. She was beginning the process of sorting through necessary official documents, forms, and legal papers that recorded who the Foresters were, where they were, who they owed, and who owed them.

She tried to jump into this necessity, all the while thinking, *Losing a loved one may be an emotional hurricane, but the paperwork is a tornado spawned from it.*

Her first step was laying the paperwork on the table, and then she took a deep breath. She was not quite ready to do any more right then, and that was okay. The first step was the hardest.

From the love seat in the study, Rand saw movement in his periphery. He peeked over the top of his glasses, spying Lexi in the doorway. He closed his book and set it on the end table.

"What can I do for you this morning, pumpkin?" he asked.

Lexi slowly moved toward him, unsure of herself, like an animal moving cautiously to take food from a stranger's hand. Rand studied her. She plopped down on the love seat and pressed herself tightly next to him. Without warning, she buried her head into his chest. He put his arm around her and felt her tears on his shirt.

Rand figured she was due for a good cry. It had been almost a week since the funeral, and he had not seen her give in to the overwhelming emotions. They all knew that she loved her father, and all she saw now was the empty space in the house where he had stood at one time or another. It was full of those empty spaces. Rand held her tightly.

She was crying because she kept thinking about all the things that were never going to happen again. Her dad was never again going to take her or pick her up from anywhere. He was never again going to be in the stands, cheering for her. He was never again going to show up at school unannounced to pick her up after he had been deployed. He was not going to be there to see her graduate from high school or college. He was not going to walk her down the aisle on her wedding day. He would not be there to meet his new grandbabies. Worst of all, he would never again wrap her up in his big bear arms and let her know that everything was going to be all right.

Rand held her and whispered, "Just let it go, sweetheart. Let it all go."

When she was exhausted and had no more tears, Rand handed her tissues from the end table.

She wiped her face and then asked, "Why did he die, PopPop?"

Rand had to think for a moment about how to answer. Lexi was smarter than her fourteen years. She had always been an excellent student, and she was extremely perceptive too. Her mother and father often said that Lexi studied people's behaviors and communication, both verbal and nonverbal, which usually gave away their truth or betrayed their lies. Rand knew his answer mattered.

He leaned his head on hers and confessed, "Honey, I don't have any answers for you. No one does. But let me say this: sometimes, bad things happen to good people. Your father was the kind of man who not only took care of you, but he looked out for others by serving his country, which meant sometimes doing dangerous things. He did not want to do dangerous things, but he knew he could not avoid them if he wanted you to be safe.

"If we avoided every risk in our lives or didn't fight for the values we believe in, we would not be doing much living at all. It would be like never falling in love because you are afraid of getting hurt. You would never get hurt if you didn't love, but you would never know how wonderful love can be.

"What I can say with certainty is that your father loved you more than anything in this world, and he would never have intentionally left you. Even though he is gone, you will always have him in your heart, and there are people who love you so much and will be here for you."

Without missing a beat, Lexi followed up by asking, "PopPop, why did my mom stop loving my dad?"

She looked straight into his eyes and saw that he was caught off guard by her question. She wondered if he was going to be honest or dance around the truth.

Rand could tell that Lexi was measuring his response. With all the conviction he could muster, he told his granddaughter that her mother never stopped loving her father no matter what Lexi saw or thought. Rand drove home his point by asking Lexi how she felt about her mother. Lexi thought about the question and answered that she hated her mother for the way she treated her father in the past few months. Rand asked Lexi if she truly hated her or if she was just very angry with her. She gazed up to the ceiling for the answer, but it was not there.

Rand told her the point was that even though a person could be very angry at someone, they could still love them. Parents got angry at children all the time, but they always loved them. He explained that even though her mom might have been angry and argumentative with her dad, she still loved him with all her heart, just like she still loved her mom.

Lexi studied him intently and got up and walked out of the study. Rand figured that when his granddaughter did not have any more questions, it usually meant she agreed with his answer or at least understood it. He picked up his book and opened it to where he left off. He read some more until the sun's warmth lulled him into a nice nap.

As much as Lexi was a daddy's girl, Cynthia was a mama's girl. She had a good and loving relationship with her father, but it was much more personal with her mother. As an adult, she talked with her mother at least two times a week; and when her parents visited, Cynthia and Linda did everything together.

Linda was there with Cynthia during the last trimester of her problematic pregnancy and delivery. Linda stayed on during Cynthia's debilitating bouts with depression after learning she would never be able to conceive again. Linda would often visit for extended periods when Tom was deployed. After Linda and Rand moved to North Carolina, she made at least one trip a month to visit her daughter, even when Rand could not go. Cynthia and Linda were as thick as thieves.

Rand did not mind that Cynthia was close with her mother. He was highly educated, but he knew his limitations when it came to understanding women and what they talked about. His hope and expectation now were that Linda's presence was helping Cynthia carry the weight of her sadness or was at least lending an ear. Rand watched his wife and daughter sequester away in corners of the house to talk. Rand had not seen Cynthia have a good cry over Tom's death, and he was thinking it was emotionally unhealthy. He found out later that Cynthia did have good cries with Linda, just like Lexi did in the study with him.

Three weeks after the funeral, Rand and Linda agreed that it was time to go home. Linda figured that her daughter and granddaughter would welcome the time alone, but she also worried that it might be a lonely, harsh reality check. Rand didn't overthink it since Cynthia and Lexi had no choice but to face a new reality. His own reality was that they had been away from the horses in North Carolina for too long, and they had their own life to resume.

Rand and Linda Templeton

Randall "Rand" Templeton was one of three boys raised on the outskirts of Harrisburg, Pennsylvania. His father, Claymont "Clay" Templeton, was an engineer in a Kennecott plant that machine-milled equipment for steel manufacturing and farming. The mill's products were in high demand worldwide. Clay had at least a dozen patents to his name for his ingenuity. His income afforded his family a fine house, a new car every few years, and the best private schools in eastern Pennsylvania.

Rand's mother, Lydia, was a churchgoing, college-educated, stay-at-home mom, who devoted her life to her family. Her parents were German immigrants who settled in Erie. She met Clay in her senior year of high school at the State Science Fair. She and Clay had engineering projects displayed next to each other, and they both won scholarship money. Coincidentally, they both attended Lehigh University in Bethlehem, Pennsylvania, where they became reacquainted, fell in love, and married after graduation.

Clay and Lydia had three boys—Roger, Randall, and Clay Jr. They were each two years apart. All three boys played sports, fished in the Susquehanna River, hunted on eastern Pennsylvania farmland, fought with one another, and defended one another with fierce loyalty. They grew up as rough-and-tumble boys, but rarely did they get into trouble or disobey their parents. One of the worst things the brothers ever did was when they tried cigarettes for the first time and accidentally burned an entire cornfield right before harvest. They were never caught, but the boys felt extremely guilt-ridden about how that farmer was going to feed his livestock that winter. Out of the goodness of their hearts, they volunteered to help that farmer with chores all winter.

Private school provided each boy with a deep and broad education, but it was the nuns' rulers across their knuckles that taught them discipline. They usually earned sore knuckles from playing practical jokes on classmates. Randall was the most mischievous of the three boys. He was also the most adventurous. He graduated from high school in 1968, during the height of the Vietnam War. Like his brothers, Rand's grades were good enough to get him into many colleges, but his interest in math and chemistry led him to Penn State University.

Scott Leland was Randall's roommate during his freshman and sophomore years at Penn. The two men became friends, and Scott started calling him Rand. The nickname stuck. Scott talked about the things he was doing in ROTC. Rand was developing informed opinions about politics and social issues, and he wanted to make a difference for the good of the nation. After hearing Scott talk so much about the ROTC program, Rand decided that it might be a place where he could be effective, so he joined. As it turned out, he excelled in his military training, military courses, and leadership. By his senior year, Rand had been promoted to cadet lieutenant colonel of the Penn State ROTC.

He graduated in 1972 and accepted a commission in the army as a second lieutenant. The US was still involved in Vietnam, but all the combat troops had been pulled out. The 90,000 US soldiers staying in-country were supporting the Army of the Republic of Vietnam's fight against the North Vietnamese communist regime. Rand's first assignments were at army bases in the US, where he underwent officer training and served in first-level leadership positions. After his officer and military occupational specialty training, he was assigned to first-line supervisory positions at Fort Benning, Georgia.

*****

Not long after pinning on his first lieutenant bar, Rand was transferred to the Advanced Weapons Research and Development Department at Fort Bliss, El Paso, Texas. It was there he met Linda

Sager, a young chemist who worked for a civilian contractor in one of the propellant research labs on Fort Bliss.

Rand was smitten by Linda the first time he saw her in her white lab coat, plastic hair cover, and goggles. He was hesitant about asking her out, but he found reasons to go to her lab several times a week even though he could have sent any one of his enlisted subordinates. He struck up conversations with her about her work, even when they had little to do with his area of expertise. Linda's older coworkers saw right through his ruse, but they thought his perseverance was admirable. Linda, however, was too absorbed in her work to notice.

When Rand finally asked Linda out on a date, she told him she would think about it. The next time he asked, she agreed. Rand smiled from ear to ear and asked what time she ate lunch. When he said lunch, she at once regretted her decision, thinking that they had different ideas about what constituted a date. With a confused look, she told him she usually ate lunch around twelve. He said that he would take her to lunch tomorrow. The next day, he arrived promptly at noon, and they walked out together.

Rand was strutting like a peacock. Linda was apprehensive but cared enough to hide it. They got into his pickup truck—or Texas limousine, as she called it—and drove to a small cantina within sight of the border crossing into Juárez, Mexico. Her first impression of the ramshackle front of the cantina was, "This is not someplace I would ever go, and definitely not on a date."

Once inside, they made their way to the only table available. Linda was surprised at how many soldiers and civilians were there. Rand assured her that it looked like a dive, but it had the best tacos in town. They ordered tacos and soft drinks. Linda was surprisingly impressed with the tacos, the service, and the cleanliness. She enjoyed the ease of their conversation. Rand made eye contact with her the whole time and asked questions like he was paying attention. She glanced at her watch, disappointed that her lunch hour was over. It was a very good date, she thought.

They drove back to work, and he asked if he could take her out again for dinner sometime.

She answered, "I would like that very much."

The following week, he arranged the date and recommended that she dress casually and be prepared to be in the night air. Her expression was one of bewilderment. He picked her up on their date night, and they drove for thirty minutes on an unlit road into the desert night. He stopped the truck in the middle of nowhere. The only thing she could see was the moon and stars. Linda half-jokingly, half-nervously told him that her coworkers knew she was on a date with him, and she was expected to be at work tomorrow.

Rand chuckled.

"First off, tomorrow is Saturday, so they aren't expecting you. Second, I'm not abducting you. And thirdly, I'm not a serial killer."

She asked, "Okay, but how many serial killers tell their victims that they are serial killers?"

He chuckled again, got out of the truck, and dropped the tailgate. Linda looked back there to see what he was doing, but the moonlight was not bright enough. Being more curious than afraid, she got out to investigate. Just then, a lantern cut through the darkness to reveal that Rand had set out two lawn chairs and a small table with a bucket of fried chicken, two veggie sides, two glasses, and a bottle of wine. Rand started to focus a small tripod telescope pointed at the stars.

Linda was pleasantly surprised and impressed, watching him set up the telescope. He said that the desert was the best place for stargazing. All she could do was smile. They spent the evening picnicking, talking, listening to coyotes, and finding stars. They exchanged stories about family, horses, camping, vacations, and dreams for the future. Around midnight, they packed up and drove to Linda's apartment. Rand walked her to the door, and they kissed good night. The next day, she kept thinking about how this Pennsylvania army guy had hit a homerun on their perfect date.

It did not take long for Linda to start thinking about Rand in a different way. She saw that there was more to him than those frat boys at Rice University, who found her to be too serious, too studious, and unwilling to let go. She rarely went on dates at school and was not used to being wooed. However, Rand was likable, charming, and had three other things going for him. He was a gentleman and a chemist, and he liked her the way she was.

Linda never had a problem with having a good time, but her idea of letting go was very different from the boys at school. She was a confident woman who knew herself and could make her own decisions. She was not the type of woman who let a man make decisions for her. But her appearance was somewhat of a disadvantage when she wanted to be taken seriously.

Linda had shoulder-length, silky blonde hair, a healthy complexion, ocean-blue eyes that appeared to sparkle behind her turtle shell frames, and a nice smile. When she walked around campus, people noticed her. However, unlike other girls on campus, Linda was not a slave to fashion, hair, and makeup. She preferred comfort. The subtle message from her appearance and body language was that she was here to get an education, not to find a husband. The resulting infrequent dating suited her just fine.

As a career chemist, Linda was focused on her work, but she started to think about the next phase of her life, like romance and family. Four of her friends were in serious relationships or married. She started to wonder if she had been too specific about the qualifications she liked in a man. Her analytical mind reasoned out that the likelihood of finding her soulmate was about one in one billion since half of the seven billion people on the planet were male, and more than half of those males were children. In other words, she was a pragmatist rather than a poet. However, societal expectations were bombarding her psyche, and the idea of finding that special someone with common interests was growing on her.

After two or three dates with Rand, Linda began to see that they had a lot in common. They excelled in chemistry and math, they liked research, and they enjoyed reading, exercising, and hiking. He liked that she could disagree with him but not treat him disagreeably. She liked that he was a serious thinker with a great sense of humor. She also did not mind his rugged good looks and athletic physique. He liked that she was attractive and healthy, almost as much as the fact that she didn't fuss about it. Neither one was a romantic dreamer, but it did not take long for Linda Sager to recognize Rand's desirability and charm. She allowed love to find its way into her heart. Two years later, in 1976, they were married in Linda's hometown of Austin, Texas.

During their engagement, Rand and Linda discussed the likelihood of having to move every few years because of his military career. She understood the demands on a military spouse from working with so many military men and women on Fort Bliss and the consequences it would have on her career. She also accepted the biological fact that she was the one in the marriage blessed with the privilege of giving birth to their children, which would take her out of the workplace for at least a few times in her life. For that reason alone, they decided that his career would be the primary one. She could find employment in her field of expertise wherever they went. Rand was likely to be assigned to army posts with military chemical research, and the likelihood of a Department of Defense contractor nearby was almost guaranteed. She also figured it would be the right time in their lives to start a family.

The military did not disappoint them, and in their first year of marriage, Rand got transfer orders to Büchel Air Base in Germany for a three-year assignment. Büchel was one of the largest weapons storage bases in Europe and a place where the newly promoted Captain Templeton could put his ability to use.

Rand and Linda loved living in Germany. Rand excelled at his job, and Linda enjoyed staying at home. The food, the beer, and the wines were excellent; and the sightseeing was amazing. In their first year, they boarded a train every month to a new destination in Germany. After seeing sites and towns in Germany, they visited other European countries west of the Iron Curtain. Rand and Linda were very happy during their three years in Europe, as evidenced by the birth of their first son, Clay, in late 1977 and then Randall in 1979.

The Cold War between east and west was at its peak during Rand's tour, causing occasional flare-ups from accidental plane border crossings and sentry post gunfire exchanges. Security of the weapons storage and handling areas was always extremely strict. Rand was exceptional and fulfilled in his work despite the high stress. He was the executive officer, responsible for daily inspections and maintenance of the stored nuclear weapons. The Air Force and the Army each had responsibility over their own weapons. The two services worked together on supporting the storage area.

In late 1979, Rand's three-year assignment in Germany was ending, and he was reassigned to Fort Belvoir, Virginia, in the Army's materials acquisitions command. The Templetons came back to the states in early 1980. Linda was six months pregnant. In April 1980, she gave birth to their third and last child, Cynthia. Rand was promoted to major and given the opportunity to attend the National War College at Fort McNair in Washington, DC.

They settled in Mount Vernon, a neighborhood near Fort Belvoir, within walking distance of George Washington's home estate. Rand was able to stay in the DC area for the rest of his career, which included two positions at the Pentagon, one year studying at the Army's War College in Carlisle, Pennsylvania, as a lieutenant colonel, and finally at the Defense Threat Reduction Agency at Fort Belvoir, from where he retired as a colonel in 2002.

Cynthia, Not Cindy

By 1986, the Templetons' youngest child, Cynthia, started grade school. Linda decided to return to work as a defense contractor for CACI International in Arlington. Over the next three years, she went to night school and earned her PhD in chemistry. She rose to an executive position in her company. Throughout the 1980s and '90s, Clay, Randy, and Cynthia grew up in the house in Mount Vernon. They attended public schools, played sports, took part in science fairs, went on exciting vacations, avoided devastating childhood illnesses, and lived privileged lives.

Of the three children, Cynthia was the most precocious. When she was in first grade, she came home angry one day because a classmate had called her Cindy. Linda hugged her and brushed her long blonde hair. She told her daughter that Cindy was a short version of Cynthia, and it was okay for people to call her that.

She turned to her mom and with a stern face said, "My name is Cynthia, not Cindy, and no one will ever call me Cindy ever again, okay, Mommy?"

Linda looked at her daughter with a small measure of pride and realized her little baby might be tougher than she thought. Perhaps her two brothers' feistiness had rubbed off on her. From that day forward, Linda fretted a little less about her daughter's fragility.

In the Washington, DC, area, a retired, well-decorated army colonel with two master's degrees in leadership and military sciences was too enticing for defense contractors to ignore. Rand had a reputation as an excellent officer—well-liked and admired by his personnel and praised by his superiors. He also had an uncanny perceptiveness and awareness of his surroundings, which usually allowed him to be one or two steps ahead of everyone else. His confidence allowed him to be as comfortable and liked in a flannel shirt, sitting around a campfire, as he was in his dress uniform at a cocktail party on Capitol Hill. Eventually, Booz Allen Hamilton offered him an executive position leading a project that interested him at a salary he could not refuse.

The American Dream

Living in a fast-paced suburban existence could make it seem like the years fly by. Rand and Linda woke up one day realizing that they were suddenly approaching the autumn of their lives. It was not one event that brought them to this realization but rather the culmination of so many rites of passage. They had watched each one of their children go off to college, start careers, get married, and start families of their own.

Additionally, Rand had retired from one career and moved into another, Linda was at the top of her career field but thinking about retirement, and they lived the best life they could. They had achieved the American dream of a comfortable life, good jobs, a house with a picket fence, financial security, and healthy children with good values, who made good choices. They raised their children on those beliefs and values. They taught them with strict rules, a firm hand, and love and patience. They raised their family believing that if you worked hard, studied hard in school, made the right choices, and were compassionate to others, then good things would come to you.

The Templetons' next phase of life was very good. When the children had left the nest, Rand and Linda began traveling again, eventually taking grandchildren with them on vacations. At home in Mount Vernon, they socialized with past associates from the military and current associates in the contractor world, they played golf together, and they stayed healthy—until 2014.

One day, while showering, Linda felt a small lump in her right breast. She was alarmed, so she scheduled a doctor's appointment. A mammogram confirmed that it was a mass, and a biopsy was scheduled. Linda and Rand were together in the doctor's office when they learned that the biopsy result was malignant for cancer. They were devastated even though the doctor assured them that they had caught it early and that the prognosis was good.

They learned this terrifying news in mid-December, but Linda insisted that they keep their Christmas tradition of having their children and grandchildren spend Christmas at Mount Vernon. The Templeton house was large enough to accommodate everyone. Every year, Rand decorated the front of the house with festive lights while Linda dressed the inside to look like Christmas town.

They put up a twelve-foot Christmas tree in the great room and decorated it with hundreds of colored lights and ornaments from past Christmases. Real pine boughs and holly were draped on the staircases and columns. The house smelled of cookies, fresh pine, and oak logs in the fireplaces. They enjoyed being surrounded by children running through the house, unable to hold their excitement and holiday cheer brought on by the season.

Linda and Rand were resolved that they should tell their children about her diagnosis and that dampening the holiday cheer was unavoidable, but they would do it after Christmas Day. On December 26, the night before Clay and his family had to return home, they asked their children to come together in the formal dining room for a family meeting. In a calm and positive voice, Linda shared her diagnosis.

Clay and Randy were not as alarmed as their wives. They did not understand what could be so terrible about a small mass in a breast. They were more interested in the treatment and next steps. Cynthia and her two sisters-in-law, on the other hand, were panic-stricken. They were more aware of the impact of that diagnosis for a woman and how devastating it could be.

Linda had hoped to not upset her children too much, but she wanted them to hear it from her sooner than later. After the announcement, the adults threw a dozen questions at her all at once. She did not have all the answers, but she assured them that they had found the mass early, and her prognosis was good. After the mood around the room improved, she explained the treatment protocol. She would have surgery at Fairfax hospital to remove the tumor followed up with chemotherapy for three to six months and then have semiannual checkups.

She took a deep breath and said, "And then when all goes well, we will retire for good, sell the house, and move someplace where we can live our lives in relaxation and no traffic."

The Templetons loved most things about the Washington, DC, area. It was the center of world politics, and it had the best museums and monuments, excellent universities, excellent public schools, a variety of cultural activity, professional sport teams, four seasons, mountains sixty miles to the west, and an ocean one hundred miles to the east. It had everything, including insufferable traffic.

Rand was typically a glass half-full kind of guy, except when he was sitting in traffic. He would arrive home most afternoons tense from the commute. He said that there were two types of drivers in DC—those who waited in line and those who cut in line. DC was full of the latter kind of people. For him, it negated all the benefits of living there. They were not leaving solely because of the traffic, but it was huge consideration.

When the holidays were over and the decorations were neatly packed away and stored in the attic until next year, Rand and Linda started to organize the small, daily details of their lives before her surgery and a new unknown. They talked about work schedules, upcoming commitments, meetings, and other arrangements. Their daily routines were about to change.

Two weeks later, with Rand at her side, Linda underwent a lumpectomy. In post-op consultations, the doctors assured her that they were happy with the procedure, but later tests would tell if they had removed all the cancerous cells. She and Rand remained positive. A week later, follow-up labs showed that the cancer had not metastasized and that her prognosis was excellent. Everything in her post-op tests looked good, allowing Linda to start chemotherapy. She shared the positive news with the children.

Linda and Rand considered themselves extremely blessed with the outcome of her surgery. They agreed that when her chemotherapy was completed, they would press ahead with their plans. Six months later, the doctors gave her a thumbs-up. They were incredibly relieved to be able to move forward. They researched areas in the south for retirement, finally narrowing the search to North Carolina.

After two road trips south, they decided they would put their house on the market and retire to an area seventy miles south of Raleigh, North Carolina. They loved the prospects of a milder climate, cleaner air, thirty-seven golf courses within twenty miles, and horse farms in the Sandhills. Their goal was to buy property and raise horses. Linda raised horses when she was growing up.

During her recovery and downtime, Linda searched the Internet to narrow down the scope of home locations and prices. Another two months later, she contacted a real estate agent and discussed their requirements. They also set up a date to tour Pinehurst and the surrounding areas. For one week, they stayed at the Carolina Hotel and enjoyed two rounds of golf, relaxation, and dining in between touring properties with their real estate agent. The house search turned into a wonderful couple's retreat and recuperation time for Linda, who spent luxurious time being pampered at the spa.

After returning to Virginia, they hired a real estate agent to sell their Mount Vernon home. Six months later, Linda was still cancer-free. She and Rand packed up their household goods and moved to a ten-acre horse farm in Vass, North Carolina. The property came with a 3,500-square-foot, single-level house and a two-story, four-stall horse stable with fenced-in property. It was exactly what they were looking for at a price they could afford. They could live debt-free in retirement and continue to do the things they loved.

Tragedy Strikes

Not long after settling in at the horse farm, they bought two horses. When Linda was completely healthy and strong, she returned to playing golf on a regular basis. They vacationed across the US and still spent time with their grandchildren when their schedules would allow. Life in North Carolina was perfect for Rand and Linda—until a phone call in 2019.

Linda answered her phone, expecting to have a chat with her daughter about her marital problems. They had been talking lately, and Linda knew about the emotional pain her daughter was experiencing in her marriage. Cynthia's words stunned Linda. She listened carefully to her daughter without interruption, and her face went pale. When Linda hung up the phone, Rand looked at his wife and knew something was terribly wrong.

She clutched Rand's arm and let out a tearful cry. Tom had been killed in an accident. Rand held her tightly, as both were in shock. Within an hour and in a panic, they packed their clothes, including funeral attire, arranged for the neighbor to care for the horses, and then drove to Virginia to be with Cynthia and Lexi.

They attended the funeral at Arlington National Cemetery and then stayed at their daughter's house. It was a family reunion under the worst circumstances. The family remembered that Cynthia had experienced a mental breakdown after Lexi's problematic birth and afterward, when she was told she could not have any more children. She underwent psychological counseling for a year, finally recovering after the benefit of time and by focusing on her daughter. Now they wondered how this traumatic loss might affect her.

Her family members subconsciously kept a watchful eye on Cynthia's behavior, knowing it would be hard to separate normal grief from a more severe fall from reality.

Lexi

Cynthia, only being able to have one child, doted over her more than other parents did with their children. She made sure Lexi had the best birthday parties, the best clothes, the best stroller, the best crib, and everything else while growing up. She also made sure that Lexi had opportunities to take part in ballet, piano, children's theater, and sports.

The unapologetic spoiling eased up when Lexi reached school-age and Cynthia went back to work. She found a position as an analyst for the US Patent and Trademark Office in Alexandria. The position suited her skill set and allowed her to have a flexible schedule to care for her grade school child. She was able to devote and balance sufficient time between her job and her family.

Tom and Cynthia realized quickly that their baby was growing so fast that if they blinked, they would miss something. This exaggeration seemed especially true around DC, where the pace of life was at whirlwind speed. The daily routine for Cynthia and Tom was 8:00 a.m. to 5:00 p.m. at the office, an hour in traffic, an hour for Lexi's activities, dinnertime, and then trying to steal a few minutes of downtime at the end of the day before getting an inadequate amount of sleep to start it all over again.

Cynthia and Tom, having lived near marine bases in the US, admitted to each other that the pace of life in the DC area was unsustainable, and they often questioned whether it was worth it. And yet the Foresters and all their friends and neighbors lived their lives the same way.

However, time marched on; and before the Foresters knew it, Lexi was a typical teenager with an increasing number of disagreements happening between mother and daughter. Lexi appreciated and usually obeyed her mother, but she began exploring her boundaries and demanding the same freedoms as her friends. She wanted to do sleepovers, dress how she liked, and date boys. Cynthia and Tom were more strict than other girls' parents. Lexi thought she was being smothered instead of appreciating the love and safety she was provided. She started to push back, which resulted in being told no more and more.

Tom and Cynthia discussed the small changes in Lexi's behavior, language, and fashion choices. Friends and family had warned Tom and Cynthia to expect behavioral changes during Lexi's teenage years, but knowing what to expect and dealing with them were two very different things. The most obvious change in Lexi was her physical growth. Her father was not happy about it. She had changed from a girl to a woman in less than a year after puberty. Even Cynthia was surprised at how quickly Lexi's growth spurt happened.

Cynthia had difficulty finding new clothes that hid her daughter's adult physique, especially since all the fashion trends were revealing. Lexi wanted to be stylish, and her preferences were the kind of clothes her mother tried to steer away from. Her father would have never allowed Lexi to go to school in the clothes that she preferred, but he rarely went shopping with them, and he was already at work when she dressed for school.

Another change in Lexi was her personal grooming. Her long, straight brown hair and clean complexion in ninth grade evolved into tinted, trending haircuts and makeup enhancements going into tenth grade. Cynthia and Tom were out of their league when it came to dealing with all the changes, especially factoring in social media, cell phone, and boys. They sought a balance between giving her enough space to grow and letting her learn from her mistakes.

When Lexi was in elementary and middle school, Cynthia had the kind of relationship where Lexi always confided in her. Sometime during Lexi's ninth-grade year, the confiding happened less, and the arguing happened more. Cynthia reminded herself that Lexi was going through one of the most difficult times in a teenager's life. Lexi was figuring out who she was and where her boundaries ended.

Her rebellious streak put a strain on her relationship with her mother. When she saw her mother's apathy toward her father right after the affair, her relationship with her mother hit new lows. And finally, Tom's sudden death threw Cynthia and Lexi's relationship past its breaking point.

Life and Friends in Vass, North Carolina

The late spring in Vass was one of Rand's favorite seasons. He enjoyed the morning chores in the stalls and the smells of renewed growth and fresh cut grass.

He fed and brushed their two horses and let them graze. Rand had cleaned their stalls, laid fresh bedding, and arranged their tack for an afternoon ride. His coffee was still warm as he finished his chores, walked toward the house, and enjoyed the serenity.

The yellow blasts of midspring pine pollen were over, so Rand was able to sip his coffee and keep his eyes open without worry of pollen overload. The temperature was pleasant, the air smelled restorative, and life was good.

He walked into the house and asked Linda what her plans were for the day. She did not have anything definitive, but she mentioned that she had hoped to get together with Aryana and Rashne sometime soon.

"Let's meet them at the club for golf," Rand suggested.

Linda made a phone call and set it up.

Aryana and Rashne Samadani were the Templetons' closest friends and former neighbors in Mount Vernon. They met years ago at a neighborhood gathering in Mount Vernon and immediately hit it off. Rashne was an executive with the World Bank. Aryana was a stay-at-home mom for their three daughters, until they were in high school, when she became a socialite and world-class Persian food caterer. She hosted dozens of parties at her home when Rashne had business partners in town. Over the years and through word of mouth, her business, Saffron & Sumac, grew into a very successful company that provided catering to some of the highest-level international events in Washington, DC.

The Samadanis became such dear friends that Aryana was at Linda's side throughout her cancer recovery, just as Linda had been there for Aryana during one of her daughter's illnesses. After Linda announced they were retiring and moving to North Carolina, Rashne and Aryana considered doing the same thing. Ironically, before Linda ever mentioned moving, Aryana had already thought about moving to North Carolina to be closer to her youngest daughter, Daria, a radiologist at Duke Raleigh Hospital.

Daria had two sons—Darius and Tyler. Aryana drove to Raleigh at least once a month to see her grandchildren. The idea of moving closer to them had been in her mind for a while. Rashne was ready to retire too, and the move appealed to him as well. He was a casual golfer, so moving to a world-famous golf resort like Pinehurst was icing on the cake.

When Linda told Aryana that they had found property in Vass, Aryana began searching for homes in the area too. Within weeks, she and Rashne had bought a large historic house in the village of Pinehurst. The house was originally built in 1910 as a boarding house, but Aryana had ideas about how to make it a grand home, with many upgrades, including a large gourmet kitchen.

Aryana's business in DC had an excellent reputation, and it could run itself. She had hired and trained enough chefs and staff that she would be able to oversee the business from Pinehurst. The best part of moving south was that she would be only forty minutes from her grandchildren. As a bonus, her house had enough rooms for them to live with her if they wanted to, and her friends could stay anytime.

Rashne learned early on in his marriage that it was always best to follow Aryana's lead, so when she made the decision to move, he agreed. After their house was remodeled and they got settled, Aryana and Rashne started to enjoy the country club lifestyle. They joined Pinehurst Country Club and took golf lessons. Rashne played golf at least twice a week, often with Rand, and Aryana played in the women's leagues.

The exercise from golfing and the low-stress environment had the added benefit of improving their health. Rashne had been in good shape all his life, eating the right food, avoiding alcohol, getting enough sleep, and exercising. But golf added another activity to his health regimen. He loved to walk the courses too. Aryana was younger than her husband and in exceptional health as well. She looked much younger than her seventy years.

Rand and Linda were delighted that their best friends moved to the area, especially when they found a house in the village. When the Samadanis were moved in, the two couples got together at least once a week, usually in Aryana's kitchen, to enjoy her cooking. Rand and Linda were like family and had an open invitation.

The Templetons' life in Vass was significantly less stressful than in DC. All their time was devoted to each other, their friends, the horses, and golf rather than work, traffic, and finances. They were members in golf groups and spent two days a week at Pinehurst Country Club. The Samadanis kept three golf carts parked at their home. One cart was for themselves, one was for guests, and one belonged to Rand and Linda.

When Rand and Linda came to the village, they parked their car at the Samadanis, visited for a while, and then used their golf cart around the village or on the golf courses. The arrangement gave Rand and Linda a way to have a personal golf cart in the village.

Pinehurst

Pinehurst Country Club's clubhouse had a large veranda overlooking the 18th hole of the famous Pinehurst course no. 2, where the US Open had been played three times in the last twenty years. Rand and Linda would sit on the veranda overlooking the 18th hole and watch the golfers finish their round. It was intimidating for even the most seasoned golfers to be watched by so many people, especially when onlookers got boisterous after too many drinks.

Often, when the husbands or wives played in their leagues, their spouses sat on the veranda, watching for them to come up the 18th hole. The two couples, along with other friends, often attended special event nights like wine tasting, trivia night, and poolside band events. Their favorites were the foreign dish nights, when Pinehurst invited international chefs to prepare Greek, German, Hawaiian, and other exotic dishes.

Aside from the country club activities, the two adjacent towns, Southern Pines and Aberdeen, shared a quaintness that drew people to them. The areas hosted thousands of guests every month. However, the character of the buildings, layout, climate, and charm kept the feel of small towns in a simpler time. Visitors were welcomed with hospitality. Personal disputes were put aside, and get-togethers were frequent.

The couples attended social gatherings in the centers of Pinehurst or Southern Pines's First Friday, held on the first Friday of every month. By late afternoon, the streets were closed except to vendors, food trucks, and entertainers; and then hundreds of people mingled in the street, circle, or plaza to enjoy the events. The Templetons and Samadanis also enjoyed seasonal events, like wine crawls, holiday parades, horse shows, car shows, an annual Christmas tree lighting festival, and a farmer's market on Wednesday and Saturday mornings.

One summer evening, when the two couples were sitting on a blanket in Tufts Park with wine and snacks, listening to a Carolina shag beach band, Linda asked rhetorically, "Were we all just too busy in DC to enjoy these kinds of outings, or did they even have things like this?"

The other three thought for a moment about her question. Their earlier lives were either too busy to enjoy the simple pleasures, or Pinehurst offered much more than other towns in the way of simple pleasures. The couples loved the atmosphere and quaintness. Linda often told Rand how much she loved being retired and living the club life. Their social calendars were full, they were getting exercise and sunshine, the nearby medical facilities were top-notch, they had great friends, and she loved having the horses.

The Sandhills Equine Center, one of the best in the South, was less than five miles from their house, and it supplied riding and horse training opportunities. Linda truly loved the area, and when she was happy, Rand was happy. The only stress in their lives usually came from their children.

They still got the occasional phone call about a sick grandchild, someone getting stitches, someone in a fender bender, or someone needing advice. However, the call from Cynthia about Tom was one they never expected. It was not the way things should be. Parents were not supposed to outlive their children, so when a child died suddenly, few parents were ever emotionally prepared or recovered. The fact that Tom was their son-in-law did not lessen the pain. They loved Tom, and they knew that his death would result in terrible suffering for Cynthia and Lexi.

Resuming Life in Occoquan

Tom's funeral was two weeks ago, and obligations demanded that Cynthia and Lexi resume living. Cynthia had informed her employer about Tom's passing, and she was given bereavement leave. She had asked her supervisor that when she returned to work, it would be less painful to not have to deal with an onslaught of sympathizers.

Lexi, on the other hand, would have to face 895 students in her school whom she had not texted about her dad's passing. Everyone would have something to say. She hated the idea of reentering the world of school drama almost as much as she hated her mother right now.

Lexi brooded for two weeks while she stayed home after the funeral, speaking to her mother only when necessary. Cynthia assumed Lexi's gloominess and rudeness was her daughter's way of dealing with grief, so she said nothing about the behavior. When it was time for Lexi to go back to school, Cynthia decided to drive her that first morning rather than have her ride the bus. She drove Lexi to the school front lobby and leaned over to kiss her goodbye. Her kiss was met with disdain. Cynthia ignored her daughter's attitude and assured her that her first day back would be all right.

Never again would anything be all right, Lexi thought as she walked away from her mother.

Lexi made her way to her locker through the gauntlet of students in the hallway reliving weekend events, burying their faces in their phones, exchanging gossip, or preening and posturing. She could see the stares and hear the whispers, but that was all it was. The return was not nearly as dramatic as she had imagined. The usual clusters of girls and even two or three boys came to her during the day and expressed their condolences. Their gestures were kind and unexpected, but then they quickly resumed their daily routines, having checked that item off their lists.

Lexi was not in a mood to talk or think today; so she nodded at people, pretended to listen, and glided through her schedule. Before she knew it, the dismissal bell rang, and she boarded the bus. She tried to remember something about the day, but it was a blur. She thought that tomorrow would be better or at least clearer in her mind.

The next day, when Lexi was in her second period class, a student entered and handed the teacher a note. He read it, called Lexi up to the front, and handed it to her. Usually, getting handed a yellow note from the principal's office meant you were in trouble. It also meant being hazed and badgered by classmates. This time was different. Her classmates knew Lexi's situation, and no one uttered a word. She grabbed her things and exited the class.

A Wallflower

When the school secretary saw Lexi approaching the office, she made an interoffice phone call and invited Lexi to have a seat. A moment later, the phone buzzed back.

The secretary answered, "Yes, ma'am, right away."

She instructed Lexi to go down the hall to the left and wait in the chairs around the corner.

Lexi had never been this deep into the school administrative spaces. Unexpected events made her weary, especially since she was still grieving. She did not need to deal with another unknown. She turned the corner and saw another girl sitting along the wall. She had seen the girl in school but had never spoken to her. She was a wallflower.

Lexi inconspicuously studied the girl. She was different from Lexi's friends. It was one of the few times Lexi had been close enough to notice her uncombed long black hair with green highlights hanging down from a scarf around her head. Lexi had seen the girl wearing a scarf before, maybe all the time. The girl's tan complexion accentuated the thick black eyeliner and her exotic eyes. Her ears had multiple piercings, and her nose had a small stud piercing.

She wore a torn black T-shirt from a random punk band tour, a knee-length black skirt, torn fishnet stockings, and midcalf black boots. Lexi remembered her friends commenting once that the girl was either making a statement, or she worked for an undertaker. Lexi imagined her smoking a cigarette right there in the office and adorned with tattoos.

After Lexi sat down, a sweet, soft, accented voice asked her, "What are you in for?"

Lexi looked up in shock. She didn't recognize the girl's accent but was taken aback by the sweetness of her voice.

Lexi moved past her shock and answered, "I'm not really sure."

The other girl nodded.

"You just lost your dad, didn't you?"

Without waiting for Lexi's acknowledgment, she continued.

"I would expect that the school will offer you grief counseling, if you want it."

Lexi did not want to talk to anyone about anything, never mind a black-nail-polish-wearing wallflower girl who was probably stoned. She wanted to ignore the girl's opinion, but she was intrigued by the girl's insight and compassion.

Finally, the girl said, "Hi. I'm Amy Demirci. I'm here because my mom is not well, like, cray-cray-for-real not well, and it's making me too sad to deal. I don't know how to feel or who to be, so the guidance counselors are trying to help me with it. They are pretty good about things like that."

The girl's openness and clarity again surprised Lexi, so much that she did not know what to say. She wondered why she had never talked to Amy before and why everyone had misjudged her, and yet she also wondered why Amy dressed this way.

Lexi said, "I'm Lexi."

Just then, one of the guidance counselors, Mrs. Jenson, opened a door, greeted the two girls, and asked Amy to come in. Moments later, Ms. Laden came out to meet Lexi and invited her into another office.

Ms. Laden introduced herself and, after inviting Lexi to sit, asked her how she was feeling. Lexi responded politely that she was fine. Ms. Laden studied Lexi's answer, causing an awkward silence. Lexi looked around. Ms. Laden looked young, but her credentials on the wall came from years of formal psychology education.

Ms. Laden could tell by Lexi's body language and facial expressions that she was nervous and uncertain about why she was there. Ms. Laden, in a gentle, scripted voice, explained that the school system offered grief counseling to any student at any time. She explained to Lexi that when a person experienced a loss or traumatic event, it usually helped to talk about their feelings to someone who was trained to not be judgmental, someone who could truly listen and validate the feelings or help the victim understand them.

Lexi suddenly looked up. She had never considered herself a victim. Laden saw Lexi's reaction and assured her that every time something traumatic happened in a person's life, they were affected and changed by it, which made them a victim.

Laden explained, "Trauma can change our brains in ways we might never realize."

She asked Lexi if she understood. Lexi shrugged her shoulders. Her crossed arms and legs revealed to Laden that she felt insecure and vulnerable. Laden had hoped that Lexi would process what was just explained to her and accept the help. However, Lexi was not yet ready to open up, so Laden asked if she would come back on Friday morning. Lexi nodded. Laden said she would make the arrangements with Lexi's teachers, so she should not worry about missing class. Lexi got up and walked out of the office, feeling no different from when she walked in, except for two things—being a victim and meeting Amy Demirci.

For the rest of the day, Lexi thought about being a victim and about Amy. The sadness about her father's death was still sucking the life out of her, but she never thought of herself as a victim. She thought of her dad as the victim. He was a victim of a tragic accident and a victim of his wife turning into a bitch. And why didn't she or her friends know Amy before now?

Lexi tried to remember the times she had seen Amy in school or if she was in any of her classes. Lexi's friends, who considered themselves normal, did not associate with weirdos, druggies, or kids in other fringe cliques. Lexi then remembered that Amy was in her science class, the last class of the day. The class was overcrowded, and Amy sat all the way in the back, away from everyone. As Lexi thought more about Amy, she realized that she dressed the way that Lexi felt inside—dark and torn.

On Friday morning, Lexi was excused from her third period class to see Ms. Laden. She knocked on Ms. Laden's door, and a voice asked her to come in. Ms. Laden arose from behind her desk, and she greeted Lexi with a warm smile. Lexi studied Ms. Laden this time. She was pretty. Lexi's eyes glanced at Laden's left hand. She was not wearing a ring. Before Lexi could make a judgment, Ms. Laden asked if she felt up to sharing her feelings about her dad. Lexi froze. The question was so to the point and so personal that it felt like an attack. Seeing her reaction, Laden at once backed off by suggesting that Lexi speak in very generic terms, if that made it easier.

Lexi had been asked a hundred times in the past three weeks how she was doing, but this was the first time someone specifically asked how she felt about her father. So many memories flooded her brain that she did not know where to start. Ms. Laden asked her to come up with just one word.

Lexi surprised herself by yelling out, "Angry!"

Laden said, "Good, Lexi! I'm proud of you. That was honest."

Laden was not surprised by the emotion. She urged Lexi to elaborate on her anger. Lexi started slowly but then rambled on about the activities she did with her dad and memories from those activities and her anger and sadness that they wouldn't ever happen again. Laden was hoping for a deeper dive into Lexi's emotions, but this was a good start. She wondered if Lexi was mature enough to understand and verbalize deeper feelings. The weary look on Lexi's face told Laden that they had talked enough for today. She asked Lexi to think about why and at whom she was angry, and they would talk about it next week.

Lexi was in her last class when she noticed Amy in the back of the room. Their assignment was to read to themselves, so Lexi moved to the back of the room and sat next to Amy. A few of her girlfriends in the class saw this and were puzzled.

Amy whispered, "So how did it go with your counselor today?"

Lexi answered, "Fine. How about you?"

Amy whispered that they talked about the same stuff every week, and then Mrs. Jenson asked how it made her feel. Amy acted out her response to Mrs. Jensen.

"My mom is so sad that she can barely get through one day without crying. All she does is pray at least five times a day. It's goes like this: praying, more crying, and then more praying. My dad has been gone for over a year, and my mom can't move on. The last time she heard from him, he said something about being illegally drafted into the army. She thinks he got killed. No one knows.

"We have no other relatives, so she feels so alone. She thinks I'm too young to help, so she tries to not burden me. So how does Mrs. Jensen think I am supposed to feel? My whole world is dissolving in front of me. Oh, excuse me, Mrs. Jensen, I feel great! Seriously, it is tearing me apart, and I cry myself to sleep at night. I feel like a stranger, even in my own nightmares."

Amy looked at Lexi and said, "I'm sorry. I didn't mean to dump on you. I know yours is much worse, but I am too consumed by my wretched life to feel anybody else's pain!"

Lexi could not conceal the shocked look on her face at hearing Amy's sad, miserable testimony in one breath. She had no words. Just then, the teacher reminded the class that it was silent reading.

After class, Lexi's friends clustered around her while walking down the hall. Jennifer asked what that was all about.

Lexi responded, "Have any of you all ever talked to her? She is actually really nice! She looks and dresses like that because she says that is how she feels."

Jennifer rolled her eyes and said, "Whatever! Like a zombie apocalypse from the trailer park."

The other girls snickered and dispersed.

Empty Spaces

After school, Lexi came home to an empty house like she did every day for the past three years, but she had felt safe knowing that her mom and dad would eventually walk through the door. Now with her dad gone, it was different. The house was just an empty space that he once filled with joy and love. Each time she entered her house after his death, it felt like a hand with long, bony fingers was reaching in and strangling her heart.

She turned on the TV to fill the house with noise and then sat down at the dining room table to do her homework. She kept looking at the clock on the wall, dreading the time when the witch got home from work. Her dad had been gone a month, but Lexi's anger toward her mother had not softened. In truth, it was intensifying because of the way her mother was going on with her life. She had not said anything about her husband since he died. In fact, she had not said much of anything, Lexi noted finally.

Cynthia arrived home from work and saw Lexi doing her homework. She changed her clothes and came back into the kitchen, talking to herself about getting dinner ready. She never said anything of substance. Lexi was thinking that her mom must have hated her dad so much that she didn't even think about him.

What a bitch! Lexi thought.

It was another quiet night at the Forester household, with little to no conversation or interaction between mother and daughter. Lexi believed that her mother did not care if they ever spoke again, and so she reciprocated the behavior in self-preservation mode.

Lexi lay in bed that night and pondered ways to punish her mother for falling out of love with her father. When she had thought enough about her mother, Lexi wondered why her friends never bothered before to get to know Amy. With those two thoughts in her head, an idea sparked in her mind, and she knew what would infuriate her mother.

Lexi's Revenge

The weekend arrived. Jennifer and Lexi had made plans to meet their friends at Potomac Mills mall in Woodbridge. It was one of the biggest shopping centers in the area, and teenagers would go there to hang out. Jennifer's mom drove the girls to the mall and told them to meet her at the food court in two hours. She allowed them to scatter to do their own shopping. Lexi and Jennifer went one way; Jessica and Shyanne went the other.

Lexi was almost running to her destination and pulling Jennifer along.

"Lexi!" she yelled. "Why are you in such a hurry?"

Lexi said she knew exactly where she wanted to go but didn't know how long it would take. Jennifer had no idea what Lexi was talking about until they arrived at a kiosk.

"Lexi, what are you going to do?" Jennifer asked in shock.

"May I help you?" a tattooed, multipierced woman asked.

Lexi asked if she could get her ears and nose pierced on the same day. The woman answered that she could get all the piercings she wanted, if she didn't mind a little pain. Then she told Lexi she would need her parents' permission.

"No problem," Lexi said. "My mom is in a wheelchair at home, but she wrote a note."

Jennifer could not believe what she was hearing. She pulled Lexi aside.

"Are you sure you want to do this?"

Lexi turned away from Jennifer.

"Here's my note," Lexi said, handing a forged permission note to the clerk, who did not even look at it.

"Okay," the clerk said. "Where do you want to start?"

Afterward, the two girls walked away from the kiosk, one in pain, one in shock.

Jennifer said, "My mom is going to kill us—me for letting you do that and you for getting it done. Your mom is going to kill my mom. Oh my god! We are in so much trouble."

Lexi looked at Jennifer and yelled, "Will you shut the hell up? I'm the one in pain. How does it look?"

Jennifer looked at the four beaded studs on the inside of Lexi's ear and then at the small diamond in the side of her nose.

"It's cute. It's sick. I love it. We are so dead!"

When Lexi and Jennifer arrived at the food court, Mrs. Johnson, Jessica, and Shyanne were sitting at a table. Their eyes opened wide as Lexi got close enough for everyone to see the piercings.

Mrs. Johnson's eyes grew wide too, and she asked in a stern voice, "Lexi Forester, what did you do? Did your mother say you could that?" And then she whispered aloud, "She is never going to let me take you anywhere ever again. Oh my god!"

Without another word, everyone grabbed their bags and headed to the car.

Mrs. Johnson dropped off Jessica and Shyanne first before heading to the Forester home. She did not want the other girls to see or hear Cynthia's reaction. When Laurie Johnson brought the girls home and opened the door, Cynthia came into the foyer and looked at Lexi's nose.

"Why did you get your nose pierced?" she asked in a deadpan voice. "You should have asked me first, especially since we have a rule about things like that."

Lexi said, "I didn't think you'd care, so I got this and these."

Lexi pulled back her hair to reveal four studs along the back rim of her ear.

Laurie Johnson closed her eyes in shame.

"I'm sorry, Cynthia. I let the girls pair up and go on their own in the mall. I didn't know she was going to get pierced."

"It's not your fault, Laurie. I don't blame you. Lexi is still trying to adjust to things, so it is what it is," Cynthia said matter-of-factly.

Laurie was suspicious of Cynthia's reaction. She wondered if Cynthia was sedated. Laurie told Jennifer that they should get home and see what her father had planned for dinner. Laurie walked out feeling troubled by Cynthia's reaction to Lexi's bold play. Laurie surmised that Lexi was aware of her mother's sedating, so she was manipulating the situation to her advantage. It was obvious that Cynthia was not herself.

All the moms in their neighborhood had an understanding that girls in the ninth grade were too young to get tattoos and piercings other than on their earlobes. Whatever one mother let her child do would put pressure on all the mothers. The mothers' groupthink was that those kind of adornments on young people often coincided with other types of behavior. And yet Cynthia hardly reacted to Lexi. Laurie became acutely aware that this was not the Cynthia she knew when Tom was alive.

Lexi went up to her room to admire herself in the mirror and apply antibacterial cream to the new holes. Sometime later, her mom from the bottom of the stairs said that she would heat up leftovers for dinner.

Lexi barely heard her but shrugged her shoulders, saying, "Whatever."

She thought that her mom had stopped caring about everything since her dad died, but this was absolute proof. She was hoping that the earrings and nose stud would be a way to punish her for not loving her father. Her mom's reaction was disappointing, but it gave Lexi the green light to push her boundaries even further.

Lexi was the talk of all her friends at school the next week. The story had made its way around on everyone's Facebook and Instagram pages, but they wanted to see the earrings and nose stud in person. The mothers were angry when their daughters came home pleading to get their noses pierced too since Lexi Forester's mom let Lexi do it. Cynthia was not popular among the PTA crowd.

Lexi's new friend Amy liked the ears and the nose. She told Lexi that she was making a statement and being her own person. Lexi appreciated the affirmation. Within weeks, Lexi was wearing shredded black jeans and boots to school. Her friends noticed the slow transformation. The mothers did too.

Is Anyone Home?

One afternoon, Mrs. Johnson picked up Jennifer and Lexi from school. The girls had stayed late to work on decorations for an end-of-year school dance. When they arrived at Lexi's house, Mrs. Johnson parked the car and came inside to talk with Cynthia. The house was quiet. Cynthia was sitting in a chair in the family room, staring at the TV. It was dinnertime, but dinner had not been prepared. Lexi and Jennifer went upstairs.

Laurie asked, "Cynthia, how are you feeling, honey?"

Cynthia looked up and finally noticed Laurie standing there.

"Oh, hi, Laurie. I didn't see you standing there. I'm not really feeling up to company right now. Please excuse the mess."

Laurie sat in the chair next to Cynthia.

"Honey, are you okay? You haven't seemed like yourself for some time now. Is there anything I can do to help? Do you want me to fix dinner for you and Lexi?"

Hearing her words, Cynthia became more responsive.

"Oh no, Laurie, I'm fine. Really! We have leftovers from the other night, and I was just going to heat them up."

When Cynthia stood up, Laurie saw that she had lost weight. She looked frail and unhealthy. Just then, Jennifer appeared at the top of the stairs, asking her mom what they were having for dinner. Laurie said goodbye to Cynthia, but she wanted to come by tomorrow afternoon. Cynthia told her that would be fine.

Laurie and Jennifer got in the car and drove home. Laurie asked Jennifer if Lexi had lost weight. She responded that Lexi looked a little bit thinner, but it was probably because of the skinny jeans she was wearing. Laurie understood that Cynthia was in mourning, but she began to question at what point a grieving widow needed professional help. She recommended that Jennifer be especially sensitive and tolerant around Lexi and Mrs. Forester.

"They are going through a difficult time, which might affect their behavior for a while."

Jennifer said, "Yeah, I've seen it already. Lexi became friends with a social outcast at school, and she is starting to dress like her. It's so weird!"

Laurie stopped by the Forester house the following day and brought over a pan of lasagna and a Crock-Pot of beef stew. Cynthia had just gotten home from work. She was grateful for the food, but she assured Laurie there was no need. Laurie opened a bottle of wine she had brought over, poured two glasses, and waited for Cynthia to come back downstairs after changing clothes. Cynthia reappeared and smiled at the sight of the wine. Cynthia was in a bad emotional place, but the social visit perked her up.

The two women sat and talked. Laurie kept the conversation light and easy by talking about their daughters and school activities. She was hoping that Cynthia would supply an opening for them to talk about her frame of mind. When Cynthia mentioned not feeling like herself lately, Laurie jumped on it.

"Cynthia, I have been meaning to ask you how you are coping. You say you are okay, but are you really? Are you talking with anyone professionally?"

Cynthia started to get teary-eyed, and then it turned into full crying as she shared with Laurie about being counseled at work today for errors and missed deadlines.

"They also suggested I see a therapist."

After saying it aloud, Cynthia was embarrassed and stopped before she said too much.

"I'm okay. Really, I am. I just need some rest. Thanks for stopping by. I appreciate your concern."

Cynthia's thanks was an indirect way of ending Laurie's visit. Laurie stood up to go. She hugged Cynthia and said that she, Lang, and Jennifer cared deeply about her and Lexi and that they wanted to help in any way they could. Cynthia thanked her and walked her to the door.

Cynthia went back into the dimly lit family room with her glass of wine and sat in her armchair. She could not stop the tears from running down her cheeks and onto her blouse.

An hour later, Lexi came downstairs for dinner. She did not see her mom in the unlit family room, but she found the lasagna on the kitchen counter. Without hesitation, she heated a serving for herself, ate it, washed her plate, and went back up to her room without a word. Earlier, Lexi overheard Mrs. Johnson talking with her mom. But by the time she came down to eat, Mrs. Johnson was gone. Lexi assumed that her mom had gone to bed early, like she had been doing lately.

The same routine happened every day for the next month. Lexi would wake up and get ready for school, fix a lunch, catch the bus, and spend her day at school. Cynthia would get up, get ready for work, and drive to Alexandria. They only spoke a few words to each other the whole month. At night, Lexi would fix herself something to eat, do her homework, go to her room, and go to bed. Cynthia would sit in the dark with a glass of wine until she dozed off.

Lexi's graduation from junior high was less than a month away. Summer vacation had always been a time of joy and excitement. Now Lexi could not stomach the thought of having to spend any part of the summer with her bitchy, pathetic mom. She had to come up with a plan to spend as little time as possible at home.

Amy's Assimilation

Amy was gradually accepted into Lexi's friend group. Lexi invited Amy to hang out with her girlfriends every chance she got after they got to know her. It did not take long for the other girls to see that Amy was kind and considerate once they got past her unusual makeup and clothes.

One day, one of the girls asked Amy about her clothes. She said that she dressed that way based on the way she felt. She was sad and lonely. She told them she had not always been a gloomy person, but she had become a casualty of her father's disappearance and her mother's despair. Amy explained how her father might have been caught up in a civil war in Eastern Europe. The girls were not familiar with the region or its politics, so they sympathized but didn't understand how that could have happened.

Amy's new friends were influencing her as much as she was influencing them. She became more talkative and sociable than anyone had ever noticed before. She enjoyed being with them, not being harshly judged anymore, and having people to share her thoughts and insecurities. Even Amy's wardrobe began to include hints of color. The girls began experimenting with more dramatic eye makeup like Amy. By the school year's end, Amy was included in all their social media and texts.

Late-Spring School Fever

On the last Friday of the school year, when testing, projects, papers, reports, and student grading were completed, it was a half day. Lexi got off the bus and let out a scream of triumph. The worst school year of her life was almost over. She hugged Jennifer and said that she would text her later to do something.

Lexi walked through the front door, and her mother was in her chair, staring at the wall.

Cynthia asked, "Why are you home so early?"

Lexi's apathy toward her mother had been festering since her father's funeral, and she had no way to release the pressure. She was at a point where she didn't want to look at her mom or talk with her.

She responded snidely, "Well, you obviously don't remember anything, but the last week of school is half days. And this is one of those, so I'm home."

Cynthia mumbled to Lexi to clean her room and bathroom because her grandparents were coming to visit for a week. The empty wineglass on the end table let Lexi know her mother's state of mind. Cynthia's drinking in the dark and vegetating in her chair had become her everyday pattern, and Lexi was disgusted by it.

Cynthia was in no mood for company, but Linda and Rand were insistent. Cynthia could not dissuade her mother from coming up from North Carolina, so she surrendered and eventually thought that the visit might be a suitable time to talk to them about the future.

"Now you know my excuse for being home. Why are you home?" Lexi asked.

Cynthia began crying.

Lexi muttered under her breath, “Jesus Christ, get ahold of yourself.”

Cynthia heard Lexi’s sassy remark. It hit her last nerve, and she snapped.

An unfamiliar voice from deep within Cynthia asked, “What did you just say to me?”

Lexi was shocked and a little scared of her mother’s tone. She did not reply.

Cynthia continued the assault.

“Why are you wearing torn hose? You look like you’re homeless!”

Lexi had been arming herself for this battle for too long.

“Oh, now you notice what I’m wearing? What the hell? I have been dressing this way because it is how I feel—tattered and torn. Why don’t you just go back to your chair, your sanctuary, and drink yourself to sleep? Or better yet, maybe you could just miss another day of work!”

Cynthia felt Lexi’s verbal jab tear into her soul, but she fired back.

“I don’t have to go to work anymore. They put me on administrative leave. You should think about that the next time you want money for a shopping spree.”

Cynthia was enraged.

“I have given you so much latitude, young lady, because you have been dealing with your father’s death, but you have become a spoiled brat who has crossed the line too many times. From now on, things are going to change.”

“Or what?” Lexi demanded as she went in for the kill. “Or you will kill me too? I know you hate me, and that’s fine because I hate you more. You hated my father, and it got him killed. Maybe you can just kill me with your own hands instead of messing with my head like you did to him!”

Before Lexi knew what happened, she was on the floor. She saw a sudden flash and then darkness. She brought her hand up to her cheek, wondering why it was burning. Seconds later, the shock wore off, and she realized her mother had slapped her. Cynthia had never struck Lexi before, and both women were shocked by it.

Lexi looked at her mom with a sadness and intensity in her eyes that said it all. The cord was cut. Any bond between mother and daughter was no more. They became two strangers in that instant. Lexi did not feel hate for her mother anymore; she felt nothing, indifference. Cynthia saw the indifference on Lexi's face. Lexi gathered herself and wiped away the tears and saliva.

She slowly got to her feet and in an unemotional, matter-of-fact voice said to her mother, "I wish you had died instead of dad!"

Then she stormed out of the front door.

Cynthia watched Lexi slam the door behind her. She was stunned by Lexi's remark and by her striking her daughter. She could not stop Lexi from leaving.

Lexi was crying uncontrollably and unable to catch her breath. She called Jennifer, but the only thing Jennifer understood was the part about Lexi coming over right now. Obviously, something horrible had just happened.

Jennifer met Lexi at the front door and took her upstairs. It took fifteen minutes for Lexi to calm down enough to explain to Jennifer what had happened.

"Your mom hit you?" Jennifer asked in disbelief.

Lexi nodded. They both looked in the mirror and could see a welt on her cheek.

"Oh my god! I think you can sue her for child abuse or at least call child protective services."

Lexi thought that Jennifer was being a little dramatic, but she appreciated her support and sympathy. Jennifer did not know that Lexi was being dramatic too. Lexi's makeup was running down her face, making things appear worse.

The two girls sat on the bed, talking about what had just happened.

Jennifer questioned Lexi, "You actually, like, told your mother you hate her? And you wished she was dead? Oh my god, Lex, that's harsh!"

Lexi knew Jennifer was right. It was harsh, and she really didn't know how to feel about it.

"I just snapped," Lexi argued. "I mean, I have been thinking it since my dad died. My mom has been in zombie land ever since. My whole world is falling apart, and she doesn't even care. All she does is drink, become one with her comfy chair, stare at the wall, barely eat, forget everything. And now she tells me she lost her job. Oh my god! How are we supposed to live?"

Just then, they heard the garage door opening. Jennifer interrupted.

"My mom is home. I'm going to ask if you can stay."

Lexi said, "Jen, I must stay! I can't live in the same house with the walking dead."

"I don't know, Lexi. When my mom hears what happened, she is going to take you home and talk with your mom."

"No!" Lexi pleaded. "I don't want to tell your mom."

Jennifer's bedroom door was ajar.

"What don't you want to tell me?" Mrs. Johnson asked firmly.

The girls looked at each other. Mrs. Johnson saw the wheels turning in the girls' heads to come up with a story. She stopped them.

"No stories! Lexi, what happened?"

Laurie pressed Lexi until she heard the whole story. It did not come as a total shock. Laurie had been extremely worried for a while, and she recognized this event as a breaking point. Even before Lexi could finish her version of the incident, Laurie was heading downstairs.

"Lexi, I need to take you home right now! Jen, you should come along too so you and Lexi can go to her room while I talk with Cynthia."

Lexi argued back, "Mrs. Johnson, I don't want to see her right now. Please, can I just stay here for a while?"

Laurie hugged Lexi.

"Honey, I know it has been very difficult for you since losing your dad, and you are trying to deal with it the best you can. But you are not alone. Your mother is struggling too. She lost as much as you did, even more. Right now, you need to be a grown-up. Okay?"

Lexi did not like what Mrs. Johnson said to her, but she knew she had lost the argument and was being taken home. Laurie shouted to her husband, who was pulling in the driveway, that she might be a while at the Foresters' house. The three females got in the car and drove the half block. Laurie jumped out of the car and headed straight for the door, not waiting for the girls. She walked into the house.

"Cynthia? Honey, it's Laurie. I'm coming in, okay?"

The downstairs was quiet.

Laurie looked around and then said, "I'm coming upstairs, okay, honey?"

She opened Cynthia's bedroom door and flipped on the light.

Lexi and Jennifer waited while Laurie was upstairs. Lexi's stomach convulsed when she heard Mrs. Johnson's shriek.

"Oh my god! Cynthia, what have you done?"

Laurie screamed for Jennifer to get her father at once! She screamed to Lexi to call 911. Lexi started crying.

"Why? What's wrong?"

Laurie yelled, "Just call 911 now and let me talk to them."

Lexi ran up the stairs while pushing 911 on her cell phone. She entered her mom's bedroom and saw her lying on the bed, unresponsive to Laurie's shaking. Crying uncontrollably, Lexi handed the phone to Mrs. Johnson.

"911. What's your emergency?"

Laurie said in a panicked voice, "Please send an ambulance. My friend has taken pills and is unresponsive. She has a faint pulse. Hurry, please!"

The neighbors watched the emergency vehicles in front of the Forester house, wondering what had happened now. They assumed that Cynthia and Lexi were struggling with the loss of Tom, but no one knew the complete story about what the Foresters were going through, not even the Johnsons, who knew them best.

The Prince William County EMTs resuscitated Cynthia en route to the emergency room of Potomac Hospital in Woodbridge. Laurie and the two girls followed the ambulance to the hospital. Laurie warned the girls it was going to be a long night.

The ER doctor forced carbon into Cynthia's stomach to absorb the antidepressants, and then they pumped out her stomach contents.

The doctor assured Lexi and Laurie that Cynthia was stable, but she would be staying overnight for routine observation and then at least two more days for a psychiatric consult. The doctor suggested that everyone go home, get rest, and come back tomorrow. Lexi asked if she could see her mom. The doctor explained that her mother was drowsy, uncomfortable, and needed rest. She would be much better tomorrow.

Lexi walked out of the hospital feeling more confused and alone than she had ever felt in her life. Her emotions were in turmoil. She had so much hate in her heart toward her mother, but at the same time, she felt love and sympathy for her too. Her thoughts were in chaos.

Jennifer wanted to say something to comfort Lexi, but she was afraid of saying the wrong thing. If she said that her mother would be okay, it might sound insincere and cliché and possibly not what Lexi wanted to hear since Lexi had told Jennifer so many times how much she hated her mother. Jennifer knew, though, that the thought of losing her mother would certainly overcome the poison in Lexi's heart.

Lexi and Jennifer were sitting in the Johnsons' back seat on the way home from the hospital, and Lexi was mumbling to herself incoherently. Laurie glanced at her in the rearview mirror with deep concern. Laurie recognized Lexi's behavior as a sign of emotional shock, possibly even a nervous breakdown. She had never seen a nervous breakdown before, but Lexi was going through something.

It was midnight when they arrived at the Forrester house. Lexi was still in a fog, so Laurie told Jennifer to take Lexi inside and help her pack a suitcase for a week. Lexi would stay with them until Cynthia got better. She reminded Jennifer to get Lexi's cell phone and charger in case they needed to contact family.

Laurie went inside the house to make sure things were turned off and the doors were locked. She switched on lights to make the house look occupied. Then Laurie yelled upstairs, reminding the girls to pack Lexi's personal items and medicines.

Jennifer yelled back in fear, "Mom, she's totally zoned out."

Laurie said, "I know, honey. She is in shock, so just pack for her."

The two girls came downstairs with a suitcase. Laurie asked Lexi for her house keys. Lexi was slow to respond.

Laurie held out her hand, saying gently, "Honey, I need to lock the front door. You had the keys when we came inside, remember?"

Lexi reached in her pocket and handed the keys to Mrs. Johnson.

Jennifer's dad, Lang, greeted them at the Johnsons' house and helped get everything inside. He asked Laurie how Lexi was holding up. Laurie whispered that they would talk after the girls went upstairs. She told Jennifer to take Lexi upstairs so she could shower and get to bed. Laurie told the girls they would figure everything out in the morning, but for now, Lexi was going to be staying with them.

After Laurie was confident that the girls were in Jennifer's bedroom for the night, she told her husband the situation.

"I don't know if Cynthia accidentally took more pills than she meant to or if it was intentional. She had been drinking, so it is possible that it could have been an accident. I hope it was an accident! Anyway, when things like this happen, the hospital keeps the patient for forty-eight hours or more for a psych evaluation."

Lang shook his head.

"I can't believe that poor girl almost lost another parent in less than six months. What was Cynthia thinking? What the hell is going on between those two?"

Laurie shook her head.

"I'm exhausted, honey. Let's not rush to judgment just yet. I will call Cynthia's mom in the morning and let her know what has happened."

Lang disagreed.

"I know it's late, but you should call now. I've talked with Rand before, and he is the kind of guy that will want to know. He and Linda can decide whether they want to come up tonight or tomorrow morning."

Laurie replied, "Yeah, I've talked with Linda before also, and you are right."

A Call in the Night

Linda was a lighter sleeper than Rand, and she heard her cell phone on its charger in the kitchen. She got up to answer her phone knowing that it couldn't be good. When Rand was on active duty, middle-of-the-night phone calls were not unusual. But nowadays, any call after midnight meant something bad.

Linda flipped on the lights and saw on her phone that Lexi was calling. She answered urgently.

"Hello, honey. What's wrong?"

A strange voice greeted her.

"Hi. Linda? This is Laurie Johnson, Cynthia's neighbor."

Linda's heart started pounding.

"Laurie, what's wrong?"

Laurie explained, "Cynthia was taken to the emergency room tonight. She is going to be okay, but they are keeping her for observation."

"What happened? Was she in an accident? Where is Lexi?"

Laurie told her, "Lexi is with us. She is safe. I think Cynthia took an overdose of medication."

"Laurie, where is Cynthia? What hospital?"

"Linda, I think it might be a good idea if you could come up here."

"Of course. I will tell Rand, and we will leave shortly. Is Lexi there so I can talk to her?"

"She and Jennifer are already in bed. She has had quite a night and is not herself."

"I understand, Laurie. Thank you for calling. You did the right thing. All right. We have a set of house keys. By the time Lexi wakes up, her grandfather and I will be at her house, waiting for her. We will talk then. Thank you, Laurie."

"I will see you in the morning."

Laurie hung up and went to bed.

*****

Linda rushed into her bedroom and shook Rand awake.

"What's the matter?" he asked.

"Cynthia is in the hospital, and we have to go."

Rand jumped up and got in the shower. Military men learned to pack and be on the move in minutes, and Rand had it down pat. He had a list in his mind of everything he would need for a week or more. Linda prepared herself and ran through her mental checklist too.

Rand called Sylvia to look after the horses. In less than an hour after Laurie's phone call, the Templetons were headed northbound to Occoquan. They arrived at Cynthia's house at four thirty that morning. Rand brought in their bags while Linda went into the kitchen to make a pot of coffee. When they were settled in, they went into the living room to wait for morning and dozed off worrying what the new day might bring.

*****

The front door opening startled Linda. She reached over and woke up Rand.

"They're here."

Rand was barely up from the couch before Lexi's arms were wrapped tightly around his waist and her head buried in his chest.

"PopPop!" Lexi exclaimed with a heavy sigh of relief.

She began to cry. Seconds later, she let go of him and reached for her grandmother. Linda hugged her tightly.

"It's okay, honey! Everything will be okay. You'll see. We are going to stay here to make sure of it. Do you want me to make you breakfast?"

Without saying anything, Rand and Linda exchanged looks about the stud in Lexi's nose. Lexi had made her fashion transformation after her grandparents' last visit. Cynthia had told Linda over the phone about Lexi's changes, but Linda had no idea that her granddaughter had metamorphosed. It was a topic for a later discussion.

Laurie and Jennifer followed Lexi into the house. Laurie greeted Rand and Linda, thanking them for coming so quickly. Linda offered coffee and breakfast. They refused breakfast politely, but coffee was fine. Laurie followed Linda into the kitchen while Lexi hugged her grandfather again. He could feel her emotion in her shaking. From the kitchen, Laurie asked Lexi if she wanted to sit with them while they talked about her mom. She didn't think there was any more to tell, so she declined and said she and Jennifer would be in the den.

Rand and Linda listened intently to Laurie's version of what happened.

"Cynthia had a bottle of vodka on the nightstand, along with an empty bottle of antidepressants, when I found her unconscious on the bed."

Laurie only described what she saw rather than surmising if Cynthia drank too much and accidentally took the pills or if she took the pills and washed them down with the vodka.

She continued.

"Lexi came to our house yesterday in tears, mad as a hornet. She said she had a big fight with her mom and that she said mean things to her. Cynthia slapped her, and Lexi ran out. After hearing this, I came back here with the girls right away and found Cynthia upstairs. I called 911. In the emergency room, they revived her, gave her a solution to drink, and pumped at least ten pills out of her. Lexi seemed to be in mild shock last night, but she is better today."

Linda cried, "Oh my god! What happens now?"

Laurie suggested that they go to the hospital this morning and get an update from the doctors. She finished by telling Rand and Linda that suspected suicides were kept under observation for several days in the psych ward.

Linda sat in the kitchen, biting her lip, as they waited for visiting hours before heading to the hospital. Everyone was on edge.

Linda and Lexi fidgeted on the way to the hospital. Linda wanted to hear Lexi's version of her argument with her mother, but she decided it was too soon, and she should let things calm down a little. She was worried that Lexi could be in a fragile state of mind. Linda wanted her granddaughter to feel their love and support first so she would not feel so alone in the world. Lexi had suffered far more than any teenager should in such a short time. Questions could wait.

They arrived at the hospital and were told that Cynthia was resting comfortably in her room, but she would be transferred to the psych ward sometime today. They found Cynthia's room on the third floor and approached it slowly so as not to awaken her. She was resting when the sound of the door caused her to open her eyes. Cynthia saw her mother in the doorway first, and she covered her face in shame, weeping into her hands. Linda went to the bedside and hugged her as if it would take away all her fears. She knew that her daughter was embarrassed and ashamed.

Linda whispered in her daughter's ear, "We're here, baby. Don't worry, we know it's been hard on you. We just didn't realize how hard. You have been putting on such a brave face, but it's time to let us help you carry the burden. It's okay. We hear you now."

Mother and daughter cried together in a long embrace. Linda finally let go, and Cynthia acknowledged her dad behind her.

"Oh, Dad!" she cried. "I'm so sorry. I'm sorry I disappoint you."

Rand bent over to hug Cynthia, and the tears rolled down his face.

"You have always made me so proud, honey. I have never been disappointed. I'm not disappointed now. I'm just so sorry we didn't see your cries for help. Can you forgive us?"

Cynthia opened her arms to her father and hugged him like she did when she was a little girl.

Lexi stood at the foot of the bed, watching them. She was relieved to see that her mom was responsive. She didn't want her mom to die, but even in this moment, she could not let go of her anger. Every feeling in her was contradictory. She didn't know how to act in this moment. The possibility of losing her mother was a wake-up call that no matter how much anger Lexi held on to, her mother was the only parent she had left.

Cynthia spent the night wrestling with her demons and her shame. In her remorse, she forgot about their argument, and she reached for Lexi. Lexi reluctantly moved to her mother's bedside. Neither one spoke, but Cynthia hugged Lexi tightly. Lexi did not reciprocate but kept her arms limp at her side. Rand saw the disparity in how they hugged each other and thought deeply about the emotional chasm between mother and daughter. He realized at that moment that a world of healing was needed.

Assumptions

It was impossible for Rand to know exactly what Cynthia or Lexi was going through in their relationship, but in the hope of helping the situation, he made assumptions and came up with his own theory.

He knew that Cynthia was devastated by Tom's affair. He assumed that she had wanted to salvage the marriage but must have struggled to forgive him. Lexi most likely saw that her mom was having difficulty relating to Tom, but Lexi did not know why. At the same time, Tom was probably on his best behavior to get back into Cynthia's good graces, which made him look like a saint in Lexi's eyes. Cynthia would never say anything disparaging about Tom to Lexi, especially about an affair, so in Lexi's eyes, Cynthia was the villain.

While both women in the house were experiencing individual anger, confusion, and uncertainty, Tom was killed suddenly in an accident. In the aftermath, Cynthia and Lexi were unable to cope with the ramifications of the death—the upheaval of their lives, the guilt, the despair, the anger, and the grief. As if all those emotions were not enough, Lexi was in, arguably, the most difficult period of her life as a teenage girl going through the social blender of her first year of high school. Finally, Rand summed up his theory that the pressure in the house became too great, and the volcano erupted.

Rand had laid it all out in his mind in a chronological sequence, and in despair, he shook his head. It was too much spaghetti for his mind to unravel completely. He would have to discuss this with his better half, Linda. She would either agree or challenge his assumptions, but at least she would have suggestions for how to handle the situation. Maybe they could come up with a plan. No, there was not a maybe about it; they had no choice. Without intervention, this broken family would not survive.

Linda, Rand, and Lexi visited Cynthia all day, even while she napped intermittently. Laurie and Jennifer came by too. Lexi sat in a corner chair farthest from her mother's bed and spent the day checking emails and social media, only occasionally looking up at her mom. When Cynthia would try to make eye contact, Lexi's eyes would dart back to her phone.

Conversation between Linda and Cynthia was light and inconsequential, speaking only about groceries, errands, appointments to cancel, and such. It was too soon and uncomfortable to talk about the elephant in the room even though Linda wanted so badly to ask Cynthia if she meant to do it. For now, the question would have to wait.

In the afternoon, a doctor came in and told Cynthia what was going to happen next. She was being moved to another floor to be evaluated by a psychiatrist. When the doctor was leaving, he asked the staff to give the family time to say their goodbyes. Five minutes later, a nurse and a technician came in, unhooked the monitors, and helped Cynthia prepare to be wheeled upstairs. Linda promised Cynthia that they would take care of Lexi for as long as it took her to get better. Cynthia was being wheeled down the hall when Linda shouted to her that they would come back tomorrow.

Lexi's feeling toward her mother was affecting other aspects of her life, including her grandparents' presence in the house. Rand and Linda wanted to make themselves at home for Lexi's sake, but after the hospital visit, Lexi's actions were not very inviting and hospitable. They understood her anger, but it didn't change the fact that they felt like intruders.

When they arrived home from the hospital, Lexi ran upstairs to her room and locked her door. She was a different person. She did not bother to help her grandparents prepare dinner or familiarize themselves with groceries in the house. Rand scowled while watching her disappear upstairs again and again.

Linda saw the scowl on his face and quietly said, "We don't know what that girl is going through, so let's go easy and give her some time."

Rand answered back, "We all are under stress right now, but it does not justify rudeness. If I did that to my parents or grandparents, my dad would have taken me to the woodshed!"

"Yes, and you had to walk to school five miles uphill each way, barefoot, through two feet of snow," Linda said, walking away from him.

Linda took it upon herself to fry up pork chops and vegetables for dinner. She wanted to make things as comfortable and normal for Lexi as she could while her mother was recuperating. Linda asked Rand to call Lexi down for dinner. He went upstairs and gently knocked on her bedroom door.

"Lexi, it's time to eat."

She answered Rand abruptly through the closed door.

"PopPop, I'm not hungry. Please go away and leave me alone!"

He stood there silently annoyed, contemplating what to do next. He knocked more firmly on the door.

"Lexi, I cannot go away until you open this door. I will give you one minute to choose."

Lexi didn't know what that meant.

Choose what? she wondered.

She put down her iPad, got off her bed, and opened the door. She intended to let her grandfather know that she was not hungry, she was not coming downstairs, and he should leave her alone. She opened her door. Before Lexi could say the first word, Rand put his index finger up to his lips. Lexi was puzzled and caught off guard.

What is he doing? she wondered.

She cocked her head, slightly curious. He extended his hand.

She thought, *Okay, I'll bite.*

So she took his hand.

Still silent, Rand carefully led her downstairs into the dining room, where her grandmother had set three lovely dinner plates at the table. He let go of her hand and pulled out a chair. Still caught in his trap, she sat and locked her eyes on him, wondering what was next. He sat.

Rand and Linda folded their hands and bowed their heads as he said a blessing. When the prayer was over, Lexi was still bewildered by the simplicity of his maneuver, having expected something much more intriguing. By this point, she could only resign herself to the fact that she was now sitting at the table. The only thing left for her to do to regain control was to act like sitting at the table had been her intention all along.

Linda spoke first, asking Lexi about the last week of school. Without looking up, Lexi shrugged her shoulders. Linda did not accept a shrug as a suitable answer. She pushed further, saying that it was highly disappointing that the Virginia school system did not inform ninth-grade students about their end-of-year progress and schedule, especially since ninth-graders could handle such information.

Lexi was amused that her grandmother directed her disappointment at the school system and not at her. Rather than fuel her grandmother's annoyance, Lexi decided to be more specific.

"Well, MomMom, they told us how we did, and they explained the schedule for the last week of school, but I did not want to bore you with it. Besides, I didn't really do as well this year because of Dad and stuff."

As soon as she said it, Lexi braced herself for the onslaught of disappointment from her grandparents. Instead, neither one of them did so much as blink! What was happening? They had no reaction. They both continued eating dinner as if she had not said a word. Finally, Rand cleared his throat.

Here it comes! Lexi thought.

"Dear, I really like the flavor of this pork chop. What did you use?"

Linda smiled.

"I'm glad. I found a pork rub in the pantry. It is tasty, if I do say so myself."

Lexi wondered if she was in bizarro world.

What the hell is going on?

She was suspicious that everything was being staged. When they finished the meal and sat to digest, Linda invited Rand and Lexi to help clean up the dishes.

Rand said, "Yep."

Lexi did not answer, but since they were doing it, she figured she might as well clear the table and bring the dishes into the kitchen.

*****

The next morning, while savoring the last few hours of sleep, Lexi was jerked out of a dream by a slightly gravelly voice saying, "Pumpkin, rise and shine. C'mon, up and at 'em."

She came out of her dream and in a sleepy voice inquired, "PopPop? What are you doing in my room? What time is it?"

Rand answered from the hallway.

"Well, sweetie, I am not in your room, but I am waking you from outside your door to give you enough time to prepare for the day. It's six thirty."

Lexi exhaled loudly in exasperation and then buried her head in her pillow as her grandfather's voice got farther away.

"Your grandmother has breakfast for us."

Lexi thought, *How long will I have to put up with crazy time?*

Forty-five minutes later, Lexi joined her grandparents at the breakfast table. They were having a quiet discussion when Lexi joined them. Linda welcomed Lexi to breakfast. Rand scanned the *Washington Post* newspaper. The table was set with fried eggs, orange slices, apple juice, toast, and bacon.

"MomMom, I can't eat all this. Do you know how fattening this is? Oh my god! Can you say cholesterol? I'll just have yogurt."

Linda smiled at her and replied, "Oh, sweetheart, you eat whatever you like. This is for your grandfather and me, but we made enough in case you wanted a healthy breakfast too."

Lexi rolled her eyes and considered the inconvenience of having to go to the fridge and get her own yogurt. This food was already on the table. She might as well save steps and eat what was in front of her. She did not mention that the eggs and bacon were cooked perfectly. She buttered a piece of toast and drank the apple juice. It was more breakfast than she had eaten in a long time, and truthfully, she didn't mind. However, if this happened every morning, she would have to buy all new clothes in a month.

Her grandfather put down the paper, took a big gulp of coffee, and asked Lexi how long it would take her to get ready. A look of confusion came over her face.

Rand explained further.

"When you get dressed, we can go for a short walk. It will get your blood and digestion juices flowing."

Rand saw that she was in her pajamas.

Lexi scowled. She had already done her hair and makeup. Obviously, her grandfather had no fashion sense. He didn't know that sweatpants rolled at the waist, a vintage Nirvana tee tucked in the front, and sneakers was dressed.

"PopPop, this is what I'm wearing today," Lexi replied snarkily.

It took every ounce of restraint for Rand and Linda not to react. They were not so old that they had forgotten the hippie generation of the sixties and what they wore then, but Lexi's clothes were still a shock.

"Oh! Well, okay," Rand said. "Let's go. It looks like it is going to be a warm, beautiful morning. Don't want to miss it. How about you escort your old PopPop around the circle so I don't get lost or fall and break a hip? I know when your ride comes, you have time."

The only walking Lexi wanted to do this morning was to the car of Jennifer's mom and through the halls of school. Instead, she got sucked in by feigned geriatric pleas for a walk to the curb and back with her old grandfather. She considered anyone over thirty to be old and frail. She did not know that her grandfather was as healthy as his horses.

Rand opened the front door, stepped out, and took in a deep, cleansing breath. Lexi was right behind him, annoyed by his exercise video dramatics, but here she was, walking a steady pace with him around the neighborhood before most kids were even out of bed.

Rand looked around the neighborhood as they walked, saying little except about the beauty of the morning. He was hoping that

Lexi would start a conversation. He could see that she was annoyed, but he hoped that the serenity would soak in and relax her mind.

"PopPop, I think we've gone far enough. This is a good place to turn back home," she said.

He looked where she pointed, and they changed direction. His decided then that Linda and his plan was going to take some time. Changes in her attitude would take a lot more subtlety on their part rather than throwing too much at her too soon.

She needed to be able to relax and trust them first before they could really help her get her life back on track. They had ideas too about what would help her, but there was no sense in talking about those now. She needed certainties. He could tell that her mind was clouded with as many questions as fears and doubts.

They walked the rest of the way in silence. When they arrived back at the house, Rand thanked her for the company.

"It is good to know that someone has your back, especially in unfamiliar territory," he said.

She gave no indications that she understood his deeper meaning, but he put it out there. They walked into the house, and Lexi ran up to her room. Ten minutes later, Jennifer knocked on the door, and Rand invited her in.

"Good morning, Mr. Templeton. Where's Lexi?"

He returned her polite greeting and pointed toward the stairs. Just then, Lexi came bounding down the stairs wearing jeans and a clean T-shirt tucked in the front. Rand looked at her quizzically.

"What?" she asked. "My clothes were sweaty from our walk. Bye, PopPop. Bye, MomMom."

The two girls were out the door, gabbing about something, before Rand could say goodbye. He kept the main door open and closed the storm door, which allowed the sunlight to come into the foyer. It was a new day.

"Well?" Linda asked, coming out of the kitchen with a cup of coffee in her hand.

"I don't know. I just don't know," Rand answered, shaking his head.

He felt out of touch with his granddaughter. He was certain that she was completely out of touch with him, and she had no desire to remedy it.

"What did she say?" Linda asked.

"Nothing."

Rand looked straight into his wife's eyes.

"She said nothing. I think it is too soon. She needs to be comfortable with us and trust us. Too many things have happened to her in such a short time. We'll give it time."

Linda and Rand were both thinking something that they were not willing to say, as if speaking it might make it truer. They thought Cynthia might not be in a state of mind where she could care for her daughter adequately. There was a high probability that Linda might have to stay in Occoquan for an extended period to help her daughter and granddaughter. Rand thought it too. Both could not stay indefinitely because someone had to take care of the horses and the farm.

They sipped their coffee and concluded that they would cross that bridge when they came to it. Now it was time to think about visiting Cynthia.

*****

In Lexi's school, by second period, stories about Lexi's mom being taken away in an ambulance last night were spreading on social media and through the hallways. The negative attention could have been worse, but Lexi's classmates were sympathetic and respectful. Her close friends expressed their love and support, but thankfully, the end-of-school-year activities kept students too busy to prod into Lexi's life.

Lexi was busy too, but she wondered why Amy had not spoken to her today. Amy interacted with one or two friends, but she seemed more like the old, reclusive Amy. Lexi, Jennifer, Shyanne, and Shannon were at their lunch table when Amy approached. Lexi moved over and patted the seat beside her. Amy sat with them.

"What up, girl?" they asked.

Amy looked down. Everyone got quiet and waited. Amy told them how much she appreciated their friendship, but right now, she didn't feel like talking about what was bothering her if that was okay. All at once, the girls told her it was fine and that they would listen whenever she felt like talking. She told them it would make her feel better if they would just keep talking about other stuff.

Lexi reached down and squeezed Amy's hand.

In a role reversal, Amy mouthed to Lexi, "Are you okay?"

Lexi nodded ever so slightly, then stopped and shook her head also slightly.

The group went back to talking about summer plans and how next year they were going to be in high school. Shannon and Jennifer squealed. Lexi had a hard time thinking that far ahead. So did Amy.

When lunch was over, the girls dispersed to their buses. Lexi caught up to Amy when no one was paying attention.

She whispered, "What's going on?"

Amy's expression was one of compassion.

"You have a few things on your plate right now, so I don't want to burden you with my shit, ya know. I hope your mom is feeling better. Did she have an accident?"

Lexi said, "Maybe we'll sit down sometime and talk about things."

Amy understood completely. Without details, the two girls acknowledged that they had something in common about their families that weighed heavy on them. They parted in the hall, feeling a tiny bit better.

Rand and Linda waited for Lexi to get home before going to the hospital. The ride in the car was quiet, because each passenger was preoccupied and in deep thought. Linda mentioned something about the heavy traffic when they passed the shopping area off the interstate highway. Rand's traffic anxiety was coming back, reminding him why he was so glad that he moved away from here.

At the hospital, they went to Cynthia's floor and inquired about her at the nurses' station. The rules on the psych floor were different from other floors. Not all patients were allowed visitors. If the patient was allowed visitors, they had to go to the lounge area. Five minutes later, Cynthia was escorted out to the lounge area. She was wearing her own clothes, but she seemed drowsy. Linda asked how she felt, how they were treating her, if she was getting enough to eat, and what the doctors said. Rand suggested that Linda give Cynthia time to answer.

They could tell that Cynthia was sedated. She looked at her mother, saying that they gave her breakfast, lunch, and dinner. She said she felt like a pin cushion because they took blood and did other tests and that they were trying different antidepressants, and it took time to figure out their efficacy and side effects.

Cynthia turned to Lexi.

"How are you, Lex? Are MomMom and PopPop taking good care of you?"

Lexi could relate to her mom at that moment because she, too, had so many questions. She never looked at her mom directly and answered that MomMom was feeding her too much and PopPop wanted to go for walks at zero dark thirty. Other than that, everything was okay. She also mentioned that they didn't know what kids wore to school these days.

Cynthia replied, "Well, it seems like we all have to learn new things and make adjustments, don't we?"

Lexi looked off into space. Cynthia reached for Lexi's hand, but she pulled it away.

Cynthia felt the rejection but offered, "Honey, I'm going to do everything I can to get better and come home soon, but I'm glad MomMom and PopPop are here to help our little broken family right now."

Tears filled her eyes.

"I love you, Lexi, and I always have, and I always will."

Lexi covered her face to hide her tears. Linda reached over and hugged Cynthia. Rand listened and was more certain about his theory. They both needed love, healing, and help.

The rest of the week was the same routine. Lexi was awakened early, offered too much food for breakfast, took walks with her grandfather, and then driven to school. In the afternoons, they would visit Cynthia and then go home to start all over again. By Thursday, Lexi had completed all her school projects and got her report card. She did well. Additionally, the doctor said that her mom was going to be discharged Friday afternoon.

Lexi's guidance counselor and teachers were still concerned about the changes they had seen in her since her father passed. Teachers often recognized subtle cries for help, but Lexi hid her pain well by coming to school every day and doing well on exams and projects. Her guidance counselor sent home with Lexi a sealed form letter about the need for professional help after tragedies or trauma. Despite her tragedy, Lexi still did well enough in her academics to be promoted to tenth grade at Woodbridge High school, with new and different challenges.

Lexi woke up on Friday morning with mixed feelings about her mother being discharged. She was harboring anger and resentment deep down for her mom's behavior toward her father and now for the assault, but another part of her was glad that her mom was coming home. Her mom had been a bitch and a train wreck for two months, but for reasons Lexi did not want to acknowledge, their house did not feel like a home without her mom in it. It was confusing.

As Lexi and her friends were leaving the school cafeteria for their last school day, she spotted Amy. She wasn't in school yesterday, and Lexi wondered where she had been. She didn't answer her texts either. She approached Amy.

"You didn't answer any of my texts last night. What gives? Are you okay?"

Amy asked Lexi if she was going to be in third period. Lexi nodded.

"I'll see you there," Amy said.

Lexi noticed that Amy dressed even more grungy than usual. She was going for the "I don't give a shit" look today.

An hour later Amy came into study hall and sat next to Lexi.

"Sorry I haven't gotten back to you, but, like, I've been totally consumed by stuff at home."

Lexi asked if there was anything she could do to help.

Amy answered, "No. Your plate is full."

She looked at Amy and told her that being a good listener and friend was not going to overload her plate. Amy smiled.

"I know your mom is having issues because of your dad and all. I get it. It is a lot to deal with. So my mom is spacing out too. I think she got a letter from someone in Georgia. My dad is gone, likely killed. No one knows where. So now I'm finding empty liquor bottles around the house, and my mom will probably lose her job. Same old shit, ya know?"

"Oh my god, Amy! Why didn't you tell us?"

She admitted how embarrassed she was about her family situation, how she didn't live in a nice house like the other girls, and how she didn't want to air her dirty laundry. Lexi did not agree with Amy's reasoning, saying that the girls would not judge her.

But Amy thought, *Everyone judges.*

Lexi hugged Amy and told her she understood. Amy didn't say anything, knowing that Lexi could not possibly understand, but she was thankful anyway. Amy said she had to bounce. Lexi asked her to call anytime she wanted to talk over the summer.

"Thanks, Lex," Amy said.

Lexi thought about Amy's problem on the way to the hospital. Linda asked her what had her so deeply in thought.

"Nothing, MomMom. I was just thinking about a friend."

When they arrived at the psych ward, Cynthia was ready and waiting to go home. They followed the orderly wheeling Cynthia down to the hospital lobby. Cynthia got up from the wheelchair, took her overnight bag, and walked to the car with her daughter and parents. Rand was surprised at how easy it was to check out of the hospital, especially the psych ward, but Cynthia was judged to be mentally stable, so he was okay with it.

As they drove away, Linda asked Cynthia, "So did the doctor talk to you today about your prognosis?"

She looked at Cynthia in the back seat and waited for an answer. Lexi listened in.

Cynthia looked out the window and asked, "Why don't we pick up something for dinner, and we can talk about it then? I feel like Korean."

Rand loved the idea and started searching a phone app for the nearest Korean restaurant. Linda held out her hand for his phone.

"No texting while driving. Bad example."

Linda finished the search and found a Korean takeout nearby. At home, Linda and Lexi laid out plates and forks on the table. Everyone spooned out their bibimbap, bulgogi, japchae, dumplings, and rice. They sat together as a family and ate. Even though it had been a week since they arrived, tension hung over the dinner table like a circus trapeze act. Linda did the talking about the meals she had prepared the past week, what she and Rand did during the day, and so on.

Lexi was quiet and disengaged. Cynthia recognized her attitude and reached out by asking Lexi how she had been. Instead of answering the question, Lexi asked what the doctors had said about her mental health. It was an awkwardly direct segue. Rand didn't approve of Lexi's tone and intent to hurt, but in all honesty, they wanted to know.

Cynthia searched for the words, trying to be funny as a means of lightening the mood.

She said, "Well, I won't be taking medication with a glass of wine anymore, if that's what you're asking."

Linda did not like seeing her daughter on the defensive. Like a mama bear protecting her cub, she softened the interrogation by explaining that they only wanted to know if she would be seeing more doctors and how often.

"Yes, Mom," she answered firmly. "I have an appointment with a psychiatrist next week. We will decide the best course of treatment to help me get through the loss of my husband."

Her voice was shaky. Linda could see in her face and hear in her voice that Cynthia was grinding through her privacy and dignity to answer the questions so they could really see her. She wanted Lexi especially to be able to see her.

Linda thought she understood how her daughter was feeling, having also endured misperceptions and misunderstandings in her life. Moms were supposed to be invincible, able to manage any adversity thrown at them. Breakdowns were not allowed. They made you feel weak and like you were a bad mother. The reality was that no one thought that way. However, mothers did so much that went unnoticed, and the recipients rarely ever acknowledged the work or expressed appreciation.

Right now, Cynthia needed to receive long-overdue appreciation and consolation, and she had to believe it. She lost her husband, and then in the middle of working through extreme emotional conflict and difficulties, she lost her daughter to anger. It was a lot to manage, even for a woman. Cynthia did not want to feel like she was failing the most important people in her life anymore.

Rand and Linda were in bed that night, each one separately contemplating their daughter's situation. In a hushed voice, Rand told Linda he had to go home, but he suggested that she should stay for a while.

Linda stared at the ceiling and without so much as a head turn said, "I know."

Rand would drive home, look after the horses and the homestead for three weeks, and then come back. They both knew that the road ahead for Cynthia and Lexi was challenging, possibly requiring drastic actions, but they would do whatever they had to. Their decisions would depend on Cynthia's psychiatric prognosis.

Rand went home to Vass and returned three weeks later. The tension and resentment in the house from Lexi had not eased. On top of that, Cynthia was beginning to experience disorientation and loss of blocks of time. Rand asked Linda in private about the situation in the house. She told him that Lexi had a deep-seated anger, and Cynthia did not appear to be responding to treatments.

There had been days when Cynthia moved about the house in a fog. Her psychiatrist was seeing her twice a week and trying to find the right combination of antidepressants. Rand was disheartened by his wife's report even though they had talked on the phone, and nothing was new. Hearing it did not have the same impact as seeing it. The situation was beyond his ability, and he was frustrated at himself for not knowing how to help. He would stay for another two weeks and pray for wisdom.

School was out for the summer, and Lexi had been sleeping in until midmorning. Rand's first morning back in Virginia, he roused her out of bed to go for their walk. She didn't want any part of it, but Rand was not taking no for an answer. Just to make him stop bothering her, Lexi threw on her sneakers, a cap, and a T-shirt while still in her pajama pants.

She came downstairs still asleep and said, "Okay, let's go!"

Rand took one look at her and told her to try again. He said she was to wash her face, brush her teeth, brush her hair, and get dressed appropriately for a workout. A half an hour later, she came downstairs in sweats, whining that she should still be in bed.

Rand opened the garage door, sucked in a deep breath, and said, "Let's go."

He started walking at a brisk pace for the first fifteen minutes, with Lexi in tow.

"PopPop," she asked. "We aren't going to do this all summer, are we?"

He replied that exercise and fresh air were good for the body and the soul, and she needed therapy for her body and soul. She did not want to know what he meant, and he did not give her time to think about it.

"Honey, I see you growing up in front of our eyes, but I can tell you that your childish disposition right now is not doing anybody any good."

He said that it was time he talked to her like an adult and expected her to act like one too. She was awake but had no idea what point he was making. She asked if she was being childish about something. He did not answer. His nonanswer was an answer.

"PopPop, you don't know what it's been like for me these past few months. My dad died! You have no idea what that is like."

He stopped in his tracks.

"Yes, honey, you lost one of the most important people in your life. I know it was your first loss, but sadly, it won't be your last. Eventually, the hurt you feel now might subside, but you will always remember him and the wonderful memories. However, you still have the other most important person in your life right in front of you. Are you are trying to lose her too?"

He told her that part of being an adult was thinking about other people and less about yourself. Lexi had been so consumed by her own feelings that she never considered how her mother felt. Her eyes squinted, her jaw tightened, and her nostrils flared.

Through clenched teeth, she said, "You don't know how she treated my father before he died, and I don't know if I can ever forgive her."

She was angry and walked twenty yards ahead of him for the rest of their walk without saying another word.

She holds on to her anger like her father, he thought.

They got back to the house, and Lexi stormed upstairs. Linda and Cynthia were in the kitchen, drinking coffee. Linda handed Rand a cup of coffee. He shook his head about Lexi. Linda understood. She sat down with Rand at the island in the kitchen and then asked Cynthia if there was anything she wanted to do today.

Cynthia continued staring out the window, answering, "No, Mom. I don't feel like going out today. I think I'll just sit and rest."

Linda looked at Rand. After forty years of marriage, their nonverbal communication was crystal clear. Linda and Rand hoped that tomorrow's appointment might help Cynthia have better clarity about her prognosis and medication options. It seemed like the pills were just keeping her sedated. Lexi needed a mother who was mentally present if she would let her in.

While the adults were biding their time in the kitchen, Lexi came bounding down the stairs, wearing earbuds and heading for the door. She still had a sour look on her face. Rand yelled to her before she was out of the door, asking what her plans were today.

"I'm going to Jennifer's. I should be home for dinner."

The door slammed behind her. Rand had no clue if this was normal behavior for a fourteen-year-old girl in this situation or new behavior for a girl at a dangerous crossroad in her life.

Another two weeks passed, and Rand needed to return to North Carolina. He and Linda talked about the near-term future. There was no sign of improvement with Cynthia, and Lexi was getting more defiant, teetering on the brink of war. Everything Lexi said and did was not the way a healthy, happy teenager would act. They decided that they would mention Lexi's behavior to the psychiatrist tomorrow after Cynthia's appointment.

When Cynthia came out of the doctor's office, Rand and Linda asked if they could talk with the doctor. She apologized that she had another appointment and that she could not speak to them about Cynthia's case unless she listed them as her HIPAA contacts. Cynthia butted in and asked the doctor if she could come back tomorrow with her parents for a chat about her daughter. The doctor agreed.

The next day, Cynthia sat in the psychiatrist's office, listening to her parents describe the situation at home. First, they wanted to know if the medications were effective other than sedating her. Then they described to Dr. Prout the current relationship between Cynthia and Lexi and what, if anything, could ease the tension. They wanted to know if Lexi could get counseling and if they could do anything to help.

During their questioning, Dr. Prout held up her hands. She was overwhelmed by everything the Templetons were throwing at her.

"Please, please, one question at a time," she pleaded.

Linda started. Her first concern was the efficacy of Cynthia's medication. What was it supposed to do for her, and how would she know if it was working? Dr. Prout explained that antidepressants took time to figure out the right dosage and blend for each patient's individual body chemistry. She explained in laymen's terms that the meds were slow-reacting in the brain, and the effects were subtle. She assured them that comatose was not the desired effect, but if the medications were overcorrecting the chemical imbalance in Cynthia's frontal cortex and hippocampus, then they were getting close to the intended target, and Prout only needed to adjust the dosage. She further suggested cognitive treatment, which she had discussed with Cynthia.

Linda asked Dr. Prout about Lexi. Prout tilted her head, trying to recall Lexi. Nevertheless, she said her immediate concern was helping Cynthia with her guilt and grief before she could begin talking about her daughter. Prout assured them that Lexi could and should get counseling. She highly recommended it for any child who suffered a devastating trauma, such as losing a parent. She reminded them too that Lexi was at a difficult age, when things like social media, peer pressure, and hormones collided, wreaking havoc on one's self-esteem and psyche. Prout asked them if her school offered counseling for Lexi after her father passed away.

Cynthia, who up to that moment had been inattentive, suddenly looked up and interjected, "Yes, they did. She met with a counselor once a week, but that was when I first noticed her clothes and attitude changing. I noticed it as clear as day, but for some reason, I couldn't do anything about it."

Cynthia's voice trailed off into her memory of the event.

"I wanted to, but I didn't have enough will to react. I couldn't say anything about it. I tried."

She put her hands over her face and sobbed. Linda put her arm around her daughter's shoulder.

Dr. Prout saw the defeat and failure in Cynthia face. When Cynthia regained her composure, Prout asked if she had thought about another type of therapy. She glanced at Cynthia for approval. Cynthia nodded.

"I recommend—and my colleagues agree—that Cynthia should seek rehabilitation-type treatment at a mental health center," Prout said.

Rand's eyes opened wide. All he heard was that they wanted to have his daughter committed. Dr. Prout was accustomed to negative reactions from family members.

"We are talking about a rest and relaxation spa of sorts with cognitive and pharmaceutical therapy treatments, not an asylum. It is completely voluntary, and Cynthia can leave anytime she wants. The doctors there will review my diagnoses and make recommendations for treatment and a prescription plan, but compliance will be up to Cynthia."

Rand crossed his arms and raised an eyebrow, asking, "For how long?"

"I can't answer that, Mr. Templeton. Cynthia has suffered a very traumatic loss compounded by overwhelming guilt and grief. You are a veteran, right?"

Rand was confused.

"Yes, but what does that have to do with this?"

Prout answered, "Cynthia's state of mind is comparable to combat PTSD, and I assume you are familiar with it?"

Rand nodded.

The doctor looked at her watch.

"Why don't you take some time, talk it over, and we can discuss it further after Cynthia's next appointment."

They thanked Dr. Prout and shook hands. Cynthia got into the back seat of the car and sat quietly as they headed home. Linda tried to have a conversation with Cynthia, but she would not respond. She was listless and looked tired. Linda faced forward and wept.

Rand looked over at his wife. Her tears tugged at his heart. He felt it too. He wanted to do whatever he could to help his daughter and granddaughter heal, but he didn't know how. He had to research the mental wellness centers that Dr. Prout mentioned. He wondered about the cost, being certain that Tricare military health insurance would not pay for that kind of private civilian treatment. If she did go away, it would also require major changes in Lexi's life.

After they arrived home, Linda went to the kitchen to prepare dinner, Cynthia went to her bedroom to rest, and Rand went to the den to begin his research. He spent hours reading about mental wellness centers in the United States. More facilities were devoted to addiction than emotional trauma, but they all sounded surprisingly successful and therapeutic. Rand was not an instant convert, but he was becoming more informed and open-minded. Later that night, he shared with Linda the things he found out about the facilities and asked her how she felt about Cynthia going to a wellness facility.

Linda had been thinking about it ever since Dr. Prout suggested it. She made the point that Cynthia probably needed some quiet time in an environment where memories of Tom were not around every corner. She mentioned too that Cynthia and Lexi clearly needed time apart, if nothing more than to give Lexi a chance to appreciate her mother and miss her.

Finally, she smiled, saying that if her battle-experienced, wise husband's opinion could be reversed in favor of something different in a couple of hours of research, then it must be the right thing to do. She kissed him good night and went to sleep. Rand sensed that Linda had made up his mind for him, and he, too, drifted off to sleep.

Sometime in the night, they decided that Linda should continue to stay in Virginia until they knew more about Cynthia's treatment plan. Additionally, if Cynthia was going away for a month or more, someone had to be there with Lexi. Linda did not have to be convinced. She would stay for as long as it took. Rand would have to return to North Carolina and come back every third weekend or as often as necessary. Neither he nor Linda could predict how long Cynthia's treatment might take. The next step was to tell Lexi.

Lexi Hears the Plan

The next evening, Rand, Linda, and Lexi sat down to dinner. Cynthia was not hungry, so she stayed in her room.

"See? This is how she gets," Lexi said with a shrug. "I don't care, though. I can fend for myself anyway, so she can just stay in la-la land for all I care. I wish I knew what kind of drugs she was taking, though."

"Lexi Lynn! That will be enough out of you, young lady!" Linda scolded.

Linda could count on one hand the times she had raised her voice at her granddaughter, but she had to put a stop to Lexi's ugliness and stewing anger. She did not like hearing her granddaughter talk about drugs either. Less than a year ago, Lexi was on a path to exceptional grades, a healthy, happy lifestyle, and opportunities. Listening to her now would make one think she was headed for trouble and a life of disappointment. Linda knew that Lexi was crying for help, but her attitude needed a serious adjustment before Linda could administer tender treatment.

Lexi was shocked by her grandmother's outburst. In defiance, she dropped her fork on her plate and got up from the table, muttering under her breath that she didn't have to deal with this either. Rand and Linda finished their meal in silence, both thinking of better ways to oversee the situation.

The next day, after Cynthia met with Dr. Prout, Linda asked how she might help her daughter and granddaughter. Prout suggested that they be patient, because Lexi was fighting an entirely separate set of demons born out of the same trauma but from her young, inexperienced perspective.

Dr. Prout did not have any new information about Cynthia getting into a wellness center, but she did have a recommendation from a colleague about a highly rated facility in Asheville, North Carolina. Linda and Rand had been to Asheville and were familiar with its reputation as an environmentally suitable area for treatment of tuberculosis in the early twentieth century. They did not know that treatment centers for other illnesses had sprung up. They enjoyed Asheville, and it was only three hours away from Vass. They could visit Cynthia often.

Rand decided that it was time, once again, for him to go home. Lexi did not care that her grandfather was leaving, but she was annoyed that her grandmother was staying. Lexi tried to convince them that she would be fine on her own and that Jennifer's mom would take her and Jen anywhere they wanted to go during the summer.

Linda explained to Lexi that she was staying to help Cynthia get better, but she would also enjoy Lexi's company, if she was amenable. Lexi rolled her eyes and wondered how the summer was going to be with her grandmother hovering while she was trying to enjoy herself with Jennifer or other friends at the pool, at the riverfront, at the mall, or at a boy's house. She did not want a chaperone, especially a senior citizen, looking over her shoulder. It could ruin her whole summer, she thought.

Champ and Pony Girl

Rand resumed his life as a retired horse owner living in the serenity of the Sandhills of North Carolina. He enjoyed his time with the horses even though they needed a great deal of care and feeding. He was relaxed around them, and he never minded the work. They were gentle animals that would respond to his commands and his attention. Sylvia, their neighbor who took care of them while Rand and Linda were away, commented on how the horses perked up whenever he came home.

The next day, Rand saddled up Champ and took him out for a long ride through the trails of the nearby equestrian center. Champ was a large black Friesian capable of carrying up to a three-hundred-pound rider. He could easily do farm chores, but Rand enjoyed the ten-year-old mount for his comfortable, smooth riding traits. When he rode by himself, Rand relished the peace and quiet, alone with his thoughts. Champ enjoyed the exercise and different grazing areas as well.

The summer days turned into weeks, forcing Rand to think deeply about the short-term and long-term plans for helping his daughter and granddaughter get past their grief and conflict. He worried about the best treatment for his daughter, the changes in his granddaughter, and especially Linda's stress trying to help Cynthia and Lexi while they were battling against each other and their own emotions. Rand's worries made it clear in his mind that his life was going to become complicated. But it did not matter, because Rand would do anything to help his family. He talked to Champ about it on their rides, but Champ had no opinions, even when Pony Girl was in tow.

Rand phoned Linda twice a week to check in and see how things were going. He drove up to see them at least one weekend a month during the summer. Linda would share with Rand whatever Dr. Prout told her. She did not go to every one of Cynthia's appointments, but she worked it out with Prout to get updates periodically.

Linda expressed disappointment to Prout about Cynthia's and Lexi's lack of progress. Cynthia had not shown any signs of emerging from her cocoon of despair. Dr. Prout agreed, telling Linda and Cynthia that she was waiting to hear from Pisgah Wellness Center in Asheville. All they needed to do was agree on a course of treatment and find an opening in the program, and Dr. Prout would set it up. Prout looked at Cynthia for a visual or verbal confirmation, but all Cynthia did was stare out of the window as if she had not heard the conversation.

In their early sessions, Dr. Prout would wait for Cynthia to start the conversation. When that failed, she would gently engage her with questions to bring her back from her self-imposed exile. Over time, Cynthia responded to questions, but she was consistently retreating into her shell. Prout was frustrated. She diagnosed that Cynthia's despair was a resulting symptom of depression and emotional trauma. She was overwhelmed and drowning in the sorrow of losing her husband. On top of that, she suffered extreme guilt of having her last two months with him entrenched in conflict and anger. She despised herself for losing that time that could have been spent loving him. She had begun to take on the blame for his affair and even his death.

When Cynthia was home, everything in the house, every corner, every chair, was an empty spot where Tom once was. She would look at each of those spots and feel an imaginary dagger plunge into her soul. If her own punishment and torture was not enough, Lexi blamed Cynthia for her father's death and hated her for it. Cynthia also felt responsible for Lexi's anger, which was so hateful and rebellious that it could affect the trajectory of her young life.

Carrying all that guilt was heartbreaking enough for Cynthia, but feeling so powerless and unworthy to do anything about it was worse. In her notes, Dr. Prout wrote that Cynthia was experiencing the hopelessness and severe anxiety of a fully conscience person trapped in a paralyzed body. She thought that Cynthia was living in her own personal hell, as if she was buried alive, screaming for someone to hear her cries, but no one was listening.

Dr. Prout did not believe her patient to be a danger to herself or anyone else. Prout could not justify having her committed and would have been reluctant to do so anyway. Cynthia was already in her own prison. Forcing her into an unknown environment might do more damage. Cynthia had to make the choice. However, if she chose to stay and continue psychiatric treatment in Woodbridge, Dr. Prout did not have the amount of time she judged that Cynthia needed. Therefore, she was urging Cynthia to voluntarily enter a mental wellness program as soon as possible. Prout reminded Linda that Cynthia had to consent to be admitted.

Linda updated Rand about Cynthia's unchanged condition and Lexi's continuing rebellion against everything and everyone. Linda had tried many times over the summer to persuade, if not demand, Lexi to see a therapist, but she seemed to be enjoying her defiance and untethered independence. Linda was ineffective at reining in Lexi from her rebellious behavior. Lexi's clothes became more torn, unkempt, and skimpier, especially her bathing suits. When Lexi came home after curfew, Linda would confront her and get no response. Linda could smell cigarette smoke on Lexi's clothes and prayed that it wasn't anything worse.

When Lexi was at home, she spent all her time in her room on her laptop or phone. Lexi would come down the stairs only to eat or when a car pulled up in front of the house. Her grandmother would ask where she was going and with whom. Lexi would say that she was going out with friends. Linda watched from the window as her granddaughter got into cars with older boys and girls. None of this behavior fazed Cynthia, who sat in her bedroom or on the couch, barely acknowledging anything or anyone. The antidepressants were making Cynthia unresponsive to life. The downward spiral was at full speed. Something had to change.

In mid-August, Rand made the four-hour drive to Virginia for Lexi's fifteenth birthday. He and Linda had decided on a bold course of action. He called Lang and Laurie Johnson and asked if he could meet with them. Rand arrived back in Occoquan with little fanfare, except for a hug and kiss from Linda.

Linda almost cried as she greeted Rand, whispering, "I hope we're not too late."

Rand asked his wife if she was ready for a big change. She nodded.

"Yes, I think it's time."

The next day, Rand and Linda walked up to the Johnsons' house to discuss their plan and ask a huge favor. There were a couple of unknowns in their scheme, so they had to rely on Laurie and Lang for support. The Johnsons promised to do whatever was necessary to help Cynthia and Lexi.

When Lexi came home from the pool, Rand asked her to come in the living room for a family discussion. She was annoyed, thinking that they had a birthday cake for her. She began to head up the stairs, saying that she had plans already and did not have the time. She was on the second step when she heard a tone that she did not recognize. It stopped her in her tracks.

Rand said, "You make the time. I am not asking. I'm telling you, young lady, to sit in this living room now!"

Lexi felt shock and fear as she backed off the steps and came into the living room.

"PopPop, what's wrong?" she asked nervously.

Rand looked at her and then her mother in the eye and said, "This family is broken. Your mother is broken, and you are broken. Neither of you has the emotional strength or the will to fix it. So your grandmother and I have made decisions for you."

Rand got up from the couch and knelt in front of Cynthia. She looked up, acknowledging his presence. He held her hands and looked into her eyes.

"Honey, I know you're in there. I remember the smiles and joy you used to feel not long ago. We are going to help you find that person again. In two days, we are taking you to Asheville, North Carolina. There is a place there that will help you find your joy once again. You will admit yourself. They will get you off the sedatives, and you may stay for as long as it takes. Okay?"

Rand was not waiting for an answer, and it was not a request. It was a directive.

Lexi reacted with a confused look on her face, wondering if her grandmother was going to be left here to take care of her. She didn't hate the idea of her mother being taken away. As Lexi's mind raced with thoughts of even more freedom to go wild, Rand pivoted toward her.

In a soft voice, he said, "Lexi, my dear granddaughter, you are broken too and need a lot more help than you think. You are harboring so much anger inside that it is destroying you. You have changed so much in six months that we don't even recognize you. So for that reason, out of love, we are taking you back to Vass to live with us while your mother is undergoing treatment. Now I'm sorry your birthday is so disappointing, but there is cake in the kitchen."

Lexi's eyes grew as wide as saucers. It took her a moment to respond.

"No. No way! You can't do that, PopPop. I have school and friends here. I can't just move away for a few months and miss school. No, I can't. I won't."

Rand was trying to be delicate and understanding with her. He did not want to be forceful. He and Linda knew she would fight this, but it was for her own good.

He answered back softly and sternly.

"You will enroll in high school in Vass. We don't know how long your mother's therapy will take, so your tenth-grade year will be in North Carolina."

No sooner had the last word left his lips than her head began shaking forcefully right and left.

"No!" she yelled out. "I'm not going. I live here. This is my home. You can't kidnap me. I won't go!"

Rand felt horrible seeing the fear and sadness in his granddaughter's eyes. He knew this would be extremely hard for her. She had lost so much already. Unfortunately, they did not have other options.

They could not leave her here indefinitely with her grandmother. It would be too much for Linda to manage on her own.

Rand spoke more assertively so she would know the issue was not open to debate.

"You have two days to say your goodbyes and get ready. This weekend, we are leaving."

Lexi, crying like a baby, jumped up, ran to her room, and slammed her door. Rand and Linda shared a look. This was going to be very difficult indeed.

The weekend arrived, and Rand wondered if his granddaughter was going to have to be dragged away kicking and screaming. She had spent her last two days crying at Jennifer's. Laurie Johnson had called Linda and asked if she could host a going away party for Lexi. Amy, Shyanne, Jessica, and Tiffany had come that Friday night to say their goodbyes. She promised to keep in touch with them every day until she got back from the boonies.

Jennifer cried too even though her mother promised she would drive her down to Vass to visit. Amy was upset about Lexi leaving. Her sophomore year was promising to be off to a great start because of Lexi and her new clique, and Amy's mother was having issues with drinking again, so she had hoped to lean on Lexi to talk about it. Lexi was the first person who reached out and helped her out of her shell, so she felt a special sisterhood. They hugged and promised to keep in touch.

On Sunday morning, when Rand and Linda began loading the car, he did not remind Lexi about their departure. He hoped instead that she would trust them to guide her through this troubling phase of her life's journey. He wanted her to come on her own accord. Cynthia followed her mother's direction and was ready to go. Not long after Rand, Linda, and Cynthia's things were in the car, Lexi appeared on the stairs, dragging a large suitcase.

"I have a few more things I'll need to bring," she said begrudgingly.

Linda could feel her granddaughter's sorrow and fear, but she was also proud of Lexi for accepting this difficult decision. She was showing a level of emotional maturity.

The Johnsons came over to get last-minute instructions about the house and to say their goodbyes. Lexi and Jennifer hugged and cried for ten minutes until it was time to get in the car. Linda sat in the back with Lexi, and Cynthia rode up front with her father. Cynthia had taken medication, so she would sleep most of the way. Lexi and Jennifer cried and waved to each other as the car pulled out of the driveway and out of sight.

The stuffed car merged onto Interstate 95 southbound within ten minutes, and Lexi asked if they were going to the loony bin first or to Vass. Cynthia was almost asleep, but she heard the verbal jab. Under medication, Cynthia was even more tolerant of her daughter's anger, but it still hurt, and each cut that Lexi delivered opened the wound deeper and more painfully. Linda was annoyed at Lexi's meanness but answered by telling her that Cynthia was coming home to Vass until they could take her to Asheville, about three hours away. Lexi pursed her lips and stared out the window.

All three women were asleep when Rand drove up the long driveway in Vass and parked in front of the garage. Except for the constant traffic between Fredericksburg and Richmond on Interstate 95, the drive was easy. It took four and a half hours, including one bathroom break. The passengers awoke when the car stopped. Rand offered to unload the luggage if they wanted to go inside and get settled.

Inside, Linda told Lexi to put her things in the bedroom that had its own bathroom, and Cynthia could take the other guest room. She said she would make dinner for everyone after they settled in. Lexi went straight to the bedroom and shut the door. Linda was not surprised. She knew that Lexi would come out in a minute or two and ask for the Wi-Fi password to set up her computer and social media.

Linda went to her bedroom for a moment, reemerged quickly, and rooted around the kitchen to scrounge up something to eat. One of her errands this afternoon would be to go to the grocery store to restock the fridge and pantry.

Linda was at the sink, staring out of the kitchen window at Rand unloading the rest of the things from the car. Cynthia came into the kitchen and hugged her mom. Linda turned to face Cynthia and saw tears running down her cheeks.

"What is it, honey?" Linda asked. "It will be okay. You'll see."

Cynthia's medication was wearing off, and she was slowly filling with apprehension and disappointment.

She whispered to her mother, "Mom, I'm so sorry I'm putting you, Dad, and especially Lexi through this. I want to feel normal again. I really do! It's been so long since I remember what happiness feels like. I'm so scared that I never will again. I'm so sorry."

She buried her head in her mother's shoulder. Linda began to cry too, hugging her daughter and telling her that she and Rand would do whatever it took for her to find joy again. And they would do the same for Lexi.

"Your father and I have been around the block a couple of times. Don't worry, you will find your joy in Asheville, and we'll help Lexi heal too, I promise. We have a plan. All you need to think about is getting better."

Linda made sandwiches and split pea soup. Rand loved split pea soup and wasted no time making his way to the kitchen table. Linda went to the back bedroom to ask Lexi to come have dinner. Lexi yelled aloud that she was on her iPad and not hungry anyway. Linda asked her again, this time telling her they would walk down to the stables after dinner.

Lexi texted goodbye to Jennifer and opened the door. She did not feel like eating, but she wanted to see the horses. She had not seen Champ and Pony Girl in a year, but her memories were good ones. Every time she came to visit, PopPop would take her to the stables, where she would help feed, clean, and walk the horses. She loved caring for them and riding even if she rode like a beginner. She remembered being afraid of Champ because he was so big, and she was younger and smaller the last time she saw them.

In the past, Lexi was more comfortable around the smaller Pony Girl. Lexi loved Pony Girl's white coat with black-and-brown patches. Pony Girl was smaller than Champ, but she had more spirit and agility. She was MomMom's horse, and Lexi remembered that they seemed almost majestic as a rider and her mount.

Lexi came out, sat at the dinner table, and attacked the soup. It was one tiny victory in the long recovery process but a good victory seeing Lexi forget her sadness for a minute and eat something. Linda and Rand had a plan to improve their granddaughter's frame of mind. Rand was an old soldier and a man's man. He could be intolerant and gruff sometimes, but Linda let him know that there would be no situation with Lexi when he would need to be like that. Rand promised that he would treat Lexi and Cynthia like injured birds in his hands.

He and Linda agreed that it was impossible for them to understand all the emotions and pain that Cynthia and Lexi were suffering through. However, they could tell that their trauma was unbearable enough, and they had no intention of compounding their problems with tough love. His and Linda's meeting of the minds reminded Rand how much he loved and depended on his wife for her exceptional guidance in these matters. Sometimes, her guidance held him back from doing something he wanted to do, but he always heeded it. He thought that she was so wise and that she made him a better person.

They finished their dinner, and Rand suggested that they take a walk to the stables and greet the horses with treats. He figured that everyone could use the fresh air. The stables were only a hundred yards down the tree-lined dirt lane with fenced paddocks on both sides. Sometimes, Rand's morning walk to the stables with a good cup of coffee was the best part of his day. Cynthia was exhausted from the drive and her angst about going to Pisgah, but she felt the tiniest glint of joy seeing Lexi's eyes light up at the mention of the horses. Cynthia's demons kept trying to darken any specks of optimism, but she fought back and let hope in. It was a baby step forward.

Linda seized the moment and told everyone to leave the dishes where they lay. She grabbed apples.

"Let's go, girls. Those horses know we are home, and they won't wait much longer."

The stroll down the path in the fading afternoon light was calming. All four people took in the rural, earthy air of the Sandhills horse country. Lexi said that she remembered the smell. When they walked into the stables, Champ and Pony Girl both stuck their heads out of their stalls to see who was coming. The horses thrust their heads up and down in excitement, having smelled Rand and Linda.

Pony Girl's eyes grew wide with suspicion and her ears folded back seeing the unfamiliar young person come toward her. Lexi slowly brought her palm up to Pony Girl's nose. She timidly sniffed and then licked Lexi's hand. Pony Girl's ears relaxed as she remembered Lexi's scent.

"She remembers me!" Lexi said.

Rand said, "Of course she does. Horses can remember people years later. She is incredibly happy to see you too. Look at how she is moving around with joy. She wants your apple."

Lexi held the apple in her palm as Pony Girl lipped it and took a huge bite. She chomped on the apple until it was completed gone. Then she licked Lexi's hand.

Rand handed an apple to Cynthia and looked at Champ.

"He wants one too."

Cynthia slowly moved her hand up to the larger horse, letting him smell her. He remembered Cynthia too and eagerly took the apple from her palm. Lexi had unknowingly backed up against the upper opening of Pony Girl's stall door while watching her mother feed Champ. Pony Girl came forward, sticking her head out of her stall, and rubbed her face against Lexi's cheek, touching gently. Lexi's wide smile said it all.

"Yeah, I think she remembers you pretty good," Rand said.

Lexi's eyes teared up.

Rand and Cynthia went into Champ's stall to clean and refresh everything while Linda and Lexi did the same for Pony Girl. They cleaned the old bedding and manure from the floor, replenished the bedding, brought in hay and oats in the hanging buckets, and filled the water bucket.

Lexi grabbed a hand brush and began grooming Pony Girl's back and flank. She remembered how to clean hooves with the hoof pick. Pony Girl stood calmly while Lexi, facing backward, straddled each one of Pony Girl's legs one at a time and drew the hoof up between her legs to pick out the matted straw, stones, and manure.

Pony Girl bent each leg at the knee easily to allow the cleaning. She enjoyed the attention.

Rand asked Lexi from across the stables if she remembered how to put on the halter. Lexi grabbed the halter off the wall, looked to her grandmother for guidance, and then put it on Pony Girl as if she had done it a hundred times before.

"Okay!" said Rand. "Let's lead them out to the paddock so they can graze for a little while we still have some daylight left."

Lexi nodded. Cynthia led Champ and Lexi led Pony Girl through the center of the stables and out to the fenced enclosure. They released the halters, and the horses knew what to do.

They had been in the fresh country air of Vass for less than two hours, and Rand was already feeling better than he had in a week. For at least the last twenty minutes, his daughter and granddaughter did not hate life. The four of them walked back to the house. Rand and Linda shared a look. A thousand thoughts were going through their heads in that five-minute walk, but not one word was spoken. The silence was all there was, and it spoke volumes.

From that day forward, Lexi got up eagerly every morning with her grandfather to tend to the horses. She liked this early-morning ritual far better than their walks around the neighborhood in Occoquan, and she was also reestablishing her relationship with the horses. Pony Girl accepted her and was even excited when Lexi entered the stables. In no time, Pony Girl was nudging Lexi for oats and hay. Rand watched the interaction between his granddaughter and the mare. He liked what he saw and told her that by next week, they would try riding. Lexi smiled widely at the idea.

Off to Asheville

The day had arrived to take Cynthia to Pisgah Wellness Center in Asheville. Knowing the day was coming, Cynthia's anxiety and depression had taken hold of her, and she was quietly apprehensive. With a little coaxing, Cynthia confided to her mother that she was afraid of going to a strange place in the mountains of North Carolina for an unspecified amount of time, unable to come home. The unknowns were too overwhelming. Rand and Linda tried to assure her that she could come home anytime she wanted.

Cynthia was aware that her depression was mostly because of her husband's death, but part of it was also because of her damaged relationship with Lexi and her lack of trying. Cynthia had been too lost in her despair to be able to have a conversation with Lexi, and Lexi was too angry and emotionally immature to accept her mother's appeals for consolation or peace offerings. The two women were stuck in a mental trench warfare, unaware that they were both in the same trench.

By midmorning, everything was packed in the car. Cynthia took her place in the front passenger seat while Linda sat in the back with Lexi. Within five miles on the interstate, Lexi was hooked up to her earbuds on her iPhone. Linda had hoped to have three hours to chitchat with her granddaughter in the back seat, but seeing Lexi plugged in and tuned out dashed all hopes of a conversation. After an hour, Rand was the only one awake in the car.

Two hours later, the mountains rose on the horizon as the car neared its destination. Rand glanced over at his cell phone navigation to ensure he would not miss the exit for Pisgah Wellness Center in Asheville. He was still unfamiliar with the apps on his phone, but he was learning. His app showed that they were five miles from the treatment center. The staff at Pisgah was not expecting Cynthia for another hour, and it was almost lunchtime, so Rand pulled into a fast-food restaurant.

All three women woke up when the car stopped. Linda appreciated the stop so she could use the restroom, eat, and enjoy a little more time with Cynthia. They went inside.

"It's just five miles up the road," Rand announced. "Isn't it pretty up here?" he asked rhetorically.

The women were either still sleepy or not talkative, but conversation was not on the menu. Finally, Linda asked Cynthia if she was feeling all right. Cynthia nodded in a half-hearted attempt to end the probing.

Cynthia looked at Lexi.

"Are you okay, sweetie?"

Lexi responded with her usual sarcasm.

"Why wouldn't I be?"

With just five words, Lexi snapped another extended olive branch and shut out her mother. Cynthia heaved a heavy sigh and frowned. Rand heard Lexi snap at her mother and stared disappointedly out at the mountains.

An hour later, they got back in the car and pressed ahead. Rand and Cynthia could see the sprawling brick structures of the facility nestled in a hillside from half a mile away. The car pulled up to a wrought iron ornamental gate and ivy-laden rock border wall. First impressions were good judging by the oohs and aahs loudly whispered in the car.

The outside of the facility looked like an exclusive spa retreat. People were strolling around the perfectly manicured shrubs and flower gardens. Others were sunning themselves or reading on the largest deck Rand had ever seen. He guessed it to be over one hundred feet long and forty feet high overlooking a forested valley below.

The iron gate opened automatically. Rand drove the car around the circular driveway, stopping at the large marble front entrance, where a woman awaited them. She was in casual office clothes and held a clipboard in her hand.

When everyone got out of the car, the woman extended her hand to Cynthia.

"Good afternoon, Cynthia. I am Mrs. Brathman. Welcome to Pisgah Wellness Center! And who else do we have the pleasure of meeting today?"

Cynthia looked at Linda standing next to her.

"This is my mother, Linda Templeton"—she pointed over to Lexi—"my daughter, Lexi, and my father, Randall Templeton."

Brathman welcomed them and suggested that they come in and enjoy refreshments after the drive. She led them up the stairs into a grand lobby and then into a well-appointed reception area with a table setting for six. A buffet table against the wall had coffee, soda, juice, fruit, assorted cheeses, energy bars, and other hors d'oeuvres. Linda was impressed. Mrs. Brathman invited everyone to help themselves to the refreshments. She told them that when they were ready, she would take the family on a tour of the facility, and then Dr. Morrell would join them for a discussion.

The selection of appetizers caught Lexi's attention so much that she disengaged from her phone, sat at the table, and sampled. Rand and Linda helped themselves to ice water. Mrs. Brathman tried to engage Cynthia in small talk. She started by asking Cynthia to call her Carole. Cynthia reluctantly chatted about the drive from Vass and her first impression of the facility. Rand and Linda listened in but suspected that the conversation was to gauge Cynthia's mental state and give Brathman insight into her feelings about being there.

Afterward, Brathman took the group on a tour of the facility, the amenities, and the services. They walked through the main building, crafted with hand-carved moldings and woodwork. The furnishings were beautiful and inviting. Linda noticed that even the colors and lighting were carefully thought out. Brathman showed them different dining rooms. One large dining room looked like a fancy food court with three different food options. Two other dining rooms had small tables, cushioned chairs, elegant settings, and subdued lighting. She said that both types of dining were available every day to suit a guest's mood, or guests might eat in their rooms.

They continued their tour of the gym, the yoga studio, the spa with massage rooms, a small, well-stocked library, and conference rooms. Brathman mentioned that counseling sessions took place in the conference rooms in group settings or one-on-one sessions depending on what the guest and doctor decided. Outside, Brathman pointed out a pool, a Jacuzzi, tennis courts, a basketball court, a volleyball court, a smoking garden, and smaller flower gardens for meditation.

The group walked along a path through a flower garden that looked over the valley below. Brathman was mentioning the restorative air of the Carolina mountains when a woman approached and introduced herself.

"Good afternoon, everyone. I hope I'm not intruding on a memorable, private moment. I am Dr. Lisa Morrell."

Dr. Morrell was in a business suit. Lexi noticed that she had a smile that could light up a room and the greenest eyes she had ever seen. Dr. Morrell appeared to be about the same age as Cynthia and had an ease about her that was completely disarming.

The doctor extended her hand.

"Cynthia? I have been looking forward to meeting you."

Cynthia forced a smile and introduced her family.

Dr. Morrell shook hands with Rand and Linda and then with a huge smile said, "And this beautiful young lady must be Lexi. It is so wonderful to meet you. Before the day is over, I'm going to give you my card with my personal cell phone number on it. I want you to keep my number in a special place, and I want you to call me day or night if you need to talk to someone about anything, anything at all. Would you do that for me?"

Lexi took the business card and did not know how to respond. It sounded like something one would say disingenuously to a child, but Lexi also heard sincerity in Morrell's voice. She was thrown off her game by a stranger giving off so much positive and loving energy, and it opened a crack in Lexi's wall of defense.

"Let's all go in and talk about the next step, shall we?" Dr. Morrell said as she gestured the group back to the main building.

They arrived at a small conference room, where Dr. Morrell asked Cynthia if she wanted to talk in private or if she wanted her family with her. Cynthia opted for her family, and Morrell was fine either way. Everyone sat in a family room setting, facing one another.

Dr. Morrell opened her folder and scanned through paperwork briefly. Everything from then on was directed at Cynthia. Morrell explained that she had read through Cynthia's medical record from her recent psychiatric care in Virginia. She was aware of Tom's death and the resulting disharmony at home. Dr. Morrell explained that Cynthia's fragile mental health was completely normal given the trauma she had been through.

She continued.

"I believe we can help you recover and become the person you were before your loss or the person you want to be. I do not know how long it will take. That is up to you. However, I want to help if you will let me."

Cynthia nodded. Dr. Morrell continued.

"Let me tell you how we do things here. I will meet with you privately the first week to develop a treatment plan. Typically, patients' mental wellness improves through scheduled one-on-one appointments, medicinal and/or cognitive therapies, group discussions, and relaxation techniques.

"I want to emphasize our philosophy: patients are our guests. You have the right to decline any treatment we suggest or offer. You have the right to leave at any time. You may use our phones, our amenities, or facilities any time you like. You may lock your door from the inside. We cannot lock you in.

"Cynthia, everything about your treatment is up to you. If you choose to go downtown to Asheville, you may call an Uber or cab or one of our scheduled shuttles. We do suggest that you do not go alone, but again, it is up to you. If at any time you feel like you are well enough and want to go home, you may. We might recommend more time depending on your progress, but everything about Pisgah Wellness Center is voluntary. However, we will ask you to leave if we find that you are using illegal drugs, abusing alcohol, or if you are disruptive to other guests. Our biggest requirements are that you respect other guests and that you allow us to help you. Can you agree to our terms?"

Dr. Morrell looked at Cynthia, waiting for an answer. Cynthia nodded tentatively.

Morrell looked at Lexi.

"Does that sound like something you would like for your mom?"

Lexi shrugged, indifferent, and then nodded.

"Great! Cynthia, you and I are going to become great friends."

Dr. Morrell made eye contact with Linda and Rand for acknowledgment and then back at Cynthia.

"Let's go talk to our business managers about the financial aspects of your care."

The group went to another smaller building off to the side and gathered around a conference table. Each person took a seat, and then another professionally dressed woman entered the room with four packets. Linda's first impression was that this woman was highly organized. Rand noticed her wavy red hair. She passed packets to Cynthia, Linda, and Rand.

"Hello. I am Mrs. Strickland, the business manager here at Pisgah Wellness Center. It is a pleasure to meet you. Cynthia, congratulations on taking a big first step. Now that you agreed to allow us to help you in your journey, Dr. Morrell and I will be your and your family's points of contact for anything. Here is my business card, which includes my office number and cell phone number. I will take your calls 24-7, no matter what. Do you have any questions at this point?"

Rand and Linda looked at each other and then at Cynthia. Nothing came to mind.

"Good! Why don't you open your packets so that I may go over the programs and costs? Please stop me when you have a question."

The group reviewed the costs, payment options, treatment plans, and emergency procedures at the center. Mrs. Strickland asked again if there were any questions or concerns and if everything met their expectations.

Rand spoke up.

"It is a bit pricey, but I think we can manage. We still don't know how long Cynthia will be here?"

Mrs. Strickland glanced at Dr. Morrell.

"It will depend on Cynthia," she answered. "We will do our very best to help Cindy find her true self, but we first must figure out how and why she lost it, where it went, and if she wants to have it back. Only then can we estimate how long it might take."

"It's Cynthia," Lexi said.

"Oh, my sincere apologies, Lexi. Cynthia. Got it. Thank you."

Dr. Morrell smiled as she made a note on her pad.

"And you may call me Lisa," she offered.

The pause in conversation suggested that the meeting was over.

As they rose from their chairs, Dr. Morrell approached Cynthia and held her hand.

"I am so glad we met, Cynthia. I believe you will love it here if you give us a chance."

Everyone had a puzzled look. Dr. Morrell perceived that there was a misunderstanding. She turned to Cynthia once again to clarify.

"As I mentioned, everything at Pisgah Wellness is voluntary. You can go home and take time to consider what we offer. You may come back at any time, or you may begin your stay with us today. It is completely up to you. And if you stay today and change your mind tomorrow, you may leave."

Cynthia had barely uttered a word the entire day.

Finally, she said to Dr. Morrell, "I'd like to stay today. We brought my things."

Morrell told her how glad she was about the decision. She said that Mrs. Strickland would need her signature on forms and that a steward would retrieve her things from the car. Dr. Morrell turned to Rand, Linda, and Lexi, assuring them they were invited to stay with Cynthia while she got settled in her room. Or they could roam the complex for the afternoon. Rand said that they had a long drive home and that they would be leaving as soon as Cynthia got settled.

For the first time in a long time, Lexi felt sympathy for her mother. She realized that her mom would be here by herself for who knew how long. What if she did not get better? What would happen then? Would they treat her well?

But Lexi's sympathies were displaced quickly by her selfishness as she realized that she would be stuck alone at PopPop and MomMom's house for who knew how long. She began to panic. What was she going to do all day? Would she have to go to school? What would happen to her friends? Would the Internet work all the time?

Lexi let go of her anger toward her mom temporarily and replaced it with the hope that she would get well soon so they could get back to their lives again in Occoquan.

When Cynthia officially became a guest, Rand, Linda, and Lexi said their bittersweet goodbyes. Cynthia felt like it was a positive step, but she would miss her family. Linda and Rand felt the same way. Lexi gave her mom a brief hug but was thinking more about how this change would affect herself.

The quiet drive home in the afternoon lulled Lexi into an uneasy sleep in the back seat. Worries about her future crowded her mind. An hour into the drive, Lexi felt the car come to a stop. Rand had pulled into a restaurant known for its wholesome country cooking. Lexi decided that she was hungry anyway and needed a bathroom break.

They sat at a window booth looking out into the countryside. The twilight sky was full of pink-and-red hues, but its beauty did not lift Lexi's spirits. A darkness was sneaking up on her, causing her to feel lonely, and her emotional roller-coaster ride was exhausting.

A New Beginning?

They ordered their food, and Lexi played a game at the table. Rand began explaining how her new life was going to be. Linda added important details when needed. Their solidarity in this decision left Lexi without options.

Rand started by explaining that they did not know how long her mom would be in Asheville for treatment, and Lexi could not sit idle indefinitely at the house. So on Monday, they would go to Union Pines High School and enroll her. Lexi listened, trying to take it all in. Rand then said she would help him with the horses every day before and after school.

Her power was gone; she had no choices. She felt like a hostage, but in resignation and clarity, she nodded. Lexi had already come to the reality that she could not miss too much school when her tenth-grade year began, and although she was hoping it would be at Woodbridge in Virginia, she acknowledged that she could not live by herself in Occoquan. She needed her grandparents for support even if it felt like she was caught between house arrest and self-exile.

What she didn't know was that she also needed them for emotional healing. The silver lining was that she enjoyed spending time with the horses even if the early-morning hours would be an adjustment. The rest of the drive home was in the dark and in silence.

An Adjustment at the Horse Farm

The first week at the Templeton farm was peaceful. When Lexi was not at the stables, caring for Champ and Pony Girl, she was in her room, texting Jennifer and Amy, or she was on social media.

Her grandparents tried several times to entice her out on the porch in the evenings for sweet tea and conversation, but she was adjusting to her new environment and needing to stay connected to her world. The horse farm had Internet, but her grandparents' cable TV channels were very limited. Lexi was not ungrateful, but she had hoped for something more like her connectivity back home; this was not it.

Lexi spent the summer taking care of the horses, relearning how to ride, adjusting to her grandparents' ways of doing things, and learning to live at a slower pace than in Virginia. She also was occasionally treated to shopping trips, outdoor music events, and days at the Pinehurst pool to work on her tan. Lexi did not want to admit to her grandparents or herself that her summer in Vass was not the worst summer she ever had, but she confided online to her friends back home that life down south was not as bad as she imagined it would be.

Back to School

The first week in September was the first week of the school year, and Lexi dreaded it. When the first day of school arrived and early-morning chores in the stables were done, Lexi got cleaned up and sluggishly got into the car with her grandparents to enroll in Union Pines High School.

The summer seemed to have flown by, and Lexi did not have a choice about going to school. She felt like one of the horses being led into a stall, except it was not her stall. The school could have been brand-new and made of gold; it would not have mattered to Lexi. She had already made up her mind that she would tolerate the temporary necessary arrangement. She had to be in school, but she did not have to like it.

She and her grandparents filled out the paperwork in the front office. Then they said their goodbyes, and Lexi was escorted to her first class. She hated the awkwardness of being the new student transferring into a new school, and being a sophomore made it even worse. Military kids transferred in more often than civilian kids, but it was never easy, especially in the middle of the school year.

The new kid was evaluated and judged the moment they entered the building. Were you cute? How did you dress? Were you smart? Were you athletic? Were you friendly? Were you shy? Were you a nerd? Where would you fall in the social pecking order? It was a universal truth in school.

Lexi followed her escort down the hall and watched him knock on the classroom door. He opened the door and introduced Lexi to the teacher. The teacher welcomed her in and, without any fanfare, asked her to take a seat. There were four empty desks available. Two or three students looked up at her, but most continued reading their assignment. It was not as awkward as she imagined. She was surprised.

At schools on military bases, new kids came and went all the time, and no one made a fuss. But this was Vass, North Carolina, so why didn't they react? Lexi did not know that Vass butted up against one of the largest army bases in the country, Fort Bragg, home of the Eighty-Second Airborne and Special Forces. Schools within a thirty-mile radius were used to military kids transferring in and out throughout the school year.

Within minutes, a girl sitting beside her whispered, "Hi. I'm Macy."

Lexi responded, "Lexi."

Macy continued.

"Did you just move here? Are you army?"

Lexi was not going to be here for more than a couple of months at most, so she was not about to give out too much personal information. She especially did not want people to know about her dad's death, her crazy mom, or that she was being held hostage on her grandparents' horse farm. She answered Macy, with convincing indifference, that her dad was a marine and that they were temporarily living in Vass. Macy said it was nice to meet her, and they would talk later if Lexi wanted to get the lay of the land.

Macy's chill attitude allowed Lexi to relax. For the time being at least, she had not set off any red flags about her completely dysfunctional life. Disarmed, Lexi judged Macy to be friendly, pretty, stylishly dressed, and studious by the way she was burning through pages in her book. She thought Macy was someone who would be a friend back in Occoquan. She continued to play it cool the rest of the day, but she welcomed Macy's friendly overtures.

When the bell rang for the next period, Macy asked Lexi about her next class. She pulled out her schedule.

"I have Algebra II with Higgins."

Macy said, "Oh, she's cool. Do you like math? I have her fourth period."

As Macy walked with Lexi through the hallways to Mrs. Higgins's class, two boys made eye contact with her and smiled. Lexi could not help but notice that everyone in Union Pines looked like the kids at her school in Occoquan. They dressed the same, they joked around in the hallways, and they huddled and gossiped. She overheard talk about upcoming sports events, clubs, and who liked whom. Everyone even had cell phones and using them in the hallways. At her old school, students were not allowed to use cell phones during school. She had imagined everyone would be less, well, metropolitan.

By the end of her first day, Lexi figured out that students in North Carolina were not very different at all. By the end of her first week, however, she was seeing one difference. The students here were less intimidating toward one another. There was more cohesiveness. It was not nearly as horrible as she wanted it to be. Lexi did not want to concede that she could get used to it and that it was tolerable for a little while.

Every day after school, Rand and Linda asked Lexi about homework. Rand asked because he wanted to know how long it would be before he and she could tend to the horses. Linda wanted to know so she could plan for dinner. Lexi started out spending her first half hour unwinding by texting Jennifer, Amy, and others to learn what was happening back home before doing her homework. Her grandparents were not happy about her priorities, but they decided not to push too hard while she was adjusting. Unwinding was reasonable. She was doing her homework every night, so they left it alone.

As soon as Lexi finished homework, Rand headed out the door to the stables, expecting Lexi to be right behind him. She was and would go right in and clean the stalls, fork out the manure, lay in fresh bedding and hay, and fill the water buckets. Rand recertified her on checking the horses' hooves by gently bending each horse's leg at the knee, face away from the horse, and pull the leg up to clean out around the frog of the hoof with a pick, check their shoes, and look for any separation between the sole and the wall. Lexi would remove all the caked debris in each hoof. He told her that she did everything right. The horses liked the attention, especially since they got a brushing too.

They filled the feed buckets with oats, and the wall feeder racks with hay. At first, Rand told Lexi to be cautious, because the horses got aggressive when the food was laid in, but he was proud of her when she pushed back the first time, letting the horses know she was there and unafraid. Lexi respected the horses' size and power, but she was kind and firm with them. They responded to her as if they knew her or because they could sense she was serious. After feeding, she let the horses go out into the paddock to graze. Around sunset, Rand, Linda, or Lexi would go out one last time and lead the horses back into their stalls for the night. Lexi learned quickly that the horses needed nearly constant care and feeding.

Linda would call Cynthia twice a week at Pisgah to check on her progress. She would ask the same questions.

"How are you doing? How are you feeling? Are you making any progress? What are the doctors telling you? What kind of treatment are you undergoing?"

Cynthia found the phone calls repetitive since she had little news to report. Occasionally, she would tell her mother about group therapy and other patients' problems. Lexi would overhear the conversations and be uninterested. Rand would talk briefly, and then Linda would put Lexi on the phone. Cynthia always wanted to talk with Lexi, but when she asked about school or how she was doing, Lexi would have little to say. Cynthia told her that she was feeling hopeful about the treatment and her prognosis.

Lexi said, "That's great, Mom, really. I gotta go."

Lexi would go back to whatever she was doing and let out a groan. She felt like it was the same annoying conversation every time. Linda tried to hide her disappointment in her granddaughter's lack of empathy, but it got more difficult each time.

After the first two weeks, Linda stopped calling Cynthia as often. She wanted to give her daughter a little space and give Lexi time to reflect. Linda expressed to Rand how disappointed she was with the way Lexi talked to her mother.

Rand echoed the same sentiment, asking Linda what they should do. She was going to give Lexi a little more time to see the positive side of things, and then she was going to point them out. Linda's tone got Rand's attention, because he never wanted to be on the receiving end of it.

A Trail Ride and Regrets

Lexi woke up promptly at 6:00 a.m. on Saturday to take care of Champ and Pony Girl. Rand was already sipping his coffee at the kitchen table, waiting for her. She noticed he had riding boots on instead of his work boots.

"Where are you going, PopPop?" she asked.

"You'll find out after we do our morning chores. I want you to wear jeans and comfortable footwear," he said.

Lexi was suspicious—not because her grandfather had ever misled her but because she still was holding on to her anger.

When they finished cleaning the stalls and grooming the horses, Rand led Champ out of his stall. Lexi watched. He went into the storeroom, brought out a saddle pad, and laid it across Champ's back. He went back in the storeroom and brought out a saddle. He threw the saddle on Champ, all the while explaining each step as he was doing it.

"Do you remember this from when you were younger?"

She shrugged nervously.

"I kinda do, but it was more than a year ago."

He ignored her nonanswer. Champ was saddled up and stomped excitedly, ready to ride.

"Well, as you can you see, Champ is ready, and I think Pony Girl is waiting on you."

"PopPop!" she exclaimed. "I don't know if I can."

"Go get her saddle pad," he said firmly.

Lexi let out a disgruntled "Ugh!" and went to the storeroom. She brought out a saddle pad.

"Now put it on her back up to her withers. Good! Now you need a saddle."

Lexi raised an eyebrow at his sarcasm.

Rand offered, "Well, if you act like you don't know, I'm going to assume that you don't."

She stomped into the storeroom and struggled with the heavy saddle.

"Now take the left stirrup and put it on the horn. Heave the saddle on Pony Girl's back."

Lexi followed his instructions.

"Reach under and pull the girth strap. Good! Cinch the strap."

He came over and showed her how to secure the saddle and drop the stirrup. Pony Girl was excited.

"Now make sure the bridle is right and the bit is in her mouth."

Lexi checked everything.

"Okay," he said. "She is ready to ride."

Lexi looked to Rand for what to do next.

He asked, "Are you going to mount up?"

"PopPop!" she protested again. "I have not done this for so long!"

He ordered her, "Mount your horse!"

Lexi grabbed the saddle horn, placed her left foot in the stirrup, and was about to mount up. Rand stopped her.

"Hold on. Get a helmet from the storeroom."

Lexi shook her head. She wasn't even sure she could do this, and her grandfather was worrying about a helmet. She came back out with her helmet and an attitude, and then she mounted Pony Girl.

When he saw that Lexi was securely in the saddle, Rand pulled Champ's reins to one side and applied pressure with his knee. Champ understood to turn and walk. Lexi did the same thing to Pony Girl. Surprisingly, she remembered the feeling in the saddle. Pony Girl moved in behind Champ. Grandfather and granddaughter were heading out to the equestrian trails for a morning ride. Rand was proud of her for overcoming her fear. Lexi smiled too because of the feeling she had not felt in a while—accomplishment.

The horses kept a slow, gentle pace under the shade of the pine trees, with only the subtlest sound coming from the occasional hawk flying above and the pine straw under the horse's hooves. Rand and

Lexi kept silent, neither one wanting to ruin the tranquility of the morning. There was an easiness to it. The fresh air and earthiness began to nip away at the jagged edges of Lexi's malignant anger.

Half an hour later, they arrived at a grassy meadow bathed in early-morning sunshine. Lexi looked up and squinted, letting the sun warm her face.

"PopPop, this feels nice. Pony Girl likes it too."

He patted Champ on the neck, saying that Champ agreed. The big horse lowered his head to sniff and pull at the grass shoots.

Then unexpectedly, Lexi asked, "PopPop, do adults regret their mistakes, or do they just rationalize and justify their actions?"

Rand wrinkled his forehead and turned down the corners of his mouth. He was taken aback by the complexity of her question, wondering if he should try to answer her or ask first why she wanted to know. He was walking a tightrope between earning her trust, getting her to drop her guard, being a parent, and setting boundaries; there were so many land mines.

He answered, "Well, honey, let me tell you what I think. I don't want to lose you in my answer, but there are so many things to first consider."

Her gaze moved away from him and to her surroundings while she listened.

He started laying the groundwork by saying, "Anything that I tell you is my opinion unless I can quote an expert or cite data. My opinion may or may not be the right answer even though it comes from years of experience consisting of millions of moments of listening, seeing, smelling, feeling, and tasting that are mine alone. No two people have the exact same experiences, because even if those two people are standing beside one another, they would have slightly different observations and perspective. And those moments have an impact on how we see things from then on. Do you understand?"

"I think so, PopPop. You are saying that your experiences over the years are uniquely yours. And even if I were standing right next to you the whole time, I would have a slightly distinct and different perspective based on my viewpoint and past experiences?"

"Exactly! You said it better than I did," he said, smiling at her precise comprehension.

"So to the point of your question, yes, adults can regret their mistakes. I have done things that I regret. People say you should never have regrets, but I think if you don't have regrets, then you are not learning, changing, or growing. I have said things that I didn't think about at the time but came to regret them later. I've done things too."

Rand turned to her.

"Can I ask you a question?"

Lexi nodded.

"Why do you ask?"

She thought for a moment before answering. She had a specific thing on her mind, but she was searching for a way to explain it in generic terms. Rand sensed that she was not ready to share.

She said finally, "I was just wondering if when you become an adult and take on all the stresses of life, do people take the time to reflect on the past?"

Rand was very impressed with her ability to verbalize her thought. It was time to turn back home, and he didn't want to get any deeper into the subject matter.

He replied, "Well, honey, one thing I know for sure is that some mistakes won't let you forget."

With that, he applied a tiny bit of knee pressure to Champ and gently pulled the reins, and the horse moved. Pony Girl followed. He would have loved to know what was going on in his granddaughter's mind, but he let the serenity of the walk home allow her time to process his answers.

When they got home and finished with the horses, Linda had a delicious breakfast waiting for them. She asked Lexi how the ride went, wondering if Rand was able to engage her in any kind of conversation. At least that was what she asked him to do.

"It was nice. Pony Girl enjoyed it. I think she likes me, although she probably was waiting for you. Anyway, the morning was quiet and peaceful, and the pine forest was pretty. I hope we can do it again."

Linda said, "Oh, I'm certain we can work something out."

She winked at Rand.

"And Pony Girl seems to like you as much as me, so I wouldn't worry about that. She likes a little less weight on her too."

She smiled at Lexi.

"MomMom, I think you are in great shape. I bet we weigh about the same."

Linda smiled.

"That is something we will never know, dear."

Rand was listening indirectly but was more focused on his eggs, sausage, and biscuits with gravy. He was smiling from ear to ear because he loved weekend morning breakfast.

Linda brought up that they were going to Pinehurst today to visit with Aryana and Rashne. It had been too long since they had seen them, but the Samadanis knew that Rand and Linda were preoccupied with family issues. Rand and Rashne had a midmorning tee time, so Linda and Aryana were taking Lexi shopping in the village.

After breakfast and cleanup, they drove to the village of Pinehurst. Lexi had been to the Samadanis' house once before, but she didn't remember it being so grand. She especially admired the soft and silky Persian rugs, which changed colors from different directions. Aryana saw Lexi admiring the rug in the foyer, so she explained how each rug was handmade by craftsmen using the finest silk and that it was a skill handed down over many generations.

Everyone entered the dining room, where Aryana had prepared a buffet. She apologized that it was just snacks for brunch but said that when Rashne and Rand returned from golf, they would have kebab, lamb, sabzi khordan, torshi, saffron rice, and Rand's favorite, tahdig, for dinner. Rand's eyes grew wide. He loved Aryana's cooking.

The two men took off in the golf cart to Pinehurst Country Club, and the women took another cart to the village center. Their first stop was Tufts Park to pick up things at the farmer's market. Then they went to the Roast Office for coffee and book browsing and then into the other shops. Their afternoon was spontaneous and exciting but relaxing as well.

Lexi was checking her phone every half hour out of habit, but she seemed more interested in absorbing the sights and sounds of her new environment rather than everyone else's life on social media. Linda saw it as a sign of progress. She hoped that Aryana's personality, combined with the village's charm, might help Lexi forget her bitterness even if it was just for an afternoon. It seemed to be working. The only other thing Linda hoped for would be for Lexi to want to talk to her mother tonight. She thought better than to mention it and risk spoiling the day.

Late in the afternoon, everyone came back together to enjoy a wonderful meal. Aryana's cooking did not disappoint. The lamb and kebab were grilled to perfection. All the other dishes and drinks were delicious. Aryana's daughter and son-in-law came too, and the group shared stories and laughed long into the evening. Lexi could not remember the last time she had such a happy time with family during a meal.

When they got back to Vass, it was almost 10:00 p.m., but Linda said that she was going to phone Cynthia. She was not talking specifically to anybody, but she hoped that Lexi might react. When she did not, Linda asked her if she wanted to say hello to her mother. Lexi hesitated and then said she would say hello when their conversation was done. Linda was not going to push the issue, but this was another small step in the right direction.

Linda talked with Cynthia for fifteen minutes, and then she asked for Lexi. Linda held out the phone.

"Your mother would like to hear your voice."

Lexi came over to the phone, took it, and went back to the recliner.

"Hi, Mom. How are you feeling? Do you think the doctors are helping you?"

These were more words than Lexi had said to her mother in a month. Cynthia started to cry at the other end.

"Mom, why are you crying?" Lexi asked, annoyed.

"I just miss you," Cynthia said. "Can't a mother miss her daughter?"

Cynthia wanted to tell Lexi about the things she was learning in therapy, but she worried that Lexi was teetering on top of a wall and could fall on either side. Cynthia did not want to push.

Lexi responded, "Yeah, I get it. I miss people too."

Cynthia felt the indirect jab.

"How was your second week at school?"

Lexi was tired of the conversation, not wanting to give her mom too much satisfaction.

She said, "It's fine, but it's not home. I gotta go."

She handed the phone back to her grandmother and went upstairs. It was enough for Cynthia to feel hopeful.

Linda came back on the phone.

"Baby steps, honey, baby steps. I will call you later this week. Take care. Love you."

Rand had overheard the conversation and shrugged in disappointment.

First Friday Spiking

Back at school on Monday, Lexi and Macy joined a group of Macy's friends at their usual lunch table. Two or three conversations were going on at once until one of the girls mentioned Trey, and then the table became quiet.

Becca whispered loudly to everyone that her boyfriend, Mitch, who was best friends with Trey, told her that Trey thought Lexi was cute. He wanted to know if she was going to be at Southern Pines's First Friday. All eyes turned to Lexi.

"What's First Friday?" Lexi asked, feigning disinterest.

Becca blurted out, "Girl, on the first Friday of every month from May to October, the town of Southern Pines closes off Broad Street to cars. And then they host bands, food trucks, and the shops stay open. People come down to hang out, including cute guys. We like to hang out around the music and then get ice cream. It's sick! We'll show you!"

Lexi shook her head.

"You have to!" Macy repeated.

Lexi admitted, "I don't think my grandparents go to things like that."

"That's even better!" Macy said. "My mom will drive us down there."

"I don't know," Lexi said.

Lexi asked her grandparents that night at dinner if she could go to First Friday with Macy. Linda thought it was a great idea. Rand wanted to think it over. Later that night, Linda talked to Rand about allowing her to go, convincing him that it was a chance for her to meet new friends and get a good impression of Southern Pines. It seemed like a safe, police-attended environment. Rand told Lexi she could go if he could talk to Macy's mom about it. Linda had already given her permission, so Rand's request was more of a courtesy than permission. Lexi was surprised and excited.

The school week was a blur to Lexi because of the anticipation of hanging out with new friends on Friday night. Once she found out who Trey was, she caught him looking at her in the hallways. His friends would nudge him every time she passed by, thinking they were being discreet.

On Thursday, Mitch and Trey were talking to Becca at her locker when Lexi walked by. Becca called her over and introduced them.

Trey smiled, saying, "I hear you are going to First Friday. Maybe we can hang out."

Lexi smiled.

"Sure. I'll be there with Becca and Macy. Should be fun."

Walking away to her next class, Lexi thought about how cute he was up close, and nice too. Her excitement about Friday night intensified.

During dinner on Thursday night, Rand dropped a bomb on Lexi. He announced that he and Linda were going to First Friday too. Lexi's eyes grew huge with disbelief. She pleaded with them not to go, saying that her arrangements had already been made.

Linda heard disappointment in Lexi's voice. She interrupted.

"Honey, nothing has changed. You can still go with Macy. Your grandfather and I just decided that we might like to go too, with our friends. So Aryana and Rashne will meet us there. We won't bother you. You don't have to acknowledge us. You probably won't even see us."

Lexi's hissy fit subsided.

"You won't linger around and try to find me?" she asked.

"No, dear. Believe it or not, we were young once, and we know what it's like to want to socialize. The only thing is that if something happens and you need us, we won't be far. Will fifty dollars be enough for you to enjoy yourself?"

Lexi liked the generous cash amount, and she was okay with them being there if they did not stalk her. She appreciated her grandparents' understanding too, and she confessed to herself that having them nearby for emergencies was not the worst idea she had ever heard.

Macy and her mom came by the house to get Lexi on Friday at 6:00 p.m. They came in to meet Linda and Rand. Lexi pointed out to Macy the stables and paddock behind the house. Macy said she loved horses and asked if she could ride sometime.

Lexi answered, "Well, I'm not much of a rider yet, not like my grandparents. The horses belong to them, so maybe we can check with them when the time comes."

"Cool!" Macy said.

Linda and Rand chatted briefly with Mrs. Radcliff, and then the girls were off.

They pulled into a parking spot on one of the side streets off Broad Street. Macy said goodbye to her mom, and the girls walked off into the crowd. Four food trucks, two beer trucks, and a wine truck were parked near the train station across from the band pavilion. A country band from Charlotte was playing, and the crowd was thick at the pavilion. Everyone was having a great time.

Macy and Lexi met up with Becca, Trish, and Lakeisha near the food trucks. The three already had soft drinks from the movie theater. Trey spotted them and walked over with Mitch, Darryl, and an older couple. Mitch introduced his older brother, Jake, and his girlfriend, Diane. They greeted everyone and said that they would be walking around.

Macy whispered to Becca that Jake's girlfriend was beautiful.

"I know, right? I want to look like that when I graduate from college. I think they are engaged," Becca said.

Lexi was taking in all the sights and sounds. Trey came over to her and started talking about school, asking how she came to be at Union Pines. She didn't want to share too much, so she told him that she was staying with her grandparents while her mom had to take care of some business in Asheville. Trey motioned for her to follow him up toward the stage. They made their way through the crowd.

Trey was seventeen, but Lexi was only fifteen and new at the nuances of navigating a relationship. The physical attraction was there, but getting to know the real person was much more subtle and complex. They both were on their best behavior, trying to camouflage their less-attractive characteristics.

Instinctively, Lexi began to sway and move her arms to the music. Trey began moving with her as if they were dancing together. He had zero rhythm and was out of his comfort zone, but Lexi smiled at his trying. By the next two songs, their dancing progressed into body parts brushing against each other and hands touching. Trey got very close. He liked her and wanted to kiss her. His face got even closer to hers. Lexi liked him, and she hoped he might try for a kiss.

The rest of their friends looked around and found Lexi and Trey dancing on the grass near the stage. Becca gave Lexi a look that said, "Sparks flying!" Lexi shot back a look that said, "Don't embarrass me!" Macy and Lakeisha picked up on it too. The girls huddled together and squealed.

An hour later, Jake and Diane rejoined the younger group to hang out with his brother, Mitch. Dusk turned into night, and Mitch brought over a tray of sodas for the group. The crowd was packed tightly enough to give Jake just enough privacy to pour bourbon into the sodas. Lexi took a sip of hers and asked what kind of soda it was. Mitch laughed, saying that it was a North Carolina brand made with real sugar.

The group meandered their way to the knee-high brick wall at the train station, where everyone sat. Trey bought hot dogs for him and Lexi. They talked, shared stories, and laughed. Before the night was over, he noticed that she was laughing a little more easily and acting silly. Trey didn't know about Mitch's brother spiking the sodas until he sipped his own. When Trey asked Mitch about it, he said that his brother wanted to see how the new girl could hold her liquor. Trey was annoyed because it was mean and made him look bad.

A little while later, Mrs. Radcliff texted Macy that it was time to go. Macy showed the text to Lexi, who turned and asked Trey if he was going to kiss her good night. He was surprised and gave her a kiss, saying that he would see her on Monday.

As soon as the girls were in the car, Mrs. Radcliff could smell the liquor on their breath. She gave Macy an angry look of disappointment. Her look also meant that they would have a talk when they got home. Mrs. Radcliff asked Lexi to find out if her grandparents were still in Southern Pines or if they had gone home. Lexi texted them and said they had just left.

When Mrs. Radcliff pulled up to the farmhouse, Lexi got out of her car and thanked her for the ride, slightly slurring her words. She was surprised when Mrs. Radcliff walked with her to the front door.

"Oh, you want to come in too?" Lexi asked.

"Yes, dear. I just need to talk to your grandparents for a second."

Lexi walked in the door and declared that she was going to bed. Mrs. Radcliff chatted with Rand and Linda.

*****

Lexi vaguely felt something tugging at her leg. She made incomprehensible noises and pulled the sheet over her head. The tugging continued. She finally stirred enough to recognize that a hand was grabbing her. She was awakening with a sour stomach and a headache, realizing that her grandfather was rousting her out of bed for Saturday morning chores and a trail ride.

"What time is it?" she uttered.

"It's time to get up and take care of the horses, missy. Let's go!"

With that, Rand walked out of the room. Lexi knew she had to get up unless she was dying. She felt a little like it, but not to that extreme. She groomed herself just enough for the stables and came down to coffee, eggs, bacon, and toast.

"Oh, PopPop, I'm not hungry right now," she complained.

"Nope, no time to waste. Ya gotta have a good, hearty breakfast to start your day," he answered.

She forced down a piece of toast, a fried egg, and juice. But her stomach was trying to reject the offering. She tried to focus on her chores while walking behind her grandfather to the stables. Both horses started moving around in their stalls in anticipation for some attention. Lexi went to work in the stall with Pony Girl. She had the routine down. Before Rand had pulled his right stirrup down, Lexi was mounted up, ready to ride.

Their pace was slow, walking between farm fence lines to the equestrian trails. Rand was enjoying this teaching moment, watching Lexi push through her first hangover.

"How ya feeling this morning?" he asked with a grin.

"I think I might have eaten something bad last night from the food truck or had too much soda. My stomach is upset. I didn't like that North Carolina soda."

Rand was intrigued.

"What kind of soda are you talking about?" he asked.

"I don't know, PopPop. The soda that Mitch bought from one of the food trucks tasted way too sweet."

"Was it in a bottle or can?"

"It was in a red solo cup. I think it might have gone bad. Can soda go bad?"

Rand knew right away what was going on, and he changed his tone. It was no longer amusing now that someone tampered with her drink. It made sense to him. He was surprised when he learned that Lexi was drinking last night, especially since her dad had been so strict about it. But now Rand was seeing a different story.

"Honey, have you ever been drunk?" he asked.

"No, PopPop. You know my dad would have killed me if I ever touched his liquor. I've never even tasted it."

"Well, you have now. Someone put something in your drink. Did you know the people you were with last night?" he asked.

"I knew all of them, except Mitch's older brother and his girlfriend. No one was drunk, though."

Rand asked, "Would you be able to tell if you were tipsy? I suspect someone thought it would be fun to get everyone a little buzzed without them knowing it. A game like that is dangerous. I'm not blaming you. I just want you to be aware that boys will try to get girls to loosen up any way they can."

"Gross! PopPop, I don't want to talk about boys and stuff like that."

"Well, honey, who else are you going to talk to that you can trust? No one is going to love you as much as your parents and your grandparents. I know it is awkward, but you are becoming an adult, so I am talking to you like an adult. It is a parent's job to prepare you for the world, which can be an unfriendly, uncaring place. It's better that you get the truth from people who love you."

Lexi did not like the conversation, but she understood what her grandfather was telling her. She slowed Pony Girl's pace to put a little distance between herself and Rand. He took it to mean that she was uncomfortable, but at least she was thinking about what he said.

Good! he thought.

When they got back to the house, Linda asked Rand what they had talked about. He shared his suspicion that someone had spiked Lexi's soda. Linda was angry that one of her friends would do something so deceitful and give her a reason not to trust them. Rand thought she was overreacting.

Unlike him, though, she understood how difficult the next few years could be for Lexi since teenage girls felt so much pressure and judgment coming at them. Mishandling incidents like this could send a teenager down the wrong path. She remembered her days as a parent of a teenage girl and how they navigated those rough waters with Cynthia.

She asked Rand later if he remembered the parent traps that they had to deal with in getting their children through their teenage years. He could not recall any specific instances, but he remembered that there were tough times.

It Takes a Village

The smell of fresh coffee and bacon the next morning woke everyone in time for chores. Rand first, then Lexi came into the kitchen, ready to work. They both poured their coffees and grabbed strips of bacon. Linda, with her coffee in hand, joined them at the stables. Rand said aloud that he had tee time with Rashne, and everyone was invited for Sunday brunch at the club. Lexi said she wanted to catch up online with Jennifer and Amy back home, but she could still do that and have plenty of time to enjoy a nice day in the village and at the Samadani house.

Lexi wanted to go to the Welcome Center to study the history of Pinehurst, then walk around and see the original cottages, stores, and hotels. She read somewhere that the Holly hotel, built in 1895, was the first hotel in Pinehurst, but she wanted to know about the other buildings too. The names Tufts, Olmstead, and Ross were displayed in the village so much that she wanted to know more about them. Anyway, it seemed to her like a good way to enjoy a Sunday.

Rand was punctual, and he began announcing aloud at eleven thirty that he was leaving for the village at noon. When noon arrived, he came out of his den, made one last announcement about his departure, and opened the door leading into the garage. He turned around to say one last time that he was leaving, and Linda was standing there with Lexi in tow.

Rand was surprised and pleased. Linda rolled her eyes at his sarcastic smirk, saying under her breath that there was no specific time to be at the club brunch buffet. Without making eye contact, he declared to anyone listening that he did not want to wolf down his lunch so he could make his one fifty tee time.

Lexi was amused at the way they fussed at each other. It was rarely about anything important, but even after forty-plus years of marriage, they still had little idiosyncrasies that annoyed the other. The nice thing was how they learned over the years to deal with differences without anger or malice. Her mind reverted to her own parents' squabbles. Nothing came to mind except the hurtful silent treatment that was in effect the last few months her dad was alive. After he died, Lexi only remembered her mom being in a semicomatose state. The memories made Lexi feel sad. She decided right then that today was not going to be a sad day. So she refocused herself on going to Aryana's after brunch, walking around the village, and enjoying the day.

The Templetons, Samadanis, and Lexi enjoyed the brunch and sitting on the veranda overlooking the 18th hole of Pinehurst course no. 2. The buffet had something for everyone, including breakfast food, lunch food, desserts, salads, and drinks. Lexi was not a big eater, but she was amazed at the choices. It would have been too easy to overindulge and walk away feeling bloated.

Rand and Rashne excused themselves when the time came for their golf round. Aryana, Linda, and Lexi got into the golf cart and headed back to the house before going around the village. It was not the first time Lexi had been in Aryana's home, but it was the first time she had been there in a good mood, which gave her a different perspective. She noticed things she had not noticed before.

The first thing she realized this time was that the house was huge. The kitchen was off to one side of the first floor, but it opened to a formal dining room and casual parlor. The rest of the first floor had other sitting rooms and a library/study. Beautiful Persian carpets covered the hardwood floors. Lexi saw how everything in the house was so well-appointed.

Aryana saw Lexi studying the decor. She and Linda joined Lexi, and she started telling Lexi stories about the furnishings and the house itself. The house was built in 1901 as a boarding house. Wealthy people from the northeast would come to James Walker Tuft's resort called Pinehurst from November to April because of the healthy air and mild winters. Guests rented rooms at boarding houses, cottages, and one of the three hotels beginning in 1895.

Aryana took Lexi upstairs to see the bedrooms. Originally, there were two guest bathrooms, at opposite ends of the long hallway. After WWII, the owners renovated the house and installed more rooms and bathrooms on both floors. In the 1980s, the electrical and HVAC systems were updated.

After seeing all the rooms in the house, Lexi was awestruck. She said to Aryana that she could open her own boarding house if she wanted.

"Your daughters and their whole families could live here with you!"

Aryana smiled, saying, "Well, my dear, Rashne and I have talked about those ideas. We would love for our children and grandchildren to live here, but they have their own lives. There is room when they come for visit. We are at the point in our lives where we don't have to work anymore, and keeping up a hotel is a lot of work. So we just go on enjoying life for the time being and trusting that whatever happens will be for the best. But you are always welcome to visit and stay whenever you want."

After the history lesson, the women got in the golf cart for a day of sightseeing and researching historic places in the village.

The Templetons did not get back to Vass until late afternoon. Everyone was exhausted from eating, shopping, and golfing and the heat. Before anyone settled down, Rand reminded Lexi about tending to the horses for the night. They had been grazing all day in the paddock. She went down to the stables, cleaned the bedding, and filled the buckets with water and oats.

Champ and Pony Girl knew what was coming. Before Lexi could fill each of their buckets with oats, the horses were nudging her out of the way. She took a quick look at their hooves and then brushed each one. It was amazing how quickly she not only got used to the natural, earthy smells of the stables but also liked it. She was beginning to find joy in things again, just a little more each day.

*****

Back in school on Monday, Lexi met Trey in the hallway after her first class. She asked him if he felt drunk on Friday night in Southern Pines.

"Not really. Why?" he asked.

Lexi said that someone had put liquor in her Coke that night, and she asked if he knew who did it. Trey said he might have seen Mitch's brother, Jake, pouring something in cups, but he did not know if she got one of the cups. She told Trey that her grandparents were cool about the whole thing but that she was not cool with it. Trey asked if she was being a bit dramatic. It bothered her even more that he didn't understand how many ways he was wrong.

"No, I don't think I'm being dramatic," she said. "Would you want your sister hanging out with guys who wanted to get her drunk so she could be manipulated? What if it was your girlfriend?"

Trey smiled at her, saying he didn't have a girlfriend, but he got her point.

The morning was not off to a good start. Rather than linger disappointingly, Lexi said goodbye to Trey and went to her class. She kept thinking to herself, though, that she already had way too much drama in her life and didn't need any more. A little bit of Trey's luster had just worn off.

She met up with Macy at lunch and asked her, "What happened when you got home?"

Macy said, "My mom was so pissed about smelling liquor that she took away my phone. I couldn't even text you. I was in major time-out for the weekend. I saw Jake pouring a little booze in our Cokes, but I didn't think it was that much. I mean, I had a little buzz."

Lexi said, "My grandparents were not angry at me because they knew it wasn't my fault. I just thought it was a weird North Carolina syrup flavor or something. They were concerned about my choice of friends, though."

"Really? You didn't know?"

Macy looked unconvinced.

"No, really! My dad would have killed me if I ever touched his liquor," Lexi swore.

She told Macy she was annoyed about the whole thing.

"Nothing happened, though, right?" Macy said. "Besides, I heard that Trey kissed you. He really likes you."

Lexi admitted that she likes him too, but she didn't want to be tipsy and lose control when she was with him. Macy told her not to worry about it because Trey was not like that, and it was just Jake being a jerk.

She promised, "It will never happen again."

The two girls chatted about other things for the rest of the lunch, and Lexi forgot about the spiked drinks. By the end of the day, the incident was forgotten. She focused on her school assignments and Trey.

Integrity

When she came home from school on Wednesday, Linda was at the table, working on a charity event at the Weymouth Center in Southern Pines. She told Lexi that her grandfather was down at the stables, waiting for her.

When she strolled down the path, she could see that the horses were saddled up and ready for a ride. Rand yelled to her to turn around, get in her riding clothes, and hurry back. She smiled and ran back to the house. Five minutes later, she came running down the path with treats for Pony Girl, who was excited to see her. Lexi and PopPop mounted their horses for their new ritual walk through the pines.

"How was school today?" Rand asked.

"It's good, PopPop. I'm making friends, and I like my teachers. I still miss all my friends back home, but this is tolerable until Mom gets better. And I love spending time with Champ and Pony Girl."

Rand said that they liked her too. He mentioned that they were going to Asheville on Saturday to see Cynthia. Lexi did not respond. He glanced at her for a reaction; there was none. He thought, at least she didn't hate the idea. After a little while, Lexi told him that she found out what happened on Friday night. She said that an older brother of one of her friends thought it would be fun to put booze in everyone's drink. Rand did not say anything. Instead, he just focused on the trail ahead.

Lexi broke the silence.

"A penny for your thoughts."

Rand continued forward on Champ, but Lexi could tell he was gathering his thoughts for an answer.

"Do you know about integrity?" he asked.

"It's being honest," she answered.

"Well, that's part of it, but it goes deeper than that. I think integrity is one of the most important characteristics a person can have. Integrity is being honest and trustworthy but also being consistent in your moral and ethical behavior. My father used to tell me that integrity is what you do when no one is looking. It is doing the right thing. Do you understand?"

"I do, PopPop, but what does that have to do with me?" she asked.

"You were victimized by someone who lacks integrity. The boy who spiked your drinks was being dishonest with everyone. He was forcing something on you without your knowledge or consent. His actions seemed harmless and insignificant, but everything has consequences. His behavior that night is a good example of how not to be. It is a good lesson for you to see the right and wrong of it. Sometimes, we can learn good and bad from the people around us."

They arrived at the meadow and dismounted to let the horses graze. Rand hugged his granddaughter. She did not say anything, but he hoped she was thinking about what he had just told her.

After enough time, Rand said, "Let's get these horses home and feed them. I'm getting hungry too."

The pair made their thirty-minute trail walk back to the house in silence. The rustling of the pine needles under the horses' hooves was peaceful. They got back to the stables and put Champ and Pony Girl up for the evening and then went up to the house. The temperature was mild, the air smelled good, and Lexi enjoyed the tranquility of the evening.

After supper, Rand went to the sink to start the kitchen cleanup, but Linda told him to relax while she and Lexi cleaned up. He wondered what he was doing that she didn't like as he tiptoed out of the kitchen to the den. When the two women were alone, Linda asked Lexi how things were going so far and if she enjoyed the trail ride this afternoon. She replied that things were okay in school, and she always enjoyed trail rides on Pony Girl.

"I think Pony Girl misses you riding her, MomMom," Lexi said.

"Oh, don't worry about that, dear. She likes you just fine. You are a little easier on her back," Linda said with self-deprecation.

"Are you missing your mom?" she asked.

"Yes, ma'am. I'm still dealing with a lot of stuff—anger, things I don't understand. But I do miss her. Deep down, I mean. And I hope she is getting better."

Linda said, "You can ask her this weekend if you want."

Without skipping a beat, Lexi said that there was a boy in school who liked her. Her grandmother's eyes gleamed with a big smile.

"His name is Trey. He seems nice, but I don't really know much about him, except that he is cute and athletic."

Linda said when she was in school a hundred years ago, those things were very important qualities in a boy.

Then Lexi blurted out another seemingly random topic.

"PopPop was talking with me about integrity and being honest. He said it is one of the most important characteristics we can have."

Lexi paused, hoping to hear her grandmother's thoughts about it.

Linda said, "I agree, sweetheart. Integrity is very important."

Before Linda could say any more, Lexi interrupted.

"But, MomMom, don't we all lie sometimes to spare people's feelings?"

MomMom thought for a moment.

"Yes, dear, we do."

Lexi was surprised by her honesty.

"How do you reconcile it? Isn't that lacking integrity?"

Her grandmother answered, "I think it is important to put things into context. Integrity is about doing the right thing. How do you decide what is the right thing?"

Lexi thought, "Well, I guess the right thing is what makes the most sense or makes people the happiest."

She wasn't satisfied with her answer.

Then her grandmother asked her, "Do people ever do things that they think will make them happy, but it doesn't?"

Lexi nodded.

"I don't know. Maybe."

Linda asked her, "Do people use drugs hoping that they will make them happy?"

Lexi nodded. Linda continued.

"Of course they do. People do all kinds of things in the pursuit of instant gratification or pleasure, even when it is not the right thing to do. I think a good rule to follow is the golden rule. In the book of Matthew, it says, 'So in everything, do unto others as you would have them do unto you.'"

"But, MomMom, the Bible also says, 'An eye for an eye.'"

Linda replied, "Exactly. Conversely, if you don't want someone to take your eye or anything else, then you should not take theirs."

Lexi asked, "MomMom, what does this have to do with lying?"

Her grandmother stopped rinsing dishes.

"Let's bring this back full circle. The golden rule says that you should not do something if you don't want someone to do the same to you, and that includes lying. When it comes to telling a lie to spare someone's feelings, it has nothing to do with truth and everything to do with opinion. Opinion is someone's thought about something. It might not have anything to do with facts or truth.

"So if your opinion hurts someone's feelings, would you still tell them? It's not a fact. It is merely what you think. Now having said that, if the situation calls for it, it is always best to tell the factual truth because it is the easiest to remember, and just one lie can ruin your credibility. But it is important to distinguish between truth and opinion. They are two different things. Does that make sense?"

"Yes, ma'am, it makes a lot of sense, but I can think of so many situations where it would be hard to decide. Like, if Jennifer's hair looked bad, I think I would tell her."

"I know, sweetheart. It is the hard part about adulthood."

After kitchen cleanup, Lexi went to her room and got online to text her friends and read about gossip from home. Jennifer, Amy, Shyanne, and others were posting pictures of one person with another person, so-and-so breaking up with someone, and who was not talking to whom. She realized that from an outsider view there was drama happening in Occoquan. What was important to her before now seemed less important. She wondered why she never noticed it before. Was it because she was looking at it from the outside now, or was she growing up?

Jennifer texted, "Where you been, BFF?"

Lexi's introspective thoughts disappeared, and she jumped right into the fray with Jennifer dishing more drama until she fell asleep.

Lexi woke up the next morning and went about her stables chores, feeling a little less weary than she had been before. There was no reason for her improved attitude other than the fresh air and the warm rays of sunshine peeking through the pine trees. She felt the calming effect of the morning. She was trying to cling to her indifference about her situation and school since it was temporary, but she could not deny to herself that her new friends at Union Pines High School had exceeded her expectations.

A First Date Ask

Her day was about to get better. Halfway through the school day, she was at her locker with friends when Trey Redmond walked over and asked if he could talk to her. Her friends sensed a need for privacy, so they scattered.

He asked her if she would go with him to the movies on Friday night. She was caught off guard, and the only thing she said was that she would have to think about it. Walking away to her next class, it hit her.

Did Trey just ask me out on a date?

She repeated it several times in her head to make sure she didn't imagine it.

An upperclassman asked me, a sophomore, out on a date.

She had gone out on group activities with her friends back in Woodbridge, but this was her first actual, one-on-one date. She walked on cloud nine for hours—until reality knocked her down to earth. As much as she wanted to say yes, yes, yes, she would have to get her grandparents' permission. Later that day, Lexi told Trey she would have to check her family situation to see if she was free Friday night. He nodded in complete understanding and walked away to class. She was unable to focus or even remember the rest of the afternoon.

On the way home, she strategized about how to ask her grandparents about going on a date. She went right into her homework when she got home and then spent time with Champ and Pony Girl. Rand thought he noticed a brighter smile and a giddiness in her step in the stalls. The horses didn't mind the extra attention either.

Rand, Linda, and Lexi sat down to dinner that evening. Linda asked her how her day went. It was not the planned segue Lexi had in mind, but it seemed like a good enough time to jump in.

"Well, since you asked, MomMom, a boy at school asked me on a date tomorrow night. He is taking me to the movies."

She tried to sneak it in as a statement rather than a question, seeing how it would go over. Rand and Linda both looked confused and were at a loss for words. It was an ambush, and they needed a time-out to respond without looking ill-prepared. Both adults slowly chewed their food while thinking over the question. It was a delicate predicament. This was clearly something her mother should decide on, and yet she was not there. They were in charge.

Lexi waited for their response, unable to think of a reason she should not be able to go. She wondered if her expression showed them that she wanted to go on the date.

Linda was the first to jump in.

"Honey, it would not be wise to be out late on Friday night since we need to be up early to go to Asheville on Saturday morning. It's a long drive, right, dear?"

Linda turned to Rand.

"Um, yes, it is a long drive, three to four hours, and that is after we tend to the horses before daybreak," Rand asserted while nodding.

Lexi was prepared for this answer.

"MomMom, I won't be out late, and it is not like I'll be the one driving. I can sleep in the car on the way to Asheville," she said with a satisfied smirk.

Rand dipped his toe into the conversation.

"Lexi, we don't know this boy, and until we meet him and his parents, I'm not comfortable with it."

"Okay, PopPop. Trey and his mother can come by to pick me up. He has his driver's license but still must have another licensed driver in the car. You can meet them then," Lexi retorted again with a smile.

Rand and Linda were becoming frustrated. They did not want to say no, but it was difficult for them to explain to her that this rite of passage should be experienced with her mother. They were not comfortable explaining to their granddaughter about the sole focus of a teenage boy. However, Lexi wanted an answer. Linda made an on-the-spot decision to ask for more time to consider it. She said that she and PopPop would have to discuss it and let her know later. It was too much for them to hope that Lexi would forget the question.

After dinner, the three of them cleaned the kitchen, and then Lexi went up to her room to go online. She could not wait to tell Jennifer. Meanwhile, in the living room, Rand and Linda looked at each other with mouths hanging open.

"What do we do?" he asked Linda.

"Rand, as far as I know, this is her first real date. And you know as well as I do, she should have her mother's permission first. We cannot let her go. We simply cannot."

Rand understood her logic and agreed.

"Lexi will not speak to us if we say no, and Cynthia will not speak to us if we say yes," he warned.

"I know. It's a no-win situation," Linda acknowledged.

They both shook their heads. After a while, Linda's eyes lit up.

"What if we take her to Southern Pines, let her be with the boy for an hour or so, and take her home at a specific time? It would be a compromise, right?"

Rand thought about it.

"I think we would be doing our duty—keeping her safe but giving her a little space at the same time. I think she should be happy with it."

They called her down to tell her their decision. Lexi's twisted facial expression upon hearing their answer said it all. It was not acceptable.

She protested, "No, PopPop! I don't want to have you and MomMom peeking over my shoulder when I'm with my boyfriend. It is too weird and creepy!"

Rand tried to convince her that she was being overly dramatic and that they would leave her alone just like they did on First Friday. She shook her head. She tried reverse psychology, forgetting that Rand and Linda had seen that play before.

"Fine! Just forget it. I'll tell Trey I can't go because my grandparents live in the puritanical age where boys and girls are not supposed to look at each other until they are married."

Rand tilted his head, wincing at her gross overexaggeration. Lexi was on the verge of tears.

Linda sympathized with her granddaughter's disappointment. She patted the cushion next to her on the couch. Lexi, angry at the world, reluctantly sat next to her grandmother, knowing that doing so meant she was accepting their decision.

Linda put her arm around her granddaughter and spoke softly.

"I know you must be so excited about going on a date with Trey. I would be! Is he handsome?"

Lexi nodded.

"Is he popular?"

Lexi nodded again.

"Is he older?"

Again, Lexi nodded.

"Does he have an older brother?" Linda joked.

"MomMom!" Lexi exclaimed. "That's way weird."

Linda welcomed the levity, then continued.

"Lexi, sweetie, we want to give you every opportunity to gain experience and learn and enjoy life in a safe and healthy manner. Our problem is that this is a special moment in your life that your mother should be privileged to experience with you. She should be the one tingling with excitement—and worry—along with you. But right now, we are treading water waiting for her to get better. While she is healing, we don't want to punish her by denying her this milestone in your life. She is missing so much already. Do you understand?"

Lexi listened and seemed mildly compassionate to what her grandmother was saying.

"I get it, but it's not fair to me either. My mom ruined my life once already, and now she is doing it from a loony bin."

Linda shut her eyes, clenched her teeth, and held her tongue. Lexi stood up.

"I'll just tell Trey I can't go this weekend. Maybe he will ask me another time, but I doubt it."

Linda frowned after Lexi went to her room.

"She is still just a fifteen-year-old after all. She understands, but that doesn't mean she likes it," Linda explained to Rand.

Rand nodded.

An Ice Cream Trust

When Lexi came home from school on Friday, without saying a word, she changed her clothes and went to the stalls to take care of the horses. She was there for nearly an hour before Rand came down to help her.

As he entered the stables, he could hear her talking to Pony Girl while brushing her. She was asking Pony Girl why she wasn't allowed to hang out with her friends on the weekend and instead was stuck doing chores with horses that belonged to her grandparents. Pony Girl was enjoying the brushing and not answering Lexi.

Rand opened Champ's stall door so Lexi could hear him. She stopped talking.

"Did you save any work for me?" he asked.

"No, PopPop. Both horses are tended to just how you showed me. Are you going to let them out again?"

He answered, "No, I think they'll be just fine until tomorrow morning. Your grandmother has fixed a fine meal, so we should get to it."

They went up to the house for dinner.

*****

Rand had cleared his plate and declared that it was a delicious meal. He looked at the two women.

"You know what would make this meal even better? Ice cream! Nothing like a fine Friday evening ice cream."

Linda was shaking her head, reminding him that he ate the last bit of ice cream three days ago.

"Well, I guess we'll just have to go out and get some," he said.

Lexi was still sore about being stuck at home, so she barely paid attention to what her grandfather was suggesting. He told Linda that he would help her clean up the kitchen, and they would head to the ice cream parlor in Southern Pines. They both looked at Lexi. Finally, she understood their scheme. Rand smiled at her.

"No, PopPop! You can't do that. You can't take me down there just so my friends can see me with you, and then we leave. It would be torturous and insulting. I'm not going."

Rand turned to Linda, almost like he had not heard Lexi.

"Mother, how long will it take us to clean the kitchen?"

Linda told Rand that they should have everything done in about twenty minutes.

"Good!" he exclaimed. "I can taste that hand-scooped waffle cone already. Do you want us to bring you back any?" he asked Lexi.

She sat with her mouth agape in total disbelief. She reconsidered in ten seconds. While running to her room, she was also yelling to her grandmother that twenty minutes was not enough time for her to wash, change her clothes, fix her hair, put on makeup, and be ready to go.

Lexi had closed her bedroom door before Linda caught the trailing end of her objections, but she got the gist of it.

"Is she going with us or not?" Rand asked with a wink.

Lexi heard the car engine and car doors shut as she was careening down the hall, carrying her purse and eyeliner. She jumped in the back seat, out of breath, thinking that her grandfather would have left her. She sat in the back seat, trying to apply her eyeliner.

Lexi begged, "Please don't say anything if we see my friends. Please!"

"I probably won't see them anyway, but if I do…"

Rand had a mischievous smile on his face. Linda interjected to ease Lexi's fear.

"You know what, darling? How about if you and I just go around the corner to that little restaurant with the outdoor seating and have a nice cocktail?"

Lexi was puzzled.

"You mean we are not getting ice cream? What is going on?"

Rand looked into his rearview mirror.

"No, dear, we are not getting ice cream. You may go wherever you like, but for the next two hours, your grandmother and I will be enjoying a cocktail."

A smile crept over Lexi's face as the plan revealed itself. Now all she had to do was text Macy to see if the group was in Southern Pines. Her phone beeped right back. All her friends, including Trey, were walking along Broad Street, heading to the ice cream shop, and then sitting outside of the train station. Lexi texted that she would meet them at the ice cream parlor. She kissed her grandparents goodbye and headed down the street.

Rand yelled to her, "We are leaving in two hours."

Lexi met up with her friends at the corner ice cream shop. Everyone was happy that she could join them, especially Trey. He hugged her and told her he was glad she came. After she ordered, she tried to pay for her ice cream, but Trey would not let her. She liked the fact that he was a gentleman. The group walked up the street to the train station, where they sat on the wall under the lights and hung out.

Lexi and Trey sat at the far end of the group and talked to each other for an hour and a half. They talked about their likes, dislikes, joys, fears, and goals. Lexi liked him more and more as they talked, except for the part about him going out with many girls at Union Pines. She kept to herself that she had never been on a date other than group dates back in Virginia.

When her two hours were up, Lexi said that she had to go. Trey and the others tried to convince her to stay longer and that they would take her home. She wanted to stay, but this was a privilege her grandparents gave her, and she didn't want to abuse it. She ignored their peer pressure and stood firm about leaving. Trey hugged her and snuck in a gentle kiss on her cheek.

Lexi walked down the street, so elated that her feet barely touched the ground all the way to the restaurant where her grandparents were waiting. Rand glanced at his watch and smiled at her punctuality and respect. They drove home, all three of them feeling victorious.

Horse Sense

The light of the next day's dawn peeked through the pines as Lexi and Rand slowly walked along the path to the stables. He was being careful not to spill his piping-hot coffee. The clean air and quiet was conspicuous and pleasant. Neither one interrupted the solitude until they heard the horses reacting to their approach.

"PopPop, how do the horses know we are coming? I mean, we are so quiet."

It was too early to explain all the science behind the animal's sensing, so he kept it simple.

"Lexi, those horses have very few things on their minds to cloud their thinking or, more accurately, their instincts. They are concerned with six things: food, water, procreation, the ability to flee when threatened, being part of a herd, and playtime. Any changes in their surroundings can be threatening. So they learn to use all their senses to flee from danger. If it is totally unfamiliar, they become cautious and defensive. In our case, they are accustomed to someone coming to feed them in the morning, so they get excited rather than afraid."

She summarized what he said to make sure she understood, saying that the horses were so uncomplicated that their senses were keen. Rand half shook his head and half nodded.

"In a manner of speaking."

The duo went to work on Champ and Pony Girl. Champ was biting on his reins, ready to go on the trail. Rand patted Champ's neck, telling him that they would ride tomorrow, but not today. They had a long road trip planned for today.

Rand, Linda, and Lexi did a final check for whatever they were bringing to Asheville before starting down the road. It was 8:00 a.m., and Rand figured they would arrive by noon. They phoned ahead to Pisgah Wellness Center and let them know they were coming to spend the day with Cynthia. Pisgah asked that all visits be scheduled ahead of time, if possible. That way, they could adjust the patient's schedule to not interrupt treatment. The weekend treatments were usually very light and flexible anyway, so Cynthia was going to be free for the day.

The Templetons pulled onto the Pisgah complex ten minutes after 12:00 p.m. They parked and went into the guest registration office. The receptionist led them to a breezeway where Cynthia was sitting in a chair, sipping tea and overlooking the mountains. Linda walked quickly to her daughter.

Cynthia saw her mother approaching and stood up to greet her. They hugged, and Linda whispered how much she missed her and asked how she was feeling. Cynthia managed a controlled smile. She said that she was very happy to see them but asked where Lexi was. Linda told her that Lexi stopped in the ladies' room.

Rand hugged Cynthia, and they all sat together. The breeze felt good, and the scenery was amazing, so he was happy just to relax with her and talk about happy things.

Lexi came into the breezeway, and Cynthia stood up to hug her. She hugged Lexi as if never wanting to let go. Lexi accepted the hug, keeping her arms at her side, not reaching back for her mother. Cynthia whispered how much she had missed her but did not get a response. She wanted to hold on to her daughter, but Lexi was barely tolerating the greeting.

Linda whispered to Cynthia, "Small steps."

They sat and talked quietly about the facility, the treatments, the group discussions, Cynthia's prognosis, the meals, and anything else that came to mind. Cynthia answered their questions but was much more interested in how Lexi was doing.

Lexi could hear small bits of the conversation from her seat on the rock wall twenty feet away from her mother, but she did not want to engage in the conversation. She was confused about how to feel. She thought she would be better around her mom when the time came, but now that she was there, angry thoughts and feelings rose inside of her that she could not let go.

Cynthia whispered to Linda, "How is Lexi dealing with everything?"

It was obvious to Linda that Cynthia, even sedated, could sense the animosity and lingering anger from Lexi. Linda told Cynthia that Lexi was like an onion, and every so often, a layer of anger peeled away. The rest of the afternoon's conversation was easy and natural. The four even strolled around the gardens, enjoying the fragrant flowers.

The afternoon waned, and Linda had in the back of her mind that soon, it would be time for them to go. As they walked together, Linda put her arm around Cynthia. Cynthia sensed that her mom wanted to say something. Linda leaned in.

"There is something we need to discuss with you."

Cynthia was concerned.

"What is it, Mother?"

Rand was listening too, and he indelicately butted in, asking if Lexi had dated boys back home in Woodbridge. Linda frowned at him, shaking her head, annoyed at how brusquely he brought it up. Lexi was trailing far behind them, but when she heard her name, she quickened her pace to eavesdrop.

Aware that her daughter was listening now, Cynthia said that Lexi's friends hung out as a group most of the time. And there might have been some boyfriend-like relationships, but no one was old enough to drive, so there was no dating per se.

Cynthia wanted to know why they were asking. Linda paused to choose her words and finally told her that Lexi had been asked out on a date. Linda quickly added that they told Lexi she had to discuss it with her mother first. Cynthia nodded vehemently. She stopped and sat on a bench along the pathway. She asked Lexi to sit.

"Honey, is there something you want to discuss with me?"

Lexi looked to the sky.

"OMG, this is not a big deal! Let's not open a federal case, okay?"

Cynthia looked down in disappointment.

Finally, she said, "My daughter going on her first date is a very big deal. Can you tell me about the boy?"

Lexi said in exasperation, "I don't know, Mom. His name is Trey. He is very cute and athletic. He is seventeen and in the twelfth grade. He has his license but can't drive alone yet, and he likes me. He invited me to hang out last night and get ice cream and take me to a movie. MomMom and PopPop told me I needed your permission. It's not a big deal!"

Cynthia asked her parents if she and Lexi could have a few private minutes. They nodded and continued down the walkway. Then Cynthia again told Lexi that dating was a big deal and that Lexi knew it.

Lexi once again said, "Oh my god! You are being mental and so melodramatic!"

Cynthia did not respond to the hurtful comment. Instead, she told Lexi that it was time for the talk. Lexi wanted to run. Cynthia grabbed her arm.

"I'm not talking about the sex talk. I'm talking about how to handle yourself around boys."

Lexi hesitated with mild curiosity. She was tempted to make an accusatory remark about how much her mother's knowledge of men worked out for her, but she bit her tongue.

Cynthia began.

"I know it is impossible for you to believe, but I was your age once, and I know how it feels. Your emotions and experiences will continue to grow and mature every day. You will learn things and then wish you had known them last month or yesterday. You and I are in a very delicate place right now in our relationship."

Lexi rolled her eyes, thinking, *No shit!*

Cynthia ignored it.

"But you are also in a very precarious place emotionally. Through counseling, I am only beginning to understand the effects that profound trauma and loss can have on us. It might cause you to do things in emotional desperation that you might not do otherwise. Lexi, I am happy that you are making friends in Vass, and I knew that dating was going to happen soon. I will not let my therapy and physical distance get in the way of your social life. You may date. I will tell MomMom."

Lexi's expression changed.

"I only wish I could be there to share those special moments with you. I want to be there when you walk in the door after a young man has treated you as if he would do anything for you, and you feel your worth. I want to hear you describe the experience of feeling like he thinks of only you. I want you to have all those amazing experiences, but I'm afraid too.

"I'm afraid that you will be with someone who does not deserve you because you feel unworthy right now. Boys go through a tough time too, and their hormones drive them to do very aggressive things, things that you might not want to do. If you don't feel good about yourself, believing that you are unworthy, it is easy to fall prey to someone who is only thinking about themselves. Just be careful! There are few things in life that only happen once. Remember that."

Cynthia reached over to hold her daughter's hands, to share the tenderness of the moment. Lexi pulled away and stood up, unaware of the piercing stab she had inflicted on her mother. Maybe Lexi's anger toward her mother was lessening, but her subconscious actions were not conveying it.

Cynthia stood up, accepting that the conversation was over. The two walked faster until they caught up with Rand and Linda in the garden. The four of them walked and talked about inconsequential things for more than an hour until it was time to go. Cynthia grabbed her mother's arm and told the other two that they would be along shortly. Rand understood that Cynthia wanted to talk with her mother privately. He and Lexi walked to the car.

Linda started.

"How is your treatment going, sweetheart?"

Cynthia was eager to talk.

"I think it's going well, Mom. They want me to stay a little while longer because I still am having bouts of depression, but they tell me it's normal. I'm also beginning to believe that Tom's death had nothing to do with me, and I don't have to carry that guilt. I had a right to be hurt and angry with him, but I never wanted any harm to come to him. I know that now. I just need to stop thinking about it.

"They also question my rationale for keeping the truth about Tom's infidelity from Lexi. They say Lexi is harboring unhealthy feelings because she doesn't understand what I was going through. My doctor wants me to consider if keeping the truth from her is doing her more harm than good. They say her love for her father will not be diminished because he made a mistake. I don't know, though. I'm not there yet, but I'm working through it.

"Okay, so listen, Mom. I don't want Lexi to suffer because I'm in therapy. She can date if you meet the boy. I'm putting a lot on you and Dad, but you were pretty good judges when it came to letting me go out at her age. Do you remember?"

Linda nodded.

"I do, but it was a long time ago, and things have changed."

Cynthia added, "I don't want her to get serious with anyone because her current situation is not permanent, but let her enjoy it while she's there. I trust you, and I love you."

"I love you too, dear. We'll see how it goes with Lex."

They arrived at the car and said their goodbyes. Lexi held back slightly, but Cynthia chose to believe that a détente was slowly occurring between them. She waved as her father, mother, and daughter drove out of sight.

On the interstate heading east, Linda asked Lexi what she and her mother talked about. Lexi was not comfortable talking to her grandmother about private conversations she had with her mother.

She responded, "Nothing much, just stuff. She told me she is feeling better and hopes to be able to come home soon. She said she would talk to you about me hanging out with my friends. We talked about Jennifer back home. You know, just stuff."

Linda asked, "Did she talk to you about boys?"

"OMG! MomMom, we are not having this conversation," Lexi protested loudly and then donned her earbuds.

Linda knew the conversation was over—for now.

Lexi and Linda slept during the drive. Rand listened to talk radio to keep him company during the three-hour drive. It was late when they arrived home. The women awoke when the car stopped in the garage. Without any words, each one headed to bed.

A Thin Veneer

Lexi came into the kitchen the next morning bright and early, anxious to take out the horses for their Sunday ride. She expected to see her grandmother making breakfast and telling her that her grandfather was already in the stables. She was surprised to find her grandfather holding a cup of coffee in one hand and a spatula in the other in front of a pan of scrambled eggs on the stove.

"Where's MomMom?" she asked.

Rand looked at her with a smile and said, "Your MomMom is in the stables right now, getting ready to go with you this morning."

Lexi's eyes nearly popped out of her head.

"What the heck! OMG, she is so wanting to talk about stuff. I don't want to."

Rand didn't so much as blink as he spooned scrambled eggs onto her plate and said that she had better eat quickly and get down there. Lexi grunted.

She reluctantly headed to the stables to face her worst fear of embarrassment. Linda had readied Champ and had mostly readied Pony Girl. Lexi checked the saddle on Pony Girl, cinched her up tighter, and walked her out of the stables. Linda followed with Champ. Both women mounted their horses and steered them between the fences toward the trail.

The sun was already above the horizon, but the serenity of the morning was consistent. The only noises were the sounds of saddle leather and the crunch of the pine needles. Nature and her splendor did not need words. All she needed was to be taken in and appreciated. Horses and riders arrived at the grassy meadow, where they let the horses feed on the sweet grass shoots. The heavy dew on the grasses quieted them even more.

Looking through the pines, Lexi could make out small pockets of steam rising from the forest floor. The silence felt awkward, and Lexi dreaded it at the same time.

"So, MomMom, what did you want to talk about?"

Linda hesitated.

"We don't have to talk about anything, dear."

There was more silence. Then Lexi heard the unmistakable sound of a preparatory inhale.

"However," Linda started, "I thought you might want to know that your mother told me it was okay for you to date."

Lexi smiled.

"I know. We talked about it, and she said she would tell you."

Linda interrupted.

"But we will have to agree to some rules."

Linda grabbed Champ's reins to begin their ride/walk back. Lexi was so relieved that the news about dating was the thing her grandmother wanted to talk about. They were minutes into their walk back when Linda asked Lexi how the talk went. Lexi felt nauseated instantly. She wanted to dig her heels into Pony Girl's ribs so hard that she would take off in flight. She would rather stick a needle in her eye than to have this conversation, muttering to herself, "Just kill me now."

"MomMom, please! I can't talk about this with you!"

Linda ignored her.

"Oh, please, don't be so dramatic. I'm not referring to your sex education. My goodness, young girls have been getting that kind of information from their friends for ages. Isn't that what sleepovers are for? Mothers know it, grandmothers know it, and big sisters know that you get all the gritty details before parents ever bring it up. Oh, we might fill in the gaps here and there, but it is just as uncomfortable for us as it is for you. No, I'm talking about how boys think."

Lexi was semi-interested but still weary.

"MomMom, I'm not sure that talk is any better."

"Well, then," Linda offered, "let me give it to you in a nutshell."

Linda looked up into the pine trees as if drawing wisdom and strength.

"Boys want to have sex as soon as they begin to understand what sex is, and what's worse, they stay that way until they die of old age."

"Gross!" Lexi shouted.

Linda continued.

"The thing is, they can't help it. It is all because of a nasty little hormone called testosterone. It drives them crazy."

Lexi giggled.

"We girls, on the other hand, mature so much faster than boys, and that inequality continues all our lives. Even though our hormones get to us too sometimes, women stay in control much better than men. We can tolerate so much more pain, do so many more things at once, we can express our emotions better, we can manage our emotions better, we raise children better, and we mostly do the small things that turn a house into a home and turn food into a meal.

"If it were left up to men, parties would have chips and beer, a furnished house would have a recliner, a sixty-inch flat-screen TV, and a remote, and no one would ever get birthday cards, Christmas cards, or thank-you notes."

Lexi let out a belly laugh. Linda giggled too.

"I guess my point is that a man only has a thin veneer of just enough charm and class to disguise his true intentions. His goal is to satisfy his urges. I'm not saying that is a terrible thing. Lord knows we have our urges too."

Lexi crinkled her nose.

"Ew! MomMom!"

"Well, we do. I'm sorry. It's nature's way. How do you think all the babies come into the world?"

Lexi replied, "I know, MomMom, but I don't want to think about my mother or grandmother having urges."

Linda laughed.

"Okay, fair enough. I never wanted to think about my parents doing those things either. Anyway, getting back to my point, boys will try to go as far as they can with you. Sadly, sometimes, boys overpower girls and go farther than girls want. Just remember, you have more control of your hormones than they do. You should always be in control of the situation too.

"Don't go anywhere with a boy if you sense he will not respect your rules. Don't do anything you are not comfortable with, and never let alcohol or drugs alter your awareness. Over time, you will realize that you have the power, and you can manipulate men without them knowing it. Women have been doing it for ages. A savvy woman can get a man to do whatever she wants and make him think it was his idea.

"Well, here we are back at the stables. Let's get the horses ready for the day and go see what I can talk your PopPop into today."

Both women smiled as they walked together back to the house.

Lexi was excited to text Macy about being allowed to date. An hour flew by, as the two girls had thumbs and fingers flying on keys, texting each other. Macy wanted to let Trey know so that he could ask Lexi out again. It did not take long before Lexi's phone was blowing up with texts from Trey and Macy at the same time.

He was already asking Lexi to hang out with him next Saturday night. He mentioned movies, bowling, driving around, or just playing video games at his house. His plans were not firm yet, but Lexi was on his mind, and it did not matter to him where they went if they were together. She was smiling the whole time while reading his texts.

*****

Fall days were relaxing in Vass. Lexi and Rand got up before sunrise to take care of the horses. Lexi was always enthusiastic and feeling better each day, in body and mind, with her horse caring routine. The tranquility and natural essence of it brought a sense of calm to her mind and simple purpose to her life. She had things in her life that still needed to be simplified, but this was not one of them. It was uncomplicated, consistent, and pleasant. She knew what the horses needed and how to provide it. They didn't ask for anything more. They appreciated her, and she found peace with them.

Lexi thought about her grandmother's "talk" and realized that Champ was more aloof than Pony Girl, trying to display his dominance. Pony Girl did not show any dominance even though she was

1,000 pounds of strength and agility. She trusted 120-pound Lexi to feed and groom her every day. Pony Girl could enjoy the care and feeding without needing to be in control. Lexi wondered how much of this contrasting behavior between the horses was personality or genetics. The only thing it affected was how much more affection Lexi showered on Pony Girl as opposed to the more cautious approach she took with Champ.

Lexi was unusually quiet on their Wednesday morning ride. The layer of dew on the pine needles that morning, brought on by the cool front that had blown in the night before, made for an especially quiet ride. The birds, squirrels, and saddles were the only things making noise that morning.

When they got to the meadow, Rand asked Lexi what was on her mind.

"I'm just wondering if you like people or animals better."

One eyebrow raised high on his forehead as he searched for an answer. He said that the question was much more complex than at first impression.

"Lexi, I don't think there is enough time left in my life to completely answer that question."

He grabbed Champ's reins and climbed onto the saddle.

"I will give you my short answer on the ride back."

Lexi climbed onto Pony Girl and strolled up beside her grandfather.

Rand did not know where to start. Finally, he said, "Like I told you before, this is only my opinion, and there are exceptions to every rule. So here goes. I've lived for many years and seen a lot of things. I have seen the good and the evil things humans can do. I can't think of examples where animals were evil, but I have seen humans be that way more times than I want to remember.

"Let me put it this way. Animals kill to eat, and they fight to breed, to protect their offspring and territory. Humans not only kill, but they intentionally inflict pain and horror for power, greed, lust, pleasure, cruelty, beliefs, and domination. Humans are so contradictory. We have the capability for extreme love, empathy, and compassion. We also have the capability for extreme evil, pain, death, and destruction.

"I've seen and read about things that humans have done to one another that are incomprehensible, things worse than death, evil things, and I have also seen things that show the deepest compassion for one another."

Lexi was listening intently until she interrupted.

"So you like animals better?"

"In the simplest of terms, I would say yes, because animals do not seem to be capable of sin. They are not corrupt, and they live within their environment. Humans, on the other hand, are predisposed to sin. Humans are like a virus. We consume everything in our path, leaving only waste and destruction in its place. But like most things, it is a very complex issue, and I am proud of you for asking the question.

"I will admit that I like these horses much better than I like a starving grizzly bear, and I have people in my life that I like and love. I might disagree or get angry at those people, but I would never commit evil against them, and they would never commit evil against me.

"So you see, your simple question is complicated. Philosophers, kings, scholars, and poets have pondered the same question throughout history. They have asked, what is evil? Why are humans so easy to give in to sin, greed, power, lust, pleasure? Why do certain people want to dominate others?"

Before Lexi realized it, the shade of the pines had given way to the open sky and direct sunlight; they were at the paddock. Lexi barely remembered the trail ride, as she had been listening so attentively to her grandfather.

"So see, dear, we are already home, and all I really did was scratch the surface and pose more questions. I want you to think about those things. If you come up with any answers on your own, you will be a better, more understanding person for it. Let me know if you do, okay?"

Lexi nodded, but she was deep in thought. They turned the horses loose in the paddock and walked to the house.

Later that afternoon, Lexi came into the kitchen. MomMom was preparing dinner, and PopPop was napping in his chair.

"Hey, honey," Linda said. "How are your friends?"

She assumed her granddaughter had been online.

"They're good," she answered.

She watched her grandmother chop vegetables until Linda asked if she would chop the rest. Lexi went to work at the kitchen counter with the knife and the chopping block.

She was chopping mindlessly and asked, "MomMom, do you like people?"

Her grandmother thought the question was especially odd and wondered why she would ask such a thing. She asked Lexi to specify which people.

Lexi clarified, "No, I mean what do you think of people in general? Do you think people are good?"

Linda didn't know how to answer, especially being suspicious about Lexi's anger toward her mother.

"Honey, you ask a very perplexing question. Off the top of my head, I guess I would say that I like people until they do something that makes me not like them."

Lexi dug deeper.

"What might they do to make you not like them?"

Linda was trying to put a meal together, so she was not completely focused on an answer, but she went on.

"Well, there are deal-breakers for me. I feel like six of the ten Bible commandments are a pretty good list. If a person murders another, I would not like them. If they steal or lie, I would not like them. If a person has no love or consideration for others, I would not like them. If they are greedy and selfish, I would not like them. If they dishonor their parents, I might not like them. There are probably more reasons, but that is a good place to start. Why do you ask, honey? Don't you like people?"

"It's not that, MomMom. I was just wondering. Do you think humans are evil?"

Linda shook her head ruefully.

"Honey, what is this all about?"

Lexi waited for an answer.

"I don't think humans are born evil, but I've read about so much evil in the world that it makes me wonder sometimes. I remember the days and weeks after September 11. We lived near DC. Everyone was so kind and compassionate to one another. It lasted for a month or so, but then people eventually went back to their selfish and inconsiderate ways.

"Humans can be so good, so loving, and so amazing. But there are people who can also be so evil. I have never experienced the horrors of war like your father or grandfather, but I listen to the news and see all the horrible things people do to each other in our supposedly civilized world. I wish everyone would act as if God were watching them all the time, because do you know what?"

Lexi leaned in close.

MomMom whispered, "He is."

The next day, in the village, Aryana and Lexi walked around the shops while Rand, Rashne, and Linda played golf. The pair strolled into the village, and sat outside of a café, enjoying coffee, and then wandered through shops until it was time to meet the golfers at the clubhouse. Aryana was genuinely enjoying Lexi's company, because it reminded her of past days with her daughters, but she didn't sense that the feeling was reciprocated. She thought Lexi would have enjoyed the day so much more if one of her friends was there instead.

Aryana had been learning the history of Pinehurst since they moved here, and she enjoyed showing Lexi the original cottages from 1895, the old photographs in the hallways of the Carolina Hotel, and other pieces of James Walker Tuft's legacy. Lexi seemed interested. Aryana would say or do something, and it reminded Lexi about what Rand and Linda said about the goodness in people. Aryana and Rashne were good people. They were so selfless and caring to everyone. Their love showed in everything they did. They joked and laughed and even got annoyed sometimes, but it was always with love in their hearts. They made Lexi feel like she was family.

Those good thoughts led Lexi to think about her mother. What had caused the love in her mother's heart to become so overtaken by anger? She hoped that when her mother was better, she would be able to talk about it. Lexi needed to know.

Her attention was redirected when Aryana mentioned something about Persian desserts and tea when they arrived back at her house. It was time for deliciousness!

*****

Rand had scheduled a veterinarian visit Wednesday afternoon, so there was no trail ride for Champ and Pony Girl. He told Lexi that instead, it would be a good day to deep-clean the stalls and hose down everything, including the horses, which would occupy the afternoon.

The veterinarian pulled up in her truck at exactly 3:30 p.m., when she said she would, knowing that Rand would have his two horses ready. She introduced herself to Lexi as Dr. Sherri Lancaster, but everyone called her Dr. Sherri. Lexi watched everything that Dr. Sherri did to Champ and Pony Girl. She approached each horse slowly, resting her hand on their left side. She listened to their hearts; took rectal temperatures; felt their muscles, bones, and joints with a trained hand; and examined their ears, eyes, teeth, and hooves. She and Rand then talked about their six-way series vaccinations and whatever else was due.

Lexi looked inquisitively at her grandfather when the doctor mentioned the six-way.

He whispered to Lexi, “It’s their seasonal vaccinations.”

Lexi then watched Dr. Lancaster take blood from the horses’ necks and give them injections there too. Neither horse reacted to anything that the doctor did, except for the temperature taking part. Lexi was grossed out by that until the doctor said that ninety-nine degrees was perfect, meaning they were healthy.

After the vet visit, Rand pulled out the hose and watered down one horse at a time. The outside temperature was dropping as the sun fell. Rand accidentally (on purpose) sprayed Lexi. She squealed.

She was scrubbing Pony Girl with a brush when, once again, out of the blue, she asked her PopPop a question.

"What do you think are the most important characteristics a person should have in addition to integrity?"

Rand was delighted she had asked.

"Before I give you my answer, I would like to know what you think."

She responded, "I think that integrity covers things like honesty and sincerity. I think that love and compassion are important. I also like humor and intellect. I think someone should not mind hard work, and understanding is good too. I'm sure there are more, but those top my list, I guess."

Rand was proud that Lexi was doing her own critical thinking. He answered her.

"You are right. All the characteristics you mentioned are important. In fact, there are a hundred books written on leadership, and they identify the most important characteristics that great leaders have in common. Not all experts agree, but they usually include integrity, compassion, confidence, courage, communication, empathy, flexibility, decision-making, and wisdom."

Rand looked over at Lexi to see if she was still listening. She tilted her head and opened her eyes wide toward him as if to say, "Continue." Rand got the hint.

"All the great prophets have written that love is the most important thing of all. I agree and would say that compassion and empathy can be in that same group. In fact, these traits are synonymous. For example, if you approach everyone with love in your heart, you will treat them with integrity, compassion, and empathy. You will talk to them, listen to them, and try to understand them. When you do that, both of you will be better for it."

Lexi nodded in deep thought. Rand went further.

"If someone has confidence and courage, they can overcome most obstacles. We have to be careful not to confuse courage and stupidity. Courage must be combined with wisdom. Wisdom comes from formal learning and a vastness of experience. You don't have to be old to have experiences. I would say that you have endured life lessons in the past year. However, extensive travel, education, and age contribute much to wisdom.

"Communication is a basic attribute that helps the other characteristics. If you are not an effective communicator, then you are not a good leader. Communication includes effective listening. You must be able to clear your mind and absorb what others are telling you. It is exceedingly difficult to do. Our brains interfere by thinking when we should be listening. Then when you have something important to say, you should be able to say it clearly and precisely so the correct idea is conveyed. It makes sense, right?"

Lexi nodded.

"Okay, I've given you things to think about, but let's play a game. You have proven to us that you have good leadership characteristics already. I have been putting twenty-five dollars a day for your hard work at the stables, showing me that you will work. I will deposit fifty dollars into your college account every day that you demonstrate one leadership characteristic. These are also the keys to success in life by the way. Okay?"

Lexi smiled in agreement.

They were back at the stables, so they led the horses back into their stalls, unsaddled them, groomed them, and went home.

Later that afternoon, Linda asked Lexi if she wanted sweet tea. Lexi loved her grandmother's sweet tea. She was on her iPad, so she responded "Yes, ma'am" to the tea and said that she would be right out. She came down the hall and spotted through the door her grandparents sitting in rocking chairs on the front porch with tea and cookies. She joined them.

Linda told Lexi that she had talked with her mother, and the prognosis was very good. She thought she might be able to finish up her treatment in a month. Lexi didn't say anything.

They sat for a while, enjoying the tea and quiet, watching the horses graze in the paddock. Rand pointed to how the horses were prancing and playing.

"Speaking of character traits."

Lexi giggled. Linda looked at him out of the corner of her eyes and wanted to know who was speaking about character traits. Lexi explained that she had asked her grandfather about good characteristics a person should have. Linda took a sip of tea, swatted a fly, and opined on the topic.

"Did PopPop mention love?"

"Yes, ma'am."

"Jesus tells us in Corinthians that of faith, hope, and love, the most important of these is love. He also gave his disciples a new commandment to love one another. If you love everyone first, you will treat them kindly and respectfully."

Lexi said, "It would be a different world, wouldn't it, MomMom?"

"It sure would. People get lost in the noise and distractions of life, and they forget how to be. There are people who never develop empathy, which prevents them from being able to feel another person's pain, fear, or love. They steal, cheat, maim, and kill others without being about to feel what it would be like if someone did the same thing to them. Those people end up in prison or the morgue. I bet your PopPop talked about courage, confidence, and intelligence."

"Yes, ma'am."

Lexi smiled.

"If you think about it, all the characteristics that lead to success support one another too. If you have empathy, you are likely to be kind also. If you have love for others, you are likely to be honest with them. I like humor too. People who can laugh at their mistakes seem to be able to enjoy the trivial things that make life special."

Lexi said, "MomMom, I guess you and PopPop have been successful because you have similar lists, and you understand what those characteristics look like. He gave me a challenge to tell him when I find or show each one of those good characteristics. I think I do it when we have these talks because I am trying to expand my wisdom."

She looked at Rand. He smiled back at her.

"You are right, but I'm not paying fifty dollars for a subtle example. I want clear-cut, specific examples. And I will tell you, not the other way around."

"Oh, no way, not fair!" Lexi protested.

All three smiled and enjoyed the tea.

The afternoon gave way to evening and dinner. Lexi had been in her room for a while, and Rand was puttering around in his garage. Linda called everyone to dinner.

In the middle of the meal, Lexi asked, "Do you think that wanting to punish or hurt somebody is the opposite of empathy, like evil?"

Rand and Linda suspected the underlying nature of her question. Lexi was doing a mental autopsy on her mother's rationale for her actions toward her father. Their suspicions made them guarded in their responses.

Linda said, "Wanting to hurt someone is never a good thing, but for me, it's all about the intent. Let's say that someone who inflicts pain on someone for pleasure is evil. However, I think hurting someone out of anger is a very human reaction. We can be so angry that we lash out without wanting to injure the person. The person can have empathy but become overwhelmed by a stronger emotion."

Lexi was absorbing her grandparents' opinions, trying to fit them into her understanding of people. The distinctions seemed nuanced to her.

She asked further, "What do you think about people that steal or destroy property?"

Linda answered, "Like I said on the porch, those people might not have developed empathy. Maybe it is because of a genetic defect, a lacking childhood, or they are overtaken by emotion. I've seen people become so outraged that they do things they would not normally do, like riot. I think people steal sometimes because they are frustrated about not having what other people have, and they don't understand why.

"Also, when people become desperate, they do desperate things. I do not think those activities are evil—wrong for sure but not evil. This is a very complicated concept and maybe worth future discussions."

Lexi agreed and went about her evening routine.

A New Shimmer

The next day, Lexi was on her iPad in her room when she heard her grandparents talking. She peeked down the hallway and saw her grandfather in a suit.

"PopPop, where are you going all dressed up?" Lexi asked.

He looked at Linda for help, but when she did not come up with an answer, he said, "Sweetheart, one of my friends passed away earlier this week, so I am attending his wake. We didn't mention it because it makes me sad, and we think you have had enough sadness for a while."

Lexi said that she was sorry his friend died and for him to be safe. She closed her bedroom door and went back online. Rand and Linda were surprised and pleased that she received that news better than they expected.

Two days later, Rand and Lexi were at the stables. Rand cleaned an empty stall, which aroused Lexi's curiosity. He asked Lexi if she wanted to go for a ride to another farm.

"Okay," she answered with mild interest.

She wanted to go to breakfast too until he backed his truck up to the horse trailer.

"PopPop, what are we doing?"

"You'll see."

They headed down the road with the horse trailer in tow.

West of Pinehurst, near Jackson Springs, Rand turned off the main road onto a dirt road through the woods. They came upon a small stables and pasture, where a younger man was standing. Rand got out of the truck to greet the man. Lexi got out and watched attentively but still unaware of what was happening. The younger man went into the stables and led out a beautiful chestnut-colored mare. He handed the lead line to Rand. They shook hands again, and Rand led the mare into the trailer. Lexi remained silent, but her eyes and mouth hung wide open in disbelief. She climbed back into the passenger side of the truck, and they drove off.

Feeling her stare, Rand turned to her.

"I guess you are wondering about the horse?"

Lexi responded sarcastically, "Uh, yeah!"

Rand was amused by her sarcasm and bewilderment.

"Her name is Shimmer. She is a two-year-old mare that belonged to John Greenley, my friend who passed away. The man we just met was his son, John Jr. He lives in Philadelphia and has no way to care for her. So at the wake, he asked me if I would take her. I made him an offer, which he refused, asking only that I come get her in the next few days, sign the papers, and love her and care for her the way his father did. I promised I would."

Lexi's eyes watered up at hearing the story. She was so happy and proud that her grandfather had the space in his stables and his heart to take in this beautiful orphan. The ride home was silent, except for the country songs on the radio. Lexi had questions she kept to herself.

When they pulled up to the horse farm and backed into the stables, she asked if she could show Shimmer to her stall. He agreed and reminded her that Shimmer was nervous and in need of love and patience to get used to her new home.

Lexi said, "I understand how that feels."

She led the mare off the trailer slowly into her stall. After disconnecting from the trailer, Rand announced that he was going to the house. Lexi heard him from a distance say not to stay out too late. For the next hour of uninterrupted calm, Lexi stroked Shimmer's mane, face, and neck. The scent and sounds of other horses made Shimmer skittish, but the tenderness of the small person beside her was soothing. Sleep came surprisingly easy for both that night.

Rand stirred in his bed to the smell of coffee brewing. Linda was asleep beside him, and the clock was showing 5:05 a.m., twenty-five minutes before his alarm. He got up, went through his morning routine, put on his glasses, brushed his teeth, and went to the kitchen. Lexi was there, bright-eyed and bushy-tailed, with breakfast and coffee ready.

"I was going to start without you, PopPop, but I figured the coffee would get you up."

He didn't question her, knowing exactly what was motivating her. They shoveled down their food and poured the coffee to go.

"Okay, let's go see how that little filly did last night," he said.

Lexi ran to the stables. All three horses were stirring with anticipation for their morning feeding and grooming. Lexi went straight to Shimmer's stall.

"You're going to make Pony Girl jealous if you are not careful," Rand advised.

"I know, PopPop. I love Pony Girl, but Shimmer needs extra care right now, and I think Pony Girl will understand. When can we let her meet them?"

From inside Champ's stall, Rand yelled, "They became aware of each other last night when we opened the trailer door and Shimmer backed out. They could smell each other. Champ and Pony Girl watched as you led Shimmer in. Shimmer knew they were here too. When we release them into the paddock, you can watch how they greet each other. Keep your eyes on Pony Girl."

Rand told Lexi to release Shimmer into the paddock. Shimmer bolted and ran along the entire fence line, investigating all four corners. He explained to Lexi that she was exploring her boundaries. Next, he released Champ. The big male slowly moved into the paddock and began grazing as if the young mare wasn't there. Lexi asked if Champ saw Shimmer. Rand explained that Pony Girl was the alpha female, and Champ was waiting for her.

Shimmer stayed on the opposite side of the paddock from Champ. Suddenly, Lexi heard the metal click release of Pony Girl's lead. The mare moved into the paddock with urgency. She trotted to the fence line toward Shimmer. The two mares met nose to nose. Lexi gasped in fear upon hearing Pony Girl let out a loud, long wheezing neigh at Shimmer. Then Pony Girl thrust one of her front legs at Shimmer, just short of jabbing her.

Lexi screamed, "PopPop!"

Rand put his hand on Lexi's shoulder and said, "It's okay. Just watch."

Shimmer turned away and walked along the fence.

Lexi asked, "What just happened?"

Rand answered, "Shimmer just learned that Pony Girl is the boss. Now they will get along."

Lexi couldn't help but think that the mares' interaction reminded her of how girls acted the first week of school. She and Rand watched the horses for five more minutes, and then they headed back to the house.

Lexi sought out her grandmother and excitedly shared every detail of how Pony Girl showed Shimmer who was in charge. Linda smiled at Lexi's joy and enthusiasm, acknowledging that horses did indeed have a pecking order just like everything else in the world. The difference was that the horses' pecking order was accepted by all and rarely challenged until they aged out. They instinctively allowed the alpha female, with her experience, to lead them to food, water, and safety. People were not so easily led, nor did they trust the ones with the most experience and wisdom. Lexi asked if that meant that Pony Girl would now care and look after Shimmer.

Linda answered, "She and Champ will look after her, and Shimmer will guard them."

Later that afternoon, the wonderful, mouthwatering smell of Southern fried chicken wafted through the house. Rand was napping in his chair with a book teetering precariously on his lap. He caught a whiff of the chicken and stirred, knocking the book off his lap and smacking the hardwood floor. He jerked awake.

"What in tarnation?"

Linda came out of the kitchen to see what had knocked over.

"You dropped your book!" she said, bemused.

He rubbed his eyes.

"Well, how can a fella read when award-winning chicken is in the fryer?"

Suppressing a smile, she turned away.

"It'll be ready in ten minutes, as soon as I mash the potatoes. Why don't you wash up and tell Lexi?"

Rand knocked on Lexi's bedroom door to let her know that supper was almost ready.

"I'll be out in a few minutes, PopPop."

She had been texting furiously with Jennifer about Shimmer until Jennifer asked about Trey. Lexi switched topics quickly and texted about how she and Trey had been hanging out at school. Jennifer wanted to know everything. Lexi almost squealed aloud while texting Jennifer that she had a date with Trey this weekend. Jennifer asked Lexi what her mom thought about it.

Lexi texted back, "My mom gave me permission, but I won't share any details. LOL."

"OMG!" Jennifer texted. "She gave you permission to date, but you haven't told her about Trey?"

Lexi's fingers were burning up the keyboard.

"No, not that! I haven't told her about Shimmer. LOL. Dinner smells delicious. Gotta bail."

The family sat down at the dinner table, Rand said the blessing, and they wasted little time digging into the meal. Lexi only weighed 120 pounds, but working on the farm gave her the appetite of a lumberjack. Considering how well she ate, her grandmother was amazed the child had not gained a pound since she had come to live with them. Linda had never been the kind of grandmother to fret about any child being too much of this or too little of that. Children changed daily, and Lexi had a high metabolism at this stage in her life.

Typically, during dinner, the three of them would talk about chores, horse farm work, schoolwork, or scheduled events. The topic today was Shimmer. Lexi had questions about the mare's future. First, she wanted to know when Shimmer could be saddled and ridden. Rand said that she had been trained and ridden already by Mr. Greenley before he got sick, but it had been a while. He suggested that they be patient. He got her saddle from John Jr. when they picked her up, but he wanted to let Shimmer become more accustomed to her new surroundings first.

Rand had an idea.

"Why don't we lead her on our trail rides behind Pony Girl before we ride her? It will let her learn the trail, and you can ride her around in the paddock a little at a time."

Lexi was excited about riding her. She also wanted to know who owned Shimmer but did not know how to ask without seeming greedy.

When there was a break in the conversation, Lexi said, "Oh, by the way, Trey asked me to go bowling this weekend."

After saying it, she plunged her fork into the mashed potatoes as if she had just asked about the weather. When she looked up from her plate, both her grandparents were wide-eyed and staring at her.

"What?" Linda asked. She tilted her head. "When were you going to ask us?"

Lexi wrinkled her brow.

"My mom said I could, right?"

Linda nodded.

"Yes, dear, she said you could date, but you still need to check with us, as a courtesy, just to make sure we do not have conflicting plans."

Rand jumped into the conversation before Lexi could give a rebuttal.

"We talked about integrity and trust, right?"

Lexi nodded. Rand continued.

"I trusted that you understood the implications of integrity, good and bad."

Lexi looked confused.

"How that applies in this case is that you should have enough integrity or honesty to not pretend you don't understand the rules, especially when doing so makes you seem innocent. Real integrity should make you feel bad when you are trying to sneak something by us. Is that what just happened?"

Lexi answered coyly, "Kinda, but also, I am so excited about Shimmer that the date thing slipped my mind a little bit."

Linda conceded.

"I get that."

Then Rand said, "I agree, and I believe you too. Also, I am proud of you for understanding and being completely honest when we called you on it. You are on the path to becoming a trusted adult."

Rand looked to his wife for her wisdom.

"Mother, what do you say?"

Linda smiled at Lexi.

"I think she's earned our trust. We still need to know the details about her date plans for safety's sake."

Lexi acknowledged their request and then asked, "Do we have dessert?"

On Friday morning, Lexi was up before the dawn, raring to go. Linda got up and fixed breakfast for the three of them. She suggested that the two of them groom the horses and then take them on a short trail ride while she cleaned the stalls. Rand was not okay with the idea, but Linda insisted, because she had not been in the stables for a while and would enjoy the quiet time.

Rand and Lexi groomed, watered, and fed all three horses. Then they saddled up Champ and Pony Girl and led them outside. Lexi put the bridle on Shimmer and led her out to Pony Girl. With Shimmer's lead in hand, Lexi mounted Pony Girl and followed Champ up the trail. Shimmer followed along without hesitation.

The ride was as relaxing and peaceful as ever. A slight breeze was blowing through the pines. Thirty minutes later, the full array of sunshine was above the horizon, giving color to all the grass varieties and fall flowers in the meadow. They stopped and let the horses graze.

Lexi and her grandfather sat down in the grass. She was the first to speak.

"PopPop, what other character traits do you want to talk about?"

He chuckled.

"Sweetheart, I think you could name as many character traits and virtues as I could. What you think is more important than what I think."

She wasn't satisfied.

"Well, tell me some," she pleaded.

He thought about it for a moment, wondering how she was going to apply this to her mother. It was too early for his brain to do amateur psychology. He spouted his free thought.

"I would say that of the many things a person needs, self-discipline, the ability to distinguish needs versus wants, the discipline to deny instant gratification, good judgment but not judging, respect for self and others, and joy are important."

Lexi took it all in and did not respond until Rand asked her about her list. She said she liked his lists, and she agreed with this one too.

"The other day, you listed communication but specifically listening."

Rand asked, "What do you think about good listening skills? Do you think people have them?"

Lexi said she assumed they did.

Rand said, "Let's do a test. To do the test correctly, you have to be completely honest."

"Okay," she said, nodding.

He said, "Two young people met and fell in love. One had blood type A– with a congenital heart ailment and a phobia. The other had blood type B+ with a V-neck sweater, lipstick, and pearl earrings." He stopped and asked her, "What did I say?"

She giggled and answered, "A boy and girl were in love. He had blood type A and was afraid of things. She had a sweater, lipstick, and pearls."

Rand smiled.

"Not bad, not bad. You missed details, though, but not bad."

Rand asked her to be honest about what came to mind when he started talking. She searched her mind for a second and said that she thought about her and Trey on a date.

"Exactly!" Rand declared. "We cannot help but to counter, rebut, or wander off in our minds when we hear words that trigger our thoughts instead of clearing our minds and listening to every word. Listening takes focus and practice. Not listening happens even more during an argument, because each person wants to express their points regardless of the other person's points. But if everyone really listened, there would be less miscommunication and misunderstandings in the world. Listening is important."

"Wow, PopPop! I never really thought about it, but you are right. It makes so much sense. I'm going to work on it."

He told her everyone should work on it, but right now, Shimmer had had a good sampling of the meadow. She agreed, and they mounted up for a quick walk home. Rand glanced back to see his granddaughter in deep thought. He turned forward and smiled.

*****

A horn honk from the driveway that evening brought Lexi racing down the hall toward the front door. Rand could see out of the corner of his eye what looked like his granddaughter in shorts, T-shirt, and sneakers. It would not have been his choice for her to wear on a date, but she was going bowling, and she was not revealing too much. All in all, he thought it wasn't unrespectable.

She yelled out that her ride was here, and she would not be out late. A voice called out from the den.

"Just a moment, dear. Why don't you bring your young man in and introduce us?"

Her grandmother's tone was more of a demand than an ask. A look of shock and horror appeared on Lexi's face.

"No, MomMom! Nobody does that anymore. It's too embarrassing. My mom wouldn't even do that to me. Please!"

Linda just smiled, answering back, "Well, she should, dear. Now the proper thing to do is to go out and tell your young man that your grandparents would like to meet him. Hurry up. He's waiting."

"Oh my god!" Lexi protested aloud while going out the door.

Moments later, the door opened, and she stepped in followed by a young man in jeans and a polo shirt.

"MomMom, PopPop, this is my friend Trey Baskins. Trey, this is my grandmother and grandfather, Mr. and Mrs. Templeton."

Trey extended his hand.

"It is nice to meet you. Lexi tells me you have horses."

"Yes, we do, son. Do you ride?" Rand asked.

"No, sir. I used to when I was little, but we moved and sold our horse. We are going to meet friends at the Aberdeen bowling center, so we should get going. It is nice to meet you both."

Lexi could not pull Trey out of the house fast enough.

From outside, she heard her MomMom yell, "No later than eleven o'clock."

Lexi gasped in embarrassment and said to Trey, "I'm so sorry!"

They got into his car, and Trey told her it was fine and was exactly what his parents did when boys picked up his sister.

She asked, "Really?"

"Yes, really! It's fine."

Back home, Linda asked Rand what he thought.

"The boy did not seem uncomfortable meeting a girl's family, so that is good. He didn't look shaggy or sloppy, so that is good. His handshake was firm, also good. His hair was groomed. I'm not disappointed."

Linda asked, "Did you see he held the door for her? Lexi was in utter humiliation, but I think she got over it by the time they got in the car."

Rand said with a smile, "We probably felt the same way in the seventies."

The couple arrived at the bowling alley at seven thirty after stopping off for a drink at the burger joint. They walked into the bowling alley and were greeted by Macy.

"OMG, you have got to help me with Becca. She heard something about Mitch, and it could get cray-cray up in here."

Lexi was taken aback by the drama already. Claire and Zing were at a table with two guys from school. Zing was a military brat who was half Chinese. Nobody could pronounce her real name, so she told everyone to call her Zing. Lexi liked her.

Mitch came back from the sign-in desk with eight pair of bowling shoes. He said that he hoped he had everyone's size, but if not, they could get the right size themselves. They laughed at the massive pile of shoes on the table. Everyone scrounged for shoes and bowling balls that fit. The eight of them were laughing and carrying on for three games. The score and sometimes even the order of bowler didn't matter. Lexi was having a great time.

When they finished bowling around 9:00 p.m., they agreed to go to the sandwich shop and hang out. They had sodas, told stories, and laughed until ten fifteen. Lexi looked at her watch and whispered to Trey that it was time for her to go home. He agreed, and they said their goodbyes.

On the way home, a short distance before the Templetons' drive, Trey pulled off the road onto an old truck road in the woods and stopped at a small clearing under the pines, just a short distance from her turnoff. Lexi asked him where they were going. He asked if she wanted to sit in the back seat for thirty minutes until her curfew.

Lexi was nervous. She wanted to kiss Trey, but she didn't want to do much more. She expected he would stop if she asked him to, but the uncertainty scared her. He could see that she was nervous. He told her he would not do anything she didn't want him to do.

Lexi reluctantly got out of the front seat and into the back seat. She made him promise that she would be home by 11:00 p.m. He promised. Trey moved close to her and started kissing her gently on her lips and neck. She leaned toward him. He reached over and pulled her closer. They kissed each other hungrily. Lexi was stirring inside with excitement that she had not felt before.

Trey slowly moved his hand onto her breast. She didn't push him away. It was her first time going beyond kissing, and she liked it. His lips and his hands were gentle and tender. He kissed her neck as she tilted her head back. He continued down to her cleavage. He almost had his mouth on a breast, and she wasn't stopping him. Soon, she felt his hand on her crotch as he fumbled for her snap.

She realized it was further than she wanted to go. She gently pushed his hand away, telling him that it was getting too close to curfew. Through his heavy breathing, he asked if she really wanted him to stop. She said that it was time to go. He was disappointed, but he slowly moved away from her, gave her a departing kiss, and slid out of the back seat. She opened her door and did the same. She saw him buckling up his pants when he got out of the back seat, and she wondered when he unbuckled them. He drove her home.

Lexi tried to fix herself to not look like she had been making out in the back seat of a car. Trey got out, opened her door, and walked her to the front porch. He ran his fingers through his hair too, trying to play it cool. He kissed her good night, and she went inside.

Linda was in the den, reading a book and enjoying a glass of wine.

She called out, “How was your evening, dear?”

Lexi responded back toward the den, “Oh, MomMom, I didn’t know you were still up. It was nice. You know, hanging with friends, bowling. It was fun. I’m kinda tired, though, so I’m going to shower and go to bed. Good night!”

“Good night, dear!” Linda said.

After showering and settling in for the night, Lexi got her iPad and saw that Macy and Jennifer had texted her already, asking about her date. She responded first to Jen that she would tell her all about it tomorrow. Then she texted Macy, who wanted to know if they went straight home. Lexi told her no, and then Macy wanted all the details. Lexi smiled and texted back that they stopped and parked in the woods.

Macy responded, “Oh, you go, girl! Slut! LOL!”

Lexi laughed to herself and texted, “I know, right? Not yet, though. We just messed around. Trey kept knocking at the door, but I’m not ready to let him in. LOL. Way late, so I’ll c u in class.”

Lexi closed her eyes and thought sweet thoughts about Trey. She wondered how he felt about her, and then she wondered what she would have done if he hadn’t been such a gentleman and stopped when she asked him to.

*****

Lexi greeted her grandfather in the kitchen the next morning with a smile and a cup of coffee. He asked her how her evening went and if she was up to the task of looking after three horses this morning. She said the evening was great and that she could not wait for the horses. They headed out, and she went straight into Shimmer’s stall and began stroking her back and neck. Lexi's soft, calm voice repeating Shimmer's name helped the young mare be at ease.

Lexi gently pulled up each one of Shimmer's legs to clean her hooves. She filled the water bucket and put new hay into the wall feeder. Then she brought around the wheelbarrow and cleaned out the manure and old bedding on the floor. After all this, she went into Pony Girl's stall to do the same thing. Rand cleaned Champ's stall and then helped her with Pony Girl's stall.

When all three stalls were done, Lexi commented, "I think she feels safe with us."

Rand responded, "Yep, I believe you're right. But don't stop giving her that first-class treatment. I think she likes it. She might even think she is your horse."

Lexi's head snapped toward him when he mumbled, "Gotta earn it, gotta earn it."

She excitedly followed PopPop into the storage room. He grabbed Champ's saddle, and she grabbed Pony Girl's. They mounted the saddles on the horses, tethered Shimmer's lead rope to Pony Girl's saddle horn, and began their ritual ride through the equestrian trails. The bristling of the pine needles was familiar and reassuring. Lexi didn't want to admit it, but she was having enjoyable experiences every day in her temporary environment.

Slowly Finding Her Way

Rand and Linda were paying attention to how Lexi was dealing with her new life, and they were glad that she was counterbalancing the unfamiliar things with her connections to familiar things. She was maturing fast and recovering from her grief right before their eyes. The last piece of their grand scheme was to help her realize that her mother was not the evil villain she made her out to be.

The easiest way to do that, they thought, would be to tell her why her mother had been so angry at her father, his betrayal, but Cynthia was adamant about not telling Lexi, even when her therapist suggested it. Another way to help Lexi was to let time and serenity erode her anger, help her realize how much she missed and loved her mother, and see her mother healthy. A lot of it would depend on Lexi, and both tactics were uncertain at best, but Rand and Linda had their fingers crossed.

Rand was quieter than usual on the trail ride the next morning, hoping that Lexi might start the conversation. She did not disappoint, coming right out and asking if Shimmer was hers and how she would be able to care for her from Woodbridge. Rand was a long-term, big-picture thinker, and he had already imagined his daughter and granddaughter staying in North Carolina. However, he was not going to mention it since it was not up to him. It would be up to Cynthia and Lexi. He responded to Lexi by saying that they would cross that bridge when they came to it.

He saw the contorted look on Lexi's face that told him she was not satisfied with his answer. So he added that Shimmer was hers to love, care for, and ride. If she did not live in North Carolina, then he and MomMom would care for Shimmer. Lexi knew that was as good an answer as she was going to get.

A Bone-Chilling Scream

On Saturdays, they usually went to the village to visit Rashne and Aryana, go golfing, sit on the porch, or go shopping. Lexi didn't mind, because she was constantly finding new items of interest at the Samadanis' house or learning something about the history of the village.

The three arrived at the Samadanis' to find Aryana's usual spread of cheeses, pita breads, hummus, fruits, and Persian treats, complimented by champagne and orange juice. These were not even her catering or party appetizers, just her normal, everyday table fare.

Linda had injured her wrist in the garden two days before, so she bowed out of the golf. And Aryana had planned to spend time with Lexi, so she wasn't golfing either. The men got in a golf cart and headed to the club. Lexi wandered upstairs to see if Aryana had done anything new to the bedrooms. Not finding anything new, she sat down in a formal chair in the hallway by a large window and scrolled through her phone messages.

Aryana and Linda were talking and drinking mimosas when they heard Lexi give out a bone-chilling cry. They rushed upstairs.

Linda yelled, "Lexi, what is it? What's wrong?"

Lexi's face was buried in her hands. The two women knelt beside her, begging to know why she screamed. Lexi handed her phone to her MomMom. The text message from Jennifer read that Amy's mom committed suicide last night and that Amy was with child protective services. She didn't know any more about it because Amy was not answering her phone. Jennifer would let her know as soon as she found out more.

Linda remembered Lexi talking about her friends in Occoquan, including one girl who was a loner and different from the other girls until Lexi got to know her. Linda did not know, however, that Lexi and Amy had become close friends. Linda hugged her granddaughter and told her how sorry she was. She wondered what Amy must be going through. She assured Lexi that if there was anything they could do, they would try. The three women hugged until Aryana suggested they go downstairs and have tea.

Lexi was too emotional to want to do anything. She insisted that Aryana and MomMom still go walking around the village. The two women stayed with Lexi on the porch. Lexi was not in a mood for talking, but she decided that their company was so much better than being alone right now. When Lexi had composed herself, Aryana asked delicately if she wanted to tell her about Amy. Lexi nodded. She told Aryana about her friend, all the while checking her phone every five minutes for news from Jennifer or Amy. The afternoon passed into evening without any further news.

The men came home from the golf course to find the women sitting on the porch. Their melancholy faces showed that something bad had happened. When Rand asked, Linda explained about Lexi's text message. Rand rushed over to Lexi to hug her and give his condolences. She was uncomfortable, because she did not like feeling this sadness and being the center of attention. She acknowledged their sympathies and redirected their attention to dinner in the hope of moving on.

The adults were acting appropriately for this situation even though they did not know Amy or her mother. Lexi's self-pity and anger left little room for her to understand that Rand, Linda, Rashne, and Aryana's love and sympathy was for her, not Amy.

Linda grew worried that this added tragedy would plunge Lexi down her ladder of emotional healing. Since Lexi had come to North Carolina, Linda and Rand had seen huge improvements in her disposition and optimism. She was climbing out of her emotional misery by changing environments, by seeing her mother get treatment, by taking responsibility for the horses, and by having meaningful life talks with her grandparents. Unfortunately, the news about Amy's mother could be a setback in Lexi's therapy. Linda could only shake her head in disappointment and hope that her granddaughter would talk about her feelings.

Aryana appeared in the doorway, announcing that dinner was ready. The mood lifted, if only for a little while.

The short drive back to Vass was solemn. Linda engaged in idle chatter with Rand about the horses in the hope of distracting Lexi. It was not working. Linda looked in the rearview mirror and could see Lexi's eyes staring out the window into the darkness. Linda repeated her remark about riding the horses tomorrow, but Lexi still did not react. She stopped trying to distract her granddaughter and accepted the fact that Lexi was processing Amy's tragedy in her own way. She would have to wait for Lexi to get through it.

Linda was in tears, wondering how much more heartache and loss her granddaughter could take. Lexi was wondering to herself how much more she was going to have to deal with before something good happened.

They arrived home more than ready to put this long night to bed.

Shimmer Saddles Up

Lexi sprung up out of bed in a panic Sunday morning knowing that she was late for her stable chores. She threw on her jeans, boots, and jacket and stumbled to the kitchen. Breakfast leftovers and empty coffee cups on the kitchen table worsened her disappointment.

She mumbled "Shit, shit, shit" under her breath, grabbed a bagel, and ran down the trail to the stables.

"Why didn't you wake me up this morning? I forgot to set my alarm!" she protested.

From inside Champ's stall, she heard her grandfather say in a sympathetic tone that he figured she could use a little more sleep this morning and that it was okay. Then Linda appeared from Pony Girl's stall with the mare in tow.

Lexi said, "MomMom! You surprised me. Are you two going riding this morning?"

Linda said, "No, we three are going riding this morning. Shimmer is waiting for you to saddle her up."

Lexi perked up.

"Oh! Do you think she is ready for a rider?"

Rand came out of the storeroom with Champ's saddle.

"I think so, but we will not know for sure unless you put a saddle on her and find out."

Lexi did not have to ask twice. She rushed into the storeroom and grabbed Shimmer's saddle and pad. Within five minutes, the three of them were coaxing the horses down the trail between the neighboring farms on their way to the equestrian trails for a Sunday morning ride.

It was a beautiful fall morning. A slight chill was in the air, pine needles were falling off the trees, and the smell of oak burning in house hearths stirred warm memories for the riders. Rand led the pack, with Linda and Lexi behind. Linda looked over her shoulder and saw Lexi tilting her face toward the sunbeams breaking through the trees. She had her eyes closed, absorbing all the energy the sun and pine air would provide. She exhaled and released the negative energy.

Linda saw Lexi's forehead wrinkle as if the weight of the world came back to rest on her shoulders.

"Just take in your surroundings, sweetheart. Let them nourish your soul. Don't think about anything else. Let your worries go."

Her granddaughter gave a barely perceptible nod and gazed forward at everything and nothing.

Rand was aware of their interaction going on behind him but decided to mind his own business. He coaxed Champ onward.

The trio arrived at the meadow, and Shimmer was excited to graze in new grasses. Everyone dismounted and let their reins fall to the ground, confident that the horses would not wander off. Rand and Linda saw the sadness and tear trails on Lexi's face. Instead of peace and tranquility, the trail ride gave her time to dwell on her woes.

Rand wanted to ignore it, but Linda decided wisely to risk asking Lexi if she was able to talk about it. Lexi thought for a moment, and then with tears welling up again in her eyes, she said that she had not heard from Amy, so there was nothing to talk about.

Linda gently prodded, "What kind of things do you want to hear from her?"

Lexi answered, "I want to know if she is okay. I want to know what is going to happen to her. I want to tell her I love her, that I'm so sorry for her. And I want her to know that I am here to help any way I can. I want to tell her all those things, but I don't even know where she is."

Linda was proud of her granddaughter's compassion, but she did not want it to be so intense that it crushed her in the process.

She told Lexi, "Amy is still probably in shock and will need time to be able to do anything, just as you are struggling with it. Give her some time, and I'm sure you will be able to reach out to her soon. Her family is with her, I'm sure."

Lexi responded, "That's the worst part, MomMom. Amy doesn't have any family. I think her dad is a prisoner of war or dead, which is why she and her mom were struggling so much. She is my age, so the state might have to take care of her."

"Oh, my word!" Linda exclaimed. "Well, let's just wait a little longer before we get sick from worry."

They mounted the horses and turned back toward home.

They were at the edge of the wood line, where pine forest turned into farm fence lines, when Lexi asked rhetorically, "How could someone ever do that?"

Rand and Linda turned around in their saddles.

"What was that, pumpkin?"

Lexi, unable to let it go, asked, "How can anyone be so selfish and end their life?"

Why Do It?

The trail ride was silent except for the pine needles. Finally, Linda spoke.

"I believe that there are so many complicated issues in a person's life that no one can answer that question. If a person is in so much anguish that the only thing they want is to not feel anything, it must be more than we have ever experienced. I can't imagine being that hopeless or unable to see through the fog of despair. But that is the thing, isn't it? We can never know what they are feeling. I would never presume to judge anybody, because we just don't know.

"Maybe she didn't have anyone to talk to. Maybe she only felt the darkness. In her mind, it wasn't selfishness. It was relief. But all she had to do was see that one more day, one more hour, one more minute might have offered the potential for something better. Also, it is important to understand that depression is a mental illness that can be treated. There are people trained to help, and they are only a phone call away."

Lexi listened and pondered her grandmother's points and her own experiences. She stopped sobbing as they strode up to the paddock. Each rider took care of their own horse. Together, they walked back up to the house, Lexi walked in step under the loving arm of her grandmother.

Rand leaned over and whispered, "It's not a good time, but I'm giving you fifty dollars for true compassion."

After dinner that Sunday night, the Samadanis came over for a glass of wine, hoping that they might get a chance to say hello to Cynthia on the video. Linda made it a point to have a video call with her daughter on Sunday nights so Cynthia could see Lexi. Linda also chatted with Cynthia during the week, but Lexi didn't participate in those calls. Talking to her mom more than once a week was still just a little too much for Lexi and her anger issues.

Linda called out to Lexi, who was in her bedroom, to join everyone for a video chat with her mother. She appeared from her room with a look of indifference. Linda saw Lexi's expression and was disappointed, but at least she was not annoyed this time.

Linda thought, *Her defensive walls are coming down one brick at a time.*

Cynthia answered the call joyfully and excitedly. She smiled when Aryana and Rashne peeked in from the background. Cynthia asked how they had been, what Aryana had been cooking and decorating, and how their golf games were.

After catching up, the Samadanis said their goodbyes because Lexi was waiting in the background. Cynthia's eyes lit up when Lexi appeared on the screen. She asked her daughter to tell her about everything—school, Shimmer, and especially dating. Lexi replied in a monotone voice that home was fine, school was fine, she was making friends, blah, blah, blah.

Her tone and inflection were mildly elated when she described how Shimmer had taken to her and was letting her ride. Lexi declared that she and Shimmer were becoming best friends and that PopPop even mentioned the possibility of her riding Shimmer in competition. Rand poked his head in the screen and smiled at Cynthia as if he had been ratted out.

"Hi, Dad," Cynthia said.

Lexi continued praising Shimmer as a beautiful quarter horse capable of championship riding.

"That's wonderful, honey! I have no doubt she can sense your kindness. I'm so happy for you. Now what about dating?"

Lexi rolled her eyes in disbelief at the invasion of her privacy, uttering through clenched teeth, "Mother!"

Linda seized the opportunity to poke her head into the screen and offer, with a heavy sigh, that Lexi had sad news to share. Lexi was unprepared at that moment to spill her emotions in a group setting. Linda had taken a chance that this détente between mother and daughter was just enough to allow Lexi to lower her war banners and lean in toward her mother.

Lexi drew a deep breath and got teary. She asked her mother if she remembered Amy, one of her newer friends back in Woodbridge. Cynthia remembered her vaguely, referring to the girl in the counselor's office who dressed differently and did not have friends. Lexi confirmed she was the one.

Cynthia asked, "What about her?"

Lexi answered tearfully, "Jennifer texted me that Amy's mom committed suicide."

Right after Lexi said it, she and her grandmother remembered Cynthia's possible suicide attempt. Lexi gulped and went silent.

"Oh my god!" Cynthia whispered, holding her hand to her mouth. "Oh, honey, I'm so very sorry. Are you okay?"

Lexi could not answer as tears rolled down her cheeks.

Seeing this, Cynthia whispered delicately to Lexi, "You can tell me about it, ya know."

Lexi eyes shifted to her periphery, where the four adults were sitting nearby.

"Not now," she answered.

Cynthia tried to supply assurances and empathy to Lexi by explaining that part of her treatment at Pisgah included exploring one's feelings and trying to communicate them to the people you loved and how much it helped you to process your emotions.

"Maybe another time, Mom."

Her tone let Cynthia know to drop it.

Cynthia asked, "So can you remind me again about Amy? Where is her father?"

Lexi was annoyed but responded, "I don't know, Mom. He disappeared two years ago, I think. Amy is my height, my weight, black hair, which she covers under a wrap, brown eyes, and a great tan. Before we met in the counselor's office, she didn't talk to anybody or have any friends. She has tats, a nose piercing, and a weird accent. But it doesn't sound like anyone I've ever heard from Georgia. Oh yeah, she's from Georgia."

Cynthia was trying to control her tears of joy about her estranged daughter talking to her. She listened carefully to Lexi's every word.

She wanted Lexi to keep going, so she asked, "How did you meet her again?"

Lexi said, "Mom, I just told you. I was sitting outside of the guidance counselor's office one day, and she was there too. We started talking. She was nice, which surprised me since she never talked to anyone. After meeting her, I introduced her to my friends, and everybody liked her. She is sweet too. She seems very kind and cares a lot about the world. It is so sad."

In the back of her mind, Lexi began imagining if her own mom had been successful in her suicide attempt. She continued.

"I think it was just her and her mom. I asked one time if she was from Atlanta, and she told me the name of her town, Table Sea or something like that. She said her dad went back there to get his family money, and he was forced into the army, I think. Her mom struggled a lot with depression because she didn't know what happened to her husband, and they didn't have a lot of money. They must be very religious because her mom prays, like, five times a day."

Cynthia did not interrupt Lexi's recollection about Amy. Lexi surprised herself at how much she had shared with her mom. Cynthia asked Lexi to call her anytime so they could talk about it privately. Lexi still had anger, but she was moved by how much her mom seemed to care and listen. Lexi wanted to hold on to her anger, but she was slowly letting it go, which made her angry at herself. She debated her dilemma in her mind but could not control how her anger toward her mother was fading.

Lexi said goodbye and retreated into her bedroom to be alone. Everyone understood and wished her a good night. Linda told Cynthia that they would talk again soon and said good night.

The four adults remained in the living room, drinking their wine and quietly discussing the video conversation. Aryana apologized for overhearing, but she explained that Muslims prayed five times a day and that Muslim women often wore head coverings, or hijabs. Rashne had the same conclusion and offered that the capital of Georgia, which was south of Russia, was Tbilisi or, as Lexi misheard, Table Sea.

He continued explaining that Georgia was in a dangerous neighborhood bordering Russia, Armenia, and Turkey. The Russians had made incursions into Georgia over the years, starting localized wars and causing bloodshed. It was probable that Amy's military-aged father got pulled into the army. Aryana said that everything Lexi described suggested that Amy was a Muslim war orphan, likely born in the US, making her a US citizen. She could be of Russian, Georgian, Armenian, Turkish, or even Persian lineage.

Rand piped in after listening, saying that Amy was most likely in child protective services right now or would be soon when they found out about her father. They wouldn't allow her to live alone for very long, and they would process her into foster homes, at least until she was eighteen. He shook his head.

"Sad, very sad, for a young girl with no one left to turn to."

Linda covered her mouth. Aryana and Rashne shared a woeful glance. The group contemplated the tragedy and sipped their wine in silence.

Later that night, after Aryana and Rashne had gone home and Rand and Linda got ready for bed, Linda went in to check on Lexi and say good night. Lexi had fallen asleep in bed with her phone in her hand. Linda gently took the phone from Lexi's hand and noticed that an app was open with photos in a collage. Lexi had been inserting selfies of her and Amy into the collage. Linda also noticed a photo file that was still open. It was titled "Me and Mom." She put the phone on the nightstand charger and kissed her granddaughter's cheek.

Lexi went right to work in the stables early the next morning despite yesterday's sad news. Rand asked if she had heard anything more from Amy, but Lexi just shook her head as she cleaned the floor of Shimmer's stall. She pulled Shimmer back into the stall and hugged her neck, and then she joined her PopPop in cleaning Pony Girl's stall. The chores were done efficiently despite the mood. The horses sensed her sadness and were especially gentle. The somber walk back to the house was accentuated by the hush of the fall morning. Lexi got ready for school.

Why Isn't Anyone Sad?

Lexi was in a woeful mood in school. Everyone was going about their routines and social interactions as if it was a normal day. Of course, no one in Union Pines High School knew Amy from Woodbridge, but Lexi was carrying such a heavy feeling that she imagined everyone else would be sympathetic or supportive. She understood that Amy was no one else's concern, but it felt to her like she should be.

Macy and Emma Jean were smiling and chatting about the homecoming dance when they approached Lexi in the hallway. Their cheerful mood annoyed her. The girls saw the troubled look on Lexi's face and asked what was wrong. She tried to play it off as if she wasn't feeling well, which was convincing until she started to cry.

Macy demanded to know why she was crying so she could help. The late bell was about to ring, so they rushed to class, and Lexi mentioned that a friend of hers from back home lost her mother this past weekend. Both girls' mouths hung open in disbelief. They hugged Lexi and asked if there was anything they could do. Their sympathy and support helped Lexi feel like she could get through the rest of the day.

Lexi's friends gathered around her at lunch, asking how she was feeling. She told them she was really sad for Amy but didn't know how to help her. Some of the girls wanted to know the details, but Macy told them that Lexi didn't want to talk about it. LeeAnne suggested that the best thing to do would be to stay in touch with Amy, let her know how much you cared, and offer to help any way you could. Lexi explained that she had been calling and texting Amy without any success.

Macy said, "You should keep trying. She is probably still in shock and doesn't know what to think right now. Give her time, but keep trying. God! I can't even imagine if I lost my mom. I'd be a mess forever."

Lexi thought about her mom. She was ashamed about how horrible she had been to her over the past months. It gave her something to think about.

Lexi was back at her locker before the last class when she felt arms wrap around her from behind and a kiss on her neck. She smiled as she turned around to meet Trey's kiss. The two were a couple now, and his surprise was welcome.

He said, "Let's hang out Friday night. My parents will be out of the house, so we could go there and watch something on Netflix."

Lexi smiled. She knew that he had more than Netflix on his mind, but so did she.

"I will have to check with my grandparents, but I'm sure it will be okay. I'll tell them we are going to hang out at the pizza place in Southern Pines."

They both went to class with differing ideas and hopes about Friday night. It was a welcome distraction for Lexi, and she felt better than she had all day.

Shimmer in a Corner

When Lexi got home after school, she went through her routine and headed down to the stables. She was enjoying getting to know Shimmer. Champ and Pony Girl were bristling as usual when Lexi came into the stalls, but there was no movement from Shimmer. The young mare did not react when Lexi approached, almost as if she was asleep.

"What's wrong, girl? Aren't you glad to see me this afternoon?"

The only time Shimmer moved was when Lexi tried to put on her halter. She turned her head and did not want it on. Lexi became worried when she had to force Shimmer out of her stall. She tried to stroke her neck, but the mare pulled away. Shimmer reached her head around toward her belly as if she had been bitten. Lexi tied Shimmer to the hook outside of the stall to clean the straw and manure. She noticed that Shimmer's droppings were soft and inconsistent. Lexi heard her PopPop coming into the stables.

"PopPop, something's wrong with Shimmer. She is not acting like herself."

Rand came out of Champ's stall and approached Shimmer calmly. He looked her over and felt her neck and back. He could see that she was lethargic and uncomfortable. He further examined her eyes and mouth, then felt her neck, legs, and belly. She was warm to the touch and had a slight mucous discharge from her nostrils.

"I'm glad you picked up on this right away," he said. "I will call the vet."

"What do you think is wrong with her, PopPop?" Lexi asked in a frightened voice.

"I don't know for sure, honey, but the vet should be able to figure it out. My guess is, she ate something that disagreed with her, or she might have a cold."

"What does that mean? I didn't know horses could get colds. Will she be all right?"

Lexi was in a panic.

"Don't worry just yet. We don't know why she is uncomfortable, but horses can get sick just like people, and they can get better too. Let's not fret. I'm sure Dr. Sherri will treat her, and she will be good as new in a few days. I'll call her now. I suspect she will be able to come by tomorrow."

"Why can't she look at her tonight?"

"Well, if it was an emergency, she would come tonight, and we would pay a lot more for that kind of service. But this is not an emergency, so tomorrow will be fine. I've taken care of horses all my life. Shimmer will be fine, and so will you. Okay? Let's just clean her stall, make sure she has clean straw, clean water, oats, and hay, and let her rest."

Lexi was not happy with his answer, but she trusted his experience. She finished her chores, promised Shimmer that they would take care of her, and went up to the house for dinner. When Lexi was washing up, she became overwhelmed with anxiety. Everything was heaped on her at once. First, there was Amy, then guilt about her mom and now Shimmer. She hated feeling this emotional and was hoping it was just hormones. Whatever the cause, she buried her head in her pillow and let the tears flow.

Linda had called her granddaughter more than once to come to dinner, and when there was no answer, she went to the back bedroom and knocked on the door. Lexi appeared without a word. Linda noticed Lexi's swollen eyes. She asked what was wrong. Lexi was embarrassed, so she lied and said that the fall pollen was irritating her eyes more than usual. Linda knew better, but she dropped it.

Right before bedtime, Lexi put on her robe and boots, grabbed a flashlight, and went to the stables. Champ and Pony Girl were alerted by the unusual arrival. She rubbed their noses, which hung out over the stall doors to investigate. Shimmer was in her stall with her head in a corner. Lexi came into the stall and rubbed her hand along the mare's back. She moved to Shimmer's front and gently hugged her neck, whispering to her that PopPop and the doctor were going to make her feel better in the morning. Lexi was upset about seeing Shimmer this way. She kissed Shimmer and went up to the house.

In bed, she checked her iPad. Jennifer was keeping her informed, but she had not heard from Amy either. She texted back to Jennifer, asking if Amy had been in school. No one in school had seen her, which was understandable for the few days she was in mourning. But Shyanne went by Amy's house, and it looked abandoned. The grass had not been cut, the fall leaves covered the yard and the porch, the mail was sticking out of the box, and the lights were off. Jennifer also heard that Amy was with child protective services until they could find foster care.

Lexi texted back that everything had turned to shit, and sometimes, she wondered if life was worth it.

Jennifer shot back in all caps, "YOU SHOULDN'T THINK LIKE THAT! Even though terrible things happen, there will always be more good things to come."

Lexi texted back, "Try to tell that to Amy." Lexi said good night and fell into a restless sleep.

The next morning, at the stables, Lexi begged PopPop to let her stay home from school to be there when the vet came. Rand was sympathetic and did not deny her request right away. He told her that he had not yet called Dr. Sherri and didn't know when or if she could come by. He asked Lexi if Shimmer would feel better with her hovering in the stall all day. Lexi didn't want to admit that he was right, but she was worried that Dr. Sherri might find something bad. MomMom was in the stables too, and she knew that Lexi was reflecting on all her recent traumas.

She hugged her granddaughter, saying, "Shimmer is not feeling well, but she will be fine, I promise. She is not going anywhere. She will be right here when you get home not only today but for years to come. Okay?"

Lexi needed that reassurance to be able to go to school without worry. She rushed up to the house to get ready. Rand looked at Linda quizzically.

Linda said, "You're a brilliant man, my love. But sometimes, you gotta read the room."

In school, Trey met Lexi in the hallway between classes. When he told her he was excited about Friday night, she saw a leery look in his eyes. Lexi was not feeling excited with the drama and worry on her plate, but Trey was not in the same place.

She wanted to be with him and be romantic so she could feel good about something, but maybe not as close as he was thinking. She told him that she hadn't heard any news about her friend Amy in Woodbridge, and it was making her gloomy. He said not to worry about it because he had ideas about making her feel good. Lexi was irritated that he was not listening to her and was only thinking of himself.

Frustrated, she finally told him, "Look, Trey, my horse is sick, and she might need me, so let's just put Friday night on pause right now."

Trey looked at her in shock.

"Your horse? You are choosing a horse over me? Wow! That's fine. I'll find something else to do this weekend."

He walked away.

"Trey. Trey!" she called out. "Great! Way to go, Lex. More drama in your life," she said to herself on the way to class.

Lexi was sitting in her history class when her phone vibrated in her pocket. If the teachers caught anyone using phones in class, they took them away. But with so much going on in her life, Lexi was desperate to see who was calling. She went up to the teacher's desk and asked permission to use the restroom. The teacher approved without hesitation.

As soon as she was in the hallway, Lexi opened her phone and read the text: "Just wanted to let you know that Shimmer is fine. Dr. Sherri is giving her medication to treat her cold. That's all it is, and it is common. Love, MomMom." Lexi was so relieved and glad that her grandmother let her know as soon as she found out what was wrong. One worry was off her plate. She wasn't going to tell Trey about Shimmer after his selfish reaction. She wanted to be with Shimmer anyway.

Lexi went straight down to the stables when she got home from school.

"Hey! What about homework?" Linda yelled from the porch.

"MomMom! I have to see her!"

Linda smiled knowing that Lexi would want to see Shimmer right away. She put down her book and followed Lexi to the stables. Linda came into the stall.

"Dr. Sherri said Shimmer will be fine. She has a cold. You shouldn't ride her until she feels better, but you can walk her. Her joints are achy, and she is stuffy just like when humans get colds. The doctor left pills for her to take once a day for five days. If we make sure she has food and water, give her the meds, and cover her at night, she will be just fine."

Lexi hugged Shimmer's neck, saying that she would take good care of her. She asked her grandmother if she could sleep in the apartment above the stables in case Shimmer needed her. Linda told her that the apartment needed repairs, including a new heating system, but Shimmer would be safe in the stables while Lexi was in the house just a short walk away. Lexi frowned.

They were sitting at the table after dinner when Linda suggested that they go to Asheville on Saturday. Lexi protested that she did not want to go because of Shimmer, and she had already talked to her mom that week anyway. Linda had hoped for a better reaction. Linda argued that they were only going for the day and that Dr. Sherri was coming by to check in on Shimmer anyway. Lexi knew that the decision had already been made.

"I guess it's a good thing I don't have any plans this weekend," Lexi said sarcastically under her breath.

On Saturday morning, Lexi woke up extra early to look in on Shimmer. She took longer doing her chores, spending more time with the mare. She told Shimmer that the doctor would be here today to check on her, and she would be back tonight. Lexi kissed her and went up to the house just in time to get in the car. By 8:00 a.m., they were heading to Pisgah Wellness Center.

They arrived at Pisgah just after 12:00 p.m. Lexi slept along the way but woke up when they neared Asheville to enjoy the full display of red-and-yellow leaves covering the mountainsides. The fall colors had peaked all the way down the Appalachians south past North Carolina to Tennessee. The harvests had been collected and farms along the way were selling their apples, pumpkins, and other goods. The smell of fall in the mountains was different from that of the pines of the Sandhills. One was not better or worse, just different.

Cynthia was waiting outside on a bench when they pulled up in front of Pisgah. She smiled widely and greeted them joyfully. Lexi got out of the back seat still listening to music in her earbuds. Cynthia went to Lexi first to give her a big hug and kiss on her forehead. Lexi gently wrapped her arms around her mother. She didn't squeeze, but the effort was better than before. Cynthia took what she could get. She held on for a minute and then let go of Lexi to greet her mother and father. She invited them all inside for lunch.

They ate lunch in a private dining room. Cynthia talked about her progress and plans. Her doctor believed that she would be ready to come home before the holidays. She was still working through issues, but she had found ways to cope and not blame herself for things that were out of her control.

She looked at Lexi.

"What?" Lexi asked.

Cynthia said that the doctor wanted to talk to her today—alone. Lexi's adrenaline rose.

"I don't know if I want to talk to anybody about anything."

Cynthia held Lexi's hand.

"Honey, that's fine if you don't. No one will force you. But I wish you would. You've had so much to deal with in your young life, and it's not fair. And I take part of the blame for it. I am trying so hard to be better for you so that we can be a family again. It would be good for both of us if you could learn new ways to help me."

"She wants to teach me how to help you?" Lexi asked incredulously.

"I'm not sure exactly, but maybe you could just talk to her and find out. It can't hurt, right?"

With her suspicions eased slightly, Lexi agreed to sit with her mother's shrink.

An attendee invited Lexi to follow him into an office down the hall. The name on the door was Dr. Judith Morrell. Lexi remembered meeting her when they dropped her mother off the first time, but the doctor did not make an impression. When Lexi entered the office, Dr. Morrell laid a folder on her desk and came over to Lexi with her hand extended.

"Hello, Lexi. I'm Dr. Morrell. I don't know if you remember, but we met when your mom first came to us for treatment."

Lexi said, "I remember."

"Wonderful!" Morrell replied. "Please have a seat. Lexi, do you know why I invited you in for a discussion?"

Lexi shrugged her shoulders.

"You want to talk to me about my relationship with my mother?"

"Yes, Lexi. Do you know why?"

"Uh, because she has convinced you she is a good person, and you want to find out why there is a disconnect," Lexi answered sarcastically.

"Lexi, do you see those certificates on my wall? They certify that I've spent a long time learning how to do what I do. I can help people understand why they think and feel the way they do. I can give them tools and methods to work through their problems. I can tell when they are being honest with me and if they are able to understand their own truth. However, I am not qualified to tell if someone is a good person or not.

"I want to talk to you because you are the most important person in your mom's life, and you will have a profound impact on your mother's mental health. I hope that impact can be positive for both of you. Now can we talk like adults?"

Lexi learned from Dr. Morrell's last statement that she wanted the best for her mom, and she was serious about her work. She also felt that Morrell was treating her with respect like an adult.

"Okay, Doc, how can I help?" Lexi asked.

"Wonderful, Lexi! Thank you so much," Morrell started. "How do you feel about your mother coming here for treatment?"

"Well, she has a lot of demons, so I am happy for her that she is coming to terms with them."

Morrell pressed her.

"Are you happy for you?"

"I guess so. I mean, it won't change what she did in the past, but maybe she will be a better person in the future."

"Lexi, do you see yourself in that future?"

"Well, she is my mom, so I guess so."

Morrell asked, "You guess so? Would it surprise you to know that 90 percent of the time your mother talks about you? I am trying to get her to concentrate a little more on her own health, but all she really cares about is you. You are everything to her."

"You mean now that my dad is gone."

"No, Lexi, I mean since the day you were conceived. I don't know of any greater love than a mother's love. One day, you will feel that joy yourself."

"Well, Doc, my mother should also have had that kind of love for my father, but she let it go, and I don't understand how a wife could just stop loving her husband."

"Lexi, do you honestly believe your mother stopped loving your father? Could you have stopped loving him?"

Lexi shook her head as if the question was ridiculous.

"Well, neither could she. People can be terribly angry at someone and still love them. It happens all the time. Your mother shared with me that your father was everything to you, and you were a daddy's girl through and through. Losing your father must be so painful for you. It is very normal to be angry about that loss. How does it make you feel now?"

"Are you serious? I would give anything to have my dad back for just one more day."

"And why is that?"

Lexi answered, "Because my dad loved me so much. He took me everywhere. We played sports together. He came to all my games. He was a hero in the military. I mean, he was everything."

"Did he make you feel safe?"

"Yes, of course! No one was going to hurt us when he was there. We always had a roof over our heads, clothes on our back, and food to eat. Anytime I was sad, he could cheer me up just with a hug. I miss him every day."

Lexi's eyes teared up.

"Lexi, when your dad died, your mom lost all that too plus the intimacy and secrets that only a couple share. She couldn't handle that loss, and her despair and demise threatened any shred of safety you had left."

Lexi nodded as she cried.

"Your mother is making enormous strides toward dealing with her loss and returning to the person she was when she was at her best. A key to her full recovery—and yours—is for you to let her back into your heart. She is a mother. Mothers need to pour out their love to their children. It's what they do. She may never love a man again, but she will never stop loving her child. Do you want to know the irony I see?"

"What?" Lexi asked.

"The irony is that you think she stopped loving your father because she was angry at him, but you have been doing the same thing to your mother by not loving her. You are angry at her, but it seems like you stopped loving her. Did you?"

Lexi shook her head.

"But you have your reason for being so angry at her, right?"

Lexi nodded.

"Well, is it possible that your mother had a reason why she was so angry with your father?"

Lexi looked up at Dr. Morrell.

"Nothing could have been so bad to make her treat him the way she did."

Dr. Morrell let out a long exhale. She thought Lexi was making a breakthrough, but her anger could not be vanquished. Morrell had suggested to Cynthia in therapy that Lexi should be told about her father's mistake, and it wouldn't matter, but Cynthia was adamant. She saw no point in tarnishing Tom's memory.

Dr. Morrell sensed that Lexi had talked enough, but before she ended the session, she asked Lexi to think about their conversation and to call anytime she wanted to talk some more. Dr. Morrell handed Lexi her business card. She pointed to the cell number, saying that it was her private number, and she would like to hear from Lexi soon.

Lexi returned to her grandparents and mother just in time to take her mom to lunch in Asheville. They spent the day walking around the city, sitting in the city center with the locals beating their drums and five-gallon buckets, window-shopping, and feeling the fall temperatures in the mountains.

Lexi told her mom that Trey had asked her to the homecoming dance. It wasn't like prom or anything, but she was excited. Cynthia was excited too and asked Rand and Linda to find vintage shops in Asheville for dress shopping. Lexi was not keen on her mother picking out her dress for homecoming, but after being pulled into a few secondhand vintage shops and seeing chic Bohemian dresses, Lexi found herself enjoying the moment. Rand stayed outside on the sidewalks, watching people and feeling good about Lexi and her mom getting along, at least for a little while.

The hours passed quickly, and it was time to take Cynthia back to Pisgah and for them to make the long drive back to Vass. Their goodbyes included an unexpected hug between Lexi and her mom as she thanked her for the outfit they bought. Cynthia told her she would be done with treatment soon and coming home for the holidays. Lexi didn't know what home she was referring to, but she didn't want to belabor the point. The car pulled away, and everyone waved goodbye.

The drive home was quiet except for the country music on the radio. The sun dropped below the mountains, giving way to the darkness and the lulling sound of the car cruising down the interstate. Everyone was tired, but Linda had to stay awake to keep Rand alert. Lexi's mind was engaged in battle between hanging on to her anger and forgiving her mom. The mental conflict took its toll, and she fell asleep.

*****

Sunday morning was a trail ride day, but Shimmer was still sick, so Lexi asked PopPop if she could skip the trail and walk with Shimmer in the paddock. He agreed that it was a good idea, so he and Linda took Champ and Pony Girl on the trail ride. Shimmer was slow to exit from her stall into the fenced area to graze. Lexi stayed alongside her, stroking the mare's flank and neck, talking to her the whole time.

She told Shimmer how she had bought the coolest dress to wear to homecoming and that her mom was being so nice, and she didn't know how to take it. She said that the doctor at Pisgah told her a few things about her mom that had been on her mind, but she still couldn't understand what went on between her parents that made her mom so angry at her dad.

She asked Shimmer if her mom could have been so angry about her dad retiring that she would hate him. Shimmer continued grazing. She asked Shimmer if it was possible that her mom had suddenly become an alcoholic or had developed a bout of manic depression. She talked to Shimmer about Trey and if she was ready to be intimate.

Lexi heard her grandparents coming off the trail toward the stables. She hugged Shimmer's neck and told her that she was a particularly good listener.

"How was the ride?" Lexi asked.

"Gorgeous, honey," Linda answered. "The chill in the morning air and crisp sounds make me feel like putting a few logs in the fireplace and curling up with a good book. We are going to Aryana's for dinner. Okay? You can show her your outfit for homecoming."

Lexi shrugged.

"We'll see."

They arrived at Aryana's house a little after 2:00 p.m. She had laid out on the table an amazing spread of cheeses, olives, meats, crackers, hummus, and other finger foods. It was so typical of Aryana.

She hugged Lexi and asked her how everything was in school, with her friends, Shimmer, everything. Lexi told her that everything was fine and that she brought along her homecoming outfit to try on.

Aryana was excited and told her to go upstairs and put it on so she could see it. Lexi appreciated the enthusiasm. She brought the bag in from the car and went upstairs to change. She came down a short while later and called Aryana from the parlor. Aryana dropped what she was doing. Linda, Rand, and Rashne followed.

"Oh my goodness! You look so cute!" Aryana said, putting her hands to her face.

"Really? You like it?" Lexi asked.

"Yes, yes, of course! You are so beautiful!" Aryana exclaimed. "Our girl is a beautiful woman!"

Lexi stood in the parlor, twirling in a two-piece sky-blue outfit. It was a strapless, half-cut top in the front and a corset back, with underlay applique all around. The pocketed satin skirt flared at the hem above the knee. While shopping in their last vintage store in Asheville, Cynthia insisted on a pair of gold-glitter, open-toe, cross-strap sandals with two-inch block heels and ankle strap closures to complete the look.

"The boy escorting you to the dance must be very special," Aryana said in an inflection that was more like a question.

Lexi's face turned red trying not to smile. Aryana gasped.

"I know what would go perfect with that."

She rushed upstairs. A minute later, she came back down holding a palm-sized blue velvet box.

"I think this will look beautiful on you," Aryana said.

She opened the box and withdrew a gold necklace with a huge pear-shaped aquamarine gemstone surrounded by crystals. She reached around Lexi's neck to put it on her.

Linda shook her head, saying, "Oh no, Aryana, it is far too expensive to loan out to anyone, and certainly not for a homecoming dance."

Lexi nodded in agreement.

"Aryana, thank you so much. I love it, but I can't."

"Nonsense! You can, and you will. I insist! It is costume jewelry, but it doesn't matter. I trust that you will take good care of it. I want to see it in your pictures."

Aryana raised her hand to show no more talk of it. Lexi looked at her grandmother, not sure what to do. Linda tilted her head and shrugged. It was decided. Lexi was borrowing the necklace. She took it off and carefully placed it in its case. She put it in her bag, along with the outfit, and took the bag to the car. When she returned, they all gathered around the table in the dining room, picking at the appetizers and watching a football game in the sunroom off the kitchen.

When the opportunity arose, Lexi whispered to her grandmother that she would only wear the necklace for pictures and then secure it in her clutch. Linda smiled and hugged her. The matter was closed, and the rest of the evening was joyful and full of Aryana's funny stories.

From that moment on, Lexi began to feel excited about the dance, especially after hearing Aryana's opinion about her outfit. She hoped that Trey and her friends would like it as much as Aryana did. Lexi was planning to hang out with them on Wednesday evening, but she wouldn't say anything about the dress and surprise them on Saturday night. When Trey came to pick her up the night of the dance, his first look would tell her everything she needed to know.

All the dance preparations that week in the school gym and around the halls and chatter among her friends were intensifying her feelings toward her date with Trey. She found herself thinking about him more.

On Wednesday, Lexi raced her grandfather to the stables. They had already agreed to shorten their morning trail ride because of the chill in the air. Somehow, though, the chill and unexpected frost on the ground made the ride that much more pleasant. They both were dressed for it, and even Shimmer seemed a little more anxious about going for a walk.

When Did You Know?

A few minutes into their trail ride and without warning, Lexi asked her grandfather when he knew he was in love with MomMom. Rand was not ready for that kind of discussion, but he stayed stoic to not give himself away. He could see her staring at him out of his periphery, waiting for an answer. His pause was awkward, but his glance told her he was forming an answer.

"Don't you think this is better answered by MomMom?" he asked.

"Maybe, but I wonder if her answer would match yours."

His throaty exhale told her that he knew he was on the hook.

After another pause and with his eyes forward, he said, "I wish I could remember if there was a thunderstruck moment. There probably was when it just hit me that I was in love with her, but I'm old and can't remember. Why are you asking?"

"I just wonder how long it takes for it to happen," Lexi said.

Rand trusted that his granddaughter's sharp intellect and mindfulness was not allowing her to be confused about being in love with her new boyfriend. She might like the boy, but it was not love, and she knew it. However, he also understood that young, healthy hormones were the most intense during a person's late-teenage years to midtwenties. He didn't even want to contemplate how sex confounded things. Giving her a nonanswer or a cliché answer would cause her to overthink it. His mind was in overdrive.

"Honey," he said, "I enjoy our talks, and I can enlighten you with facts, figures, history, and evidence to support my opinions. But love is the most complex thing we've ever talked about."

"Why?" she asked.

"For hundreds of reasons. Philosophers, poets, writers, saints, and dreamers have tried to define it since Adam and Eve. It is so individualized that no two people experience it the same way. And it can be easily confused by other things."

"What other things?"

"Lexi, you are old enough to talk about these things as an adult. I get that. But it might be better to talk with MomMom because I believe that women think about love differently than men."

"I agree, which is why I want your opinion."

Rand let out a short laugh.

"I'm not getting out of this, am I?"

"Nope."

"All right. In a nutshell, I believe that the purest form of love is the bond between a mother and a child. It's nature's biological way to ensure survival of her offspring. Her love toward that child supplies nourishment, security, emotional growth, confidence—all the things necessary for the brain and body to grow healthy and productive. It is so instinctive that mothers will give their lives to protect their offspring.

"Fathers, on the other hand, are not as physically connected to their children, so the love develops differently. It grows and becomes almost as strong and equally as necessary, but there is a difference, in my opinion.

"So as we grow into adulthood, hopefully with a healthy childhood filled with love, we seek the same fulfillment with others and eventually with a mate. Society has acknowledged that love and fulfillment is not only between members of different sexes, and that's okay. However, I don't believe science has been able to improve upon egg and sperm reproduction yet, but after thousands of years of social constructs, we have finally come up with some healthy workarounds. Are you following?"

"I'm with you the whole way, PopPop, but I think it is time to head back. Keep talking, though."

"Okay, so what you are wondering is, when does all the magic, all the stars and fireworks, all the arguing and making up that comes with dating, liking, and lusting, turn into love."

"Yep," Lexi answered.

"You are the only one that can answer that question, sweetheart."

"PopPop!" she pleaded in disappointment.

"No, Lexi, I mean it, and here's why. There are so many things that will be so unique to only you in your experiences with romance. Your young, healthy hormones will confuse the heck out of you and cause you to make decisions that you may regret later, but you will find your way through them. Everyone does. Well, some people don't, and it's called divorce.

"And then, too, people change over time. The person you couldn't live without when you were twenty will not be the same person when he or she is forty. Our bodies change. Our experiences change. Our hopes and dreams change. Responsibilities of life weigh us down. And when you spend years with someone, the spit shine wears off, and you see the real person for who they are, not the pristine, on-their-best-behavior, perfect dream of a person. It gets real. And when you go through all the worst times and see the flawed person for who they really are and you still like them and want to be with them, that is love."

"Wow, PopPop. That is a great definition! I guess to know if you're in love takes a long time?"

"I would say so. People say love at first sight, and that may be possible, but there is a lot of time between that first sight and that last first kiss."

Rand put a knee into Champ's flank to bring him to a trot for the last one hundred yards. Lexi and Shimmer followed closely behind. In short order, they put the horses up, and Lexi got ready for school.

Trey Date

In school, Trey met Lexi at her locker. They kissed and talked about plans for the evening with their friends. They were going to get pizza in Southern Pines and then catch a movie at the theater. Trey would pick her up and bring her home right after the movie. However, it was also getting close to Thanksgivings. So midsemester testing was over, the homecoming was this weekend, and class demands were winding down for a week. He was hoping that her curfew was going to be a little less restrictive.

Rand welcomed Trey into the living room early that evening and waited with him for Lexi. She didn't take long. Linda asked when she would be coming home. She explained that classes were dialing down for the holiday break, but she would still be home right after the movies, probably around ten thirty. Linda nodded and told them to be careful. The young couple headed out.

They arrived at the pizza house, and the gang was already there. The girls hugged, the guys bumped fists, and then everyone dug into two large pizzas. The talk around the table was the usual gossip, football and lacrosse talk, and movie banter. No one was especially gung ho for comic book hero movies, but it was the newest movie in the theater. They finished eating with time to catch the 8:00 p.m. showing. After the movie, the couples paired off and went their separate ways while the three others jumped in one car and headed home.

Trey talked about the movie on the ride to Lexi's house but quickly switched topics to homecoming and how excited he was to be taking her to the dance. Before reaching her driveway, he pulled off the road onto the old truck trail where they had parked before. He stopped the car and moved close to her. They began kissing. Lexi only wanted to hang out at first base, but she could tell by his rapid breathing that Trey was swinging for a home run. She did not want nor was she mentally or emotionally prepared for a wham-bam rendezvous.

When Trey had completed what he considered the proper amount of kissing, he reached under her blouse. Lexi didn't say stop, but Trey was acting like he was racing the clock, which didn't sit well with her. When he tried to slip his hand down the front of her jeans, she stopped him. He asked what was wrong, and she tried to explain that she was not feeling it, especially since she had to be home in fifteen minutes. He said that was why he was rushing, and he thought she wanted to do it.

He was annoyed again, which made Lexi feel disappointed, guilty, and angry all at once. She told him that she didn't want her first time to be a quickie on the side of the road. In anger, he got back into the driver's seat and started the car. Neither one said anything until she opened the door in front of her house and got out. She said goodbye, but he just backed up and drove away. This was not the way she wanted her relationship to be going right before homecoming.

When she went inside, Rand and Linda were up.

Linda asked, "How did your date go, dear?"

Lexi was not about to share the slimy details of the last half hour.

"It was fine. All the gang was together, and we watched a movie. No big deal. I'm going to my room for the night. Good night."

They both answered back, "Good night, sweetheart."

Lexi took her shower, got into bed, and texted Jennifer about how badly Trey behaved the last half hour of their date.

Jennifer texted, "So he really expected you to hook up your first time in the front seat of the family sedan? That's so shady! I don't even know him, but he is a tool, and I already don't like him."

Suddenly, a text popped up from Amy.

"Hi, my BFFs. I've missed you!"

Lexi was so excited.

"Amy! Where have you been? How have you been? Are you okay? We've missed you!"

Jennifer was texting her similar things at the same time. Texts were flying back and forth in a three-way conversation.

Amy answered back, "I'm good now. Things were a little unsettled in the child protective services, going from different foster situations, but I'm settled now. I'm with a nice couple who have fostered other kids besides me. It's temporary if something more permanent comes along or until I'm 18. They are nice. Enough about me. What's up with you?"

Lexi explained everything to Amy that she had texted Jennifer. It was all about living at her grandparents' place, the horses and riding, school, and Trey.

Jennifer then texted back, "Right? What a dirtbag! I thought you said he was a babe. IMHO, seems like a red flag to me. Maybe little selfish, ya think?"

Lexi answered back, this time to both Jennifer and Amy.

"Yeah, he lost big points tonight. He didn't even say goodbye when he dropped me off. He's my date to the homecoming dance this Saturday. OMG, you should see the outfit we put together in Asheville. My mom even helped. It wasn't the worst experience in my life. It is so vintage and sick. I'll send pics. Well, I got an early morning with my pony, so chat later. Hugs. So glad you are okay, Amy, I miss you."

Before Lexi closed her iPad, Jennifer texted one more line.

"Hmm, I didn't get my invitation to homecoming. I would have been your plus one. LOL."

Lexi drifted off to sleep, tossing and turning all night.

*****

5:00 a.m. came early. Rand had a cup of coffee waiting for her, but Lexi's sour face and groans sent out a clear message.

"Didn't sleep well, Lex?" he asked. "Are you ill?"

"No, PopPop, I'm not ill. But I have a lot on my mind, so I couldn't sleep for more than an hour at a time. I don't think Shimmer and Pony Girl care, though, so we should give them their morning routine, and maybe they will give me a kick-start."

"Right behind you, barrel rider," he said, following her out the door.

Lexi was right. Shimmer made her feel better by being extra cuddly. She kept gently rubbing her nose and face against Lexi's head. Rand took care of Champ and Pony Girl to lighten his granddaughter's chores for today. When they finished and were walking back up to the house, she grabbed his hand and thanked him for being so perceptive.

"It's what we do for the people we love, Lex. We all have those days."

Lexi was not looking forward to seeing Trey at school. This was their first official fight, and she was about to find out how he acted afterward. Her answer did not take long. She waited for him at her locker, just like every day for weeks. He would meet her and walk with her to class, but today, he didn't show up.

She went with her girlfriends to her first class, but his no-show was heavy on her mind. They had not been dating very long, but she didn't like the way he was dealing with their first argument, especially when it was over something so important to her. Jennifer was right, this was a red flag. In a moment of sympathy and caring, she hoped he wasn't sick at home.

Right after class, she got her answer. He strode by her in the hallway with his friends. She looked right at him in bewilderment, but after their eyes first met, he looked away. She felt like someone had just punched her in the gut, but she was too angry to cry. She was upset and could not pay attention in her classes. The teachers could have been teaching Greek for all she could tell. Her mind was too full of the unfolding drama.

At lunch, Lexi went out to the bleachers to be alone. Other couples and small groups were taking in the crisp fall air. The lunch period was almost over when three upperclassmen girls came over to her. They were giggling.

"Aren't you Trey's newest girlfriend?" one of the girls asked. "Sophomore, right?"

The other girls laughed.

"New here too, right? A horse girl from a broken home?"

As soon as Lexi saw them approach, she knew this was not a friendly visit. She nodded to the first question, but the comment about a broken home turned her face into a squinty-eyed "What did you just say, bitch?" look.

The girl continued.

"Well, we heard he was taking you to homecoming, which is sweet, but you might want to ask Cassie Long where she took him last night. He might've had an early homecoming, if you know what I mean."

Then another girl leaned in and whispered to Lexi, "Look, I don't know you, but I hear you are nice. He burned me once too, so we thought you should know."

Lexi said, "He was with me last night."

"I heard he went to Cassie's late last night."

The girl backed away, giving a sympathetic glance. Lexi overheard one of the other girls ask her what she whispered to Lexi.

She said, "I wanted to know where she got her shoes."

The revelation was breaking Lexi's heart while at the same time stirring in her the kind of anger she had only felt toward her mother. She gathered her things and stormed back into the school. She knew where Trey would be after lunch, so she headed straight to him. He was at his locker with his friends. Lexi stood behind him. He turned around and saw the teary-eyed look on her face.

"What did you do after you dropped me off last night?" she demanded loudly.

"Hey, chill, Lex. Keep your voice down. What are you talking about?"

He was stuttering because he knew that a shitstorm was about to hit him.

"Answer the question, Trey."

"I went home, Lexi. I was a little pissed, so I went home. Okay?"

"Did you go to your home or Cassie's?"

Trey's buddy sucked in a deep breath through his teeth as he backed away.

"Lexi, where are you getting this from? Who told you this bullshit? Someone is lying to you. I wouldn't touch Cassie. She's a slut, and everyone knows it."

Trey's bad luck was about to get worse. Their lovers' spat was being noticed both ways down the hall. Students were recording the argument. A moment later, Cassie approached.

"A slut? You didn't mind me being a slut last night when you came over, did you? I wasn't a slut when we dated last year and you cheated on me. You are the only guy I've been with, and this is the way you treat me. Piss on you and shame on me! You are so not worth it."

Cassie didn't even look at Lexi. She held an open palm to Trey, gesturing that she was through with him, and she stormed off.

Lexi glared at Trey. He didn't want to face her, but everyone was watching and recording, so his pride wouldn't let him look away. Her expression revealed all the anger she felt toward him at that moment. She walked away without a word. The chatter in the hall relived the drama for the next hour. Lexi texted her grandmother to come and pick her up.

Linda dropped everything and went to pick up her granddaughter. She checked her out of school for the afternoon on the pretense of a sudden illness. Lexi had been crying. Linda asked her if she needed to go to urgent care. Lexi told her that she was physically fine, but something happened today that made her emotionally sick. Linda asked if she wanted to talk about it. She assumed it had something to do with Trey. She asked if they had a fight about the homecoming dance.

"There isn't going to be a homecoming dance, MomMom, at least not for me. I wouldn't go with that pig if he was the last boy on earth!" Lexi cried.

Linda said, "Oh, honey, I'm so sorry. Sometimes, couples argue during stressful times. Maybe one or both of you were stressed out about the dance."

"No, MomMom, this has nothing to do with the dance. This has to do with a boy being a scumbag cheater," Lexi yelled, surprising herself.

"Oh, dear!" Linda whispered.

She wasn't prepared for her granddaughter's revelation but knew better than to make a bigger deal out of it. She didn't think Lexi was sexually active but also didn't know what it meant when she said he was a cheater. She hoped that in tenth grade, cheating could mean lesser offenses.

Lexi asked her grandmother if she could stay home from school tomorrow. Linda could not say no. When they got home, Linda told Lexi that a nice cup of tea would make her feel better. She thanked her grandmother but said she just wanted to go to her room and be alone.

Lexi took a nap for the rest of the afternoon. Rand knocked on her door around 5:00 p.m. to ask if she was going to join him in the stables. The knock awakened her, and she asked him to give her a minute. She got up, got changed, and walked with him down the path.

Rand said, "MomMom says you are not feeling well. Is there anything you want to talk about?"

His question meant that he knew it was not a physical illness.

Lexi answered, "No, PopPop, I don't really want to talk about it. Maybe later."

"Okay. Just letting you know I might not be as good a listener as Shimmer, but I won't give you a long face."

Lexi smiled at his dumb humor. They finished their chores quickly, returned to the house, and ate dinner. The conversation at the table was light and carefully avoiding Lexi's school day. She appreciated their respect of her privacy. Everyone cleaned up after dinner, and then Rand and Linda sat in the family room to watch TV while Lexi went to her room.

Texting with Jennifer and Amy would make her feel better. She checked social media first and saw that the hallway scene at school had gone viral, even before school let out. She grabbed her pillow to her face and screamed into it as loudly as she could.

School was going to be unbearable. All the kids were going to praise Trey for being a macho player but slut-shame her for being a tease. Heaven only knows what they would say about Cassie, although Lexi had her own opinion on that matter. Only three people knew what happened between her, Trey, and Cassie. But that did not matter on the Internet. Every coward hiding behind a keyboard found enough courage to put out their own comments, opinions, and memes no matter who it hurt. Even at her young, still-impressionable age, Lexi was almost too far gone to have any faith left in the goodwill of humanity. People were selfish and cruel. Period!

After calming down, she reached out to Jennifer, Amy, and Shyanne to tell them what had happened. Her friends all responded similarly with love toward her, vitriolic hostility toward Trey, and shame and regret about the Internet. She appreciated and needed to feel their compassion for her situation.

Jennifer texted that since Lexi had such a cute outfit for the homecoming, she should go anyway and shine. She would show them that she was above the pond scum that they swam in. Lexi appreciated that kind of support from Jen, but she responded that if she went by herself, it would just look pitiful and desperate.

Amy butted in that it would be so dope if they all could come down and go to homecoming with her. Lexi loved that idea, texting, "If only." They said their goodbyes, sent her their love, and shut down for the night. Lexi tossed and turned for a while but finally drifted off to sleep, thinking about her friends back in Woodbridge.

Lexi stayed home from school on Friday, and it was just like Saturday. They all went to the stables to care for the horses, spending extra time with them. All three went for a trail ride, which included easy trotting along the way. Rand and Linda were letting Lexi take a short recess from her troubles. It might have been a cool mid-November day, but the warmth of the sun was beaming down on them like a lantern of hope. Lexi closed her eyes, sitting atop Shimmer, and soaked it all in. There it was in the quiet, the sound of pine needles crunching under Shimmer's hooves. The serenity was cleansing her soul of the anger and despair of yesterday. After their meditative ride, they returned to the stables, set the horses up for the day, and went in for good old Southern breakfast/brunch.

During breakfast, Lexi noticed her PopPop glance at her MomMom. She asked what was going on. Linda told Lexi that they got good news yesterday but were too occupied about whatever happened at school yesterday to say anything. Finally, she said that Cynthia would be finished with her treatment and would be home for Thanksgiving.

Lexi's expression did not give away how she felt about the news. Linda had hoped that her granddaughter would be excited, but she also understood that Lexi might be clinging to her resentment at the moment. Lexi stared into her cup of coffee. Rand and Linda didn't know what to say. They let Lexi think on it. After a pause, Linda said it was so wonderful that Cynthia was doing so well and was able to find happiness in life again. Linda was trying to be so careful with her words to not incite Lexi's anger but instead to elicit a response.

Lexi finally spoke.

"I'm truly happy that Mom is out of that dark place she cocooned herself into last summer. I still do not understand how or why she got there, but deep down in my heart, I was sad for her, and I'm glad she is better. But now I wonder about our future. How will she be when we go back to Occoquan? It'll just be me and her with all those memories. Will I be able to fit back into my school? What about Shimmer? What will you do? I knew this was coming, but it is here, and now it will change everything again. It scares me."

Linda put her hand on Lexi's.

"Sweetheart, all those things will work out one at a time, when that time comes. But enjoy this day, and we will be right beside you when we cross those other bridges one at a time. It will all work out for the best, I promise you. It always does."

Lexi tried to force a smile, but the serenity of the morning was just displaced by the weight of the world once more on her shoulders. She hoped this day couldn't get any worse.

Surprise Guests

After dinner, Rand was cleaning the kitchen when he heard a car pull up out front.

He yelled to Lexi in the family room, "Lex, are you expecting anybody?"

"No, sir," she replied.

Rand started swearing under his breath that if it was a solicitor this time of night, he was going to slam the door in their face. He was already expecting the knock and was heading toward the door in a foul mood. He opened the door to three screaming teenage girls and two adults.

Lexi recognized Jennifer's scream at once. She jumped up and scrambled to the door. She hugged Jennifer, Amy, Shyanne, and Mr. and Mrs. Johnson. The roar and high-pitched screams lasted five minutes until someone was finally able to explain to Rand what was happening.

Last night, Jennifer told her mom about what happened between Lexi and her boyfriend and that Lexi wasn't going to her homecoming dance. Jennifer also mentioned she wished she could go with Lexi to spite the boy. Jennifer's mom, Laurie, told her husband, Lang, about it, and he said that he would not be opposed to making a quick trip to Pinehurst for a round of golf over the weekend. After hearing her parents' idea, Jennifer called Amy and Shyanne. They arranged with Shyanne's parents and with Amy's foster parents for them to go also. The three girls were escorting Lexi to her homecoming.

Rand and Linda had tears of joy as they hugged the girls and the Johnsons for being so generous with their time and love. Lexi couldn't stop her tears of joy. She was so excited to see her friends again and even more amazed that they would make such a trip to help her in this way.

After the shrieks subsided, Rand said that they would make up the pullout sofa in the den and find room for everyone to stay the weekend. He would even clean up the apartment above the stables. Mr. Johnson told him not to worry about it, because they had reservations at the Pinehurst Manor. They just wanted to stop over for the evening, let Lexi know their plans, and go check in at the hotel.

They hoped the surprise wouldn't be too much of an inconvenience, but the girls wanted to spend the day with Lexi tomorrow and do all their makeup and hair with her, if that was okay. Rand shook Mr. Johnson's hand again with enthusiasm and gratitude, saying it was much more than okay.

The four adults sat and talked for an hour while the girls went into Lexi's room to catch up on gossip, see their dresses, and make plans for tomorrow. While the adults were talking, Rand remembered that he had made golf plans with Rashne for tomorrow, so he excused himself to call and cancel. Aryana answered the phone.

Rand explained to her about Lexi's friends coming down. She was so happy for Lexi and asked about their plans for tomorrow as far as getting ready for the dance. Rand put Linda on the phone to explain the details. Linda hung up the phone and came back into the family room. She yelled to the girls in the back bedroom to pack up, because they were going into the village. Rand looked at her, confused.

Linda said, "Aryana insisted that the girls stay together in one of her upstairs suites tonight and that she will arrange for two stylists to come tomorrow to do the girls' hair and makeup at her house. She wants us all to come over now for a party."

The Johnsons didn't know what to say. They remembered hearing about the Samadanis' generosity, but this was too much to offer.

Linda said, "When Aryana gets an idea in her head, there is no refusing it. Besides, she is two streets over from the Manor. You and Laurie can have a nice evening alone, and the girls will be right around the corner. You can golf tomorrow and not worry about a thing. All the women will go shopping and touring in the village."

The girls screamed even more excitedly about the posh turn of events. Within minutes, they packed up everything they needed for a grand sleepover.

In the twenty minutes it took to drive to the Samadanis' house, Aryana had laid out her usual table fare of appetizers and beverages. When everyone arrived, she led the girls upstairs to the largest suite in the house and told them it was theirs for the night. She also said that her hairdresser would come by tomorrow with a makeup girl to do their hair and makeup. She invited them to get settled in and then come down for refreshments.

It seemed like a dream come true for the girls, especially Amy. All she had known for the past year, except for meeting these new friends, was tragedy and loss. She could not help but wonder if Lexi, Jennifer, and Shyanne accepted this weekend event as the kind of good fortune that landed on them every so often. Amy did not think of them as unappreciative or shallow, but it could not possibly mean as much to them as it did to her. She found herself barely suppressing her tears about this opportunity, because for her, the magic spell would end on Monday.

While the girls were upstairs, deciding the sleeping arrangements, working out toiletries space in the bathroom, and gossiping, Aryana took the time to speak with Lang and Laurie Johnson, thanking them for being so supportive of the girls. She asked Laurie if she thought Amy would be comfortable talking privately about her situation.

Aryana loved Lexi like her own daughter, but this weekend, she wanted to focus more on Amy. Aryana could only imagine the lack of love and sense of abandonment that Amy must be feeling in her heart. Her mother died only a short while ago, she had not had time to grieve, and she was tossed into child protective services without any family support system or hope of a future. The other connection for Aryana was that Amy was a Muslim, and Aryana understood that culture better than anyone else in the room.

Laurie knew about Aryana's compassion, generosity, and wisdom. So she easily agreed that it would be wonderful if Amy bonded with Aryana.

All four girls, each with their individual personalities, came bouncing down the stairs as one entity wrapped in the promise of a magic weekend. The girls came to support their best friend and present a united front to the betrayers. For the rest of the evening, these beautiful and strong young women ate, drank, laughed, whispered, and created a memory with their loving and supportive adults.

Aryana seized the opportunity when she saw Amy admiring one of the Persian carpets in the sitting room. She asked Amy if she knew much about Persian rugs. Amy said that they had a few handmade rugs in their home, but she didn't know what would happen to any of those things now. Aryana reached for Amy's hand and told her how sorry she was about her mother. Amy stared at the rug, not knowing how to respond. She was awash with joyful emotions and did not want to go to her dark place by talking about her mom's death.

"I would rather not talk about it tonight, if that's all right," she whispered to Aryana.

Aryana said, "Of course, dear. It's a happy time right now, and you should enjoy it. But I would like to be there for you if you ever do want to talk about anything. Okay?"

Amy nodded. Then Aryana asked if she remembered anything about Tbilisi. Amy was puzzled, asking how Aryana knew about her birthplace. Aryana said that Lexi mentioned it. Amy laughed, acknowledging that most of the kids in school didn't even know that Georgia was a country in Europe. She didn't think that Lexi even understood her when she talked about her home.

Aryana laughed and agreed that many Americans didn't know much about world geography. However, she and Rashne did. She told Amy that she and Rashne were Muslim. They did not go to mosque, but occasionally, they prayed. She told Amy that there was a small bedroom upstairs where the carpet and window faced east for prayer. She invited Amy to use it if she wanted to pray. Amy understood her meaning.

Amy admitted that her mother and father were much more Muslim than she was, if that was a thing. Her mom especially would go through periods where she prayed five times a day for the return of Amy's father. They thought he was forced into the army to fight against Russia when he went back there to claim his family money. Her mother received phone calls from him that would break up, and then he disappeared. She said her mother was inconsolable.

Amy mentioned that she lived in Tbilisi as a child even though it had a very small Muslim population. She said that the Sunni Muslims in Georgia mostly lived near Turkey, but her dad's job took him to the capital. They moved to the US when things became bad and people started disappearing.

Aryana listened to every word and heard the hopelessness in her heart. This young woman was alone. She hugged Amy tightly, asking her not to think anymore and to enjoy the love that now surrounded her. They rejoined the group.

The next morning, the four young women stirred in their beds to the aromas of Rashne's famous coffee and Aryana's full buffet spread of eggs, fruits, breads, tomatoes, cucumbers, yogurt, and other breakfast treats. They got dressed and rushed to the dining room to find all the adults already eating the food. Aryana called Laurie and Lang Johnson this morning to invite them over from the Manor, and Rand and Linda already knew what to expect, so they were there at 8:00 a.m.

The men had plans for golf, but the women talked about what they wanted to do and at what time. Rashne suggested that they start off the morning at the spa. The girls squealed at the idea. Pinehurst's spa was only a few streets away, and it didn't take the women long to get there. All seven women were pampered with facials, waxing, skin treatments, and massages. By early afternoon, they were so relaxed that they had to be poured back to the house. They were met in the driveway by two hairstylists and another woman who did makeup.

There was plenty of time to prepare for the homecoming, so Aryana had arranged to have a late lunch and sangria on the patio. The spa treatments had put everyone in relaxed, peaceful moods. They sat and talked for hours, first about their outfits, then their relationships, evolving into their hopes and goals.

By 4:00 p.m., the hairstyling process began. The four young women came out of the suite at 6:30 p.m. dressed in their homecoming attire and looking and feeling on top of the world. The adults commented how each one looked so confident, so poised, and so beautiful. They took pictures, and Shyanne did a video chat with her parents so they could see them. Aryana asked Amy if she would take a picture with her and Rashne. Amy smiled between the two of them.

A limousine pulled up the driveway in front of the mansion at 6:50 p.m. Aryana announced that the car was waiting to take them to Elliott's for dinner, then to Union Pines High School and then back home. The women headed out the door, squealing, whooping, and promising to crush the night.

The four of them strode confidently into the gymnasium, where music and dancing were already rocking the gym. Everyone in the gym looked beautiful and was having a fun time. Lexi had no illusions that her entrance would command anyone's attention, but neither did she think it would be routine. Her four-girl posse surprisingly turned heads, and Lexi felt a small victory and satisfying revenge. However, her confidence shrank when she realized that she would face Trey eventually. She hoped her friends would have her back, but only she could have the confrontation.

The four girls crossed the dance floor to the refreshment table. Lexi saw Macy and Leanne coming toward her.

Macy said, "Hey, girl. I saw what happened. It sucks. Trey is a tool."

Lexi replied, "Yeah. He left me hanging out there in the wind. Oh, these are my best friends from home. So how come you ghosted me the last two days?"

"You know I don't do drama. But you were the lightning rod for only a day, and it was over before the next breakup, so we're cool, right?"

Shyanne leaned in and said, "Yeah, she's cool. Lexi came from a place where real friends stand by each other. Oh, look, and here we are!"

Shyanne glared at Macy, who acted like she was confused by the comment. Amy and Jennifer laughed as Macy and Leanne walked away.

"We got you, girl!" Shyanne told Lexi. "Let's show some Jagger moves."

The girls got out on the dance floor. They danced and laughed with one another for the next three songs. Amy spun Lexi around, and she bumped into Trey. He saw her and came over to talk with her. Lexi froze.

Jennifer said, "Let me guess. You're Tree?"

He looked at Jennifer with a smirk on his face.

"It's Trey. Who are you?"

"I'm one of the best friends."

He looked at Lexi.

"Can we talk? In private?"

Her friends hoped that Lexi would find her strength right now, and they waited for her answer.

Lexi said, "I'm pretty sure we don't have anything to talk about, but I'm sorry I ruined your Trey Tap program. Uh, this song is my jam, so if you would excuse us. Oh, my grandfather knows a lot about being a man and what trust looks like. You should talk to him."

Trey replied, "Your grandfather? Oh, I see, but not your father?"

Just then, Amy threw her drink in Trey's face.

Trey yelled, "You stupid bitch!"

He raised his hand toward Amy. Shyanne stepped between them.

"I wish you would, you pathetic, cheating redneck!"

Trey saw the fire in her eyes and stopped dead. He lowered his hand, smiled, wiped the punch off his face, and backed away. Classmates watched as he tried to regain his dignity by acting like he made the decision to back off. Everyone knew otherwise. Shyanne turned to her girls, winked, and resumed dancing. For the next two hours, Lexi danced the night away and introduced her friends to other people she had met in Union Pines.

As the evening wore on, Lexi felt more and more victorious about standing up to Trey and was so proud of her girls. However, there was a small feeling inside that she couldn't shed. Before Trey showed his true self, she was drawn to him, she liked him, he was charming, and she wanted him to like her too. Lexi also felt alarmed at how wrong and gullible she was about him. She questioned her judgment. She thought he was a nice guy, but when she finally saw behind the curtain, he was selfish and thoughtless.

In the limo ride home, the girls cheered and celebrated their evening. They relived the Trey drama, they chided one another about slutty dance moves, and they applauded their sisterhood. Amy asked Lexi about the Trey Tap program. The other girls leaned in as Lexi explained.

Cassie, the other woman, had called her Thursday night after the hallway incident. She was apologetic, contrite, and sad about what had happened. Cassie admitted to Lexi that she, too, was taken in by Trey Baskin's charm and good looks. They dated for a short while last year, and she really liked him. But right after he got what he wanted, he broke up with her. She was devastated, especially when she heard that Trey had bragged to his football pals about scoring one for the Trey Tap program.

One of Trey's earlier conquests let Cassie in on the secret. Trey told the guys in the locker room during his sophomore year that his goal in high school would be to tap as many virgins as he could before graduation. He called it his Trey Tap program.

The girls shook their heads in disgust upon hearing just one more thing about this human garbage. Amy, Jennifer, and Shyanne started tossing out ideas all at once about how to hurt him and his car. Lexi laughed at their revenge suggestions but said that he was off her radar forever.

"Besides," she said, "I don't want to burn any bridges, because he might be flipping my hamburgers one day."

They laughed all the way back to Aryana's.

The adults were around Aryana's kitchen table when the girls crashed through the front door, giggling. It was after 11:30 p.m., but everyone was wide awake and excited to hear how the night went. The girls did not disappoint, spilling all the details about the wondrous and glorious victory of the night. They talked about the atmosphere in the gym, the decorations, the outfits, the music, the dancing, and the love they shared between one another.

Amy brought up how proud she was of Shyanne for standing up to Trey. Lexi's wide-eyed look let them know to skim on the gritty details. She did not want her grandparents to know specifically why she broke it off with Trey. It would be too much information.

The talk about the evening events finally settled down, and the adults hugged and congratulated each of the girls for a successful evening. Aryana hugged Amy and reminded them that they had one last night together in the suite before they turned back into pumpkins. The women went upstairs, got ready for bed, and enjoyed the remaining sleepover. Tomorrow, they would have breakfast and do a little shopping around the village; and then Jennifer, Shyanne, and Amy would have to go home.

They all said their good nights, each girl clinging to the fading euphoria of the night while simultaneously trying to keep at bay that feeling that came at dusk on Sunday nights—the sadness that tomorrow was back to five days of toil, stress, and discontent.

Although it was only Saturday night, it felt like Sunday, because tomorrow morning would be here before they knew it, the girls would go home, and the weekend would be a memory. Lexi kept reminding herself what her grandfather had said once about being in the moment, but her anticipation of a lonely tomorrow was ruining her mood tonight. The girls tried to extend the evening for as long as they could with chitchat and reminiscing about the homecoming until exhaustion caught up with them, and each one drifted off to sleep.

*****

The morning flew by, just as the girls had dreaded, and with the conclusion of lunch, it was time to go. The good news was that Lang had enjoyed golf at Pinehurst so much that he promised to come back often if invited. Rashne and Rand extended an open invitation. Each girl took turns thanking the Samadanis for their extreme graciousness and then hugging Lexi goodbye, promising to text every day.

They waved as the car pulled out of the village for their four-hour drive back to Occoquan. Lexi loaded her things into her grandparents' car and thanked Aryana and Rashne. She told them she had no words to express what their generosity and love meant to her this weekend. It was the best weekend she ever had in North Carolina.

With tears in her eyes, Lexi hugged Aryana tightly, thanking her again and again. Rand told her to break it up because she still had chores to do. Lexi smiled and got in the car. This weekend would be hard to beat.

New Construction

They pulled into the drive, and Lexi saw a construction truck and two pallets of lumber sitting on the side of the trail leading to the stables.

"What is that, PopPop?" she asked.

Rand answered nonchalantly, "I guess the contractor is finally starting that long-overdue refurbishment project above the stables. I forgot to tell you. For the next month, we will be boarding the horses at Steadman's. It will be safer for them. Nothing will change except their location. We will still be tending to them each morning and evening and taking our trail rides. I'll get the golf cart from Aryana's to go back and forth to the Steadman stables."

Lexi did not take long to put away her things and get dressed for the stables. She was anxious to see Shimmer. Rand, Linda, and Lexi took the truck down the lane to Steadman's. The horses seemed content in their temporary boarding, especially since other horses were there. Champ, Pony Girl, and Shimmer were excited when their family arrived. They were waiting to be fed. Lexi hugged Shimmer and whispered into her ear about the amazing weekend. Shimmer was more interested in her feed bucket.

Later that afternoon, Linda and Rand were cleaning up the dinner dishes when Linda announced down the hall that they were going to call Lexi's mom.

"Lexi, I'm sure you want to tell your mother about your weekend. Come out, dear."

Linda's laptop screen lit up with Cynthia answering the video call.

"Hi, Mom! Did you all just finish dinner? Is dad right there? Hi, Dad!"

Cynthia's voice was gentle and pleasant.

"Hi, dear," Linda answered. "We have had a very excited weekend."

"I can imagine. Where is Lex?"

Lexi plopped on the couch beside her grandmother.

"Hi, Mom."

"Hi, honey! I've been trying to keep busy all weekend, waiting to get this call. Tell me everything about homecoming. What did your friends say about your dress? How was your date? Did you have the best night of high school so far?"

Lexi held her palms up toward her mom.

"Whoa, Mom, slow down. Things have happened in the past few days. One thing at a time."

Lexi opened up completely and shared each event in chronological order. She started the story with her terrible date with Trey and finished with saying goodbye to the three best friends in the world as they went home after an exhausting, amazing weekend. She told her mom how wonderful and generous Aryana and Rashne were, how Grandma and Grandpa were so supportive, and how grateful she felt about everything, except Trey.

She glossed over the specific details about her date with Trey, but Cynthia understood what happened. It was the longest conversation Lexi had with her mother since before her father died. Lexi even described the events that went viral on social media, including the drink in the face and how Shyanne stood up to Trey. He was brutally chastised online.

When Lexi finally stopped to take a breath, she asked her mother how she was feeling. Cynthia was wiping tears from her eyes and said that she was just so happy to hear that her daughter's weekend went so well. Lexi said goodbye and that grandma wanted to talk with her.

After she left, Linda and Cynthia talked a while longer about the weekend and about them coming to pick her up on Thanksgiving Day. Cynthia was flooded with emotions about Lexi. She was exceedingly happy for Lexi getting to experience the weekend but equally saddened that she wasn't there to share it with her. Her feelings were conflicting, but it made her that much more resolved to stay positive and continue her healing journey with Lexi hopefully willing to forgive.

*****

The last week at school before Thanksgiving break was fun and easy. Lexi enjoyed being the object of adulation for how she and her friends treated Trey. The video of the homecoming confrontation was online, causing Trey to have to endure razzing in the hallways. He took the abuse in stride, pretending to ignore the comments, and he steered clear of Lexi.

She could not deny that she liked it when he met her at the locker and kissed her sometimes, but that was over, and her routine would be different now. Also, she was not sure how much longer she would be at Union Pines now that her mom was well. She assumed that she would be returning to Woodbridge after the Christmas break. The truth was that the students at Union Pines were just as cool as the students back in Virginia, maybe even a little more close-knit, and she was going to miss Shimmer. Things were mixed up in her head.

Lexi came home early on Wednesday because of an early dismissal. The temperature was perfect for a trail ride. Lexi, Rand, and Linda climbed into the golf cart and headed to Steadman's. Other boarders were with their horses. A young woman was leading her mare out of a stall three stalls down from Shimmer when Lexi noticed her.

"Cassie?" Lexi asked.

Cassie turned around to see Lexi leading Shimmer out as well.

"Uh, hi, Lexi," Cassie answered, flustered. "I didn't know you boarded here."

"My grandfather's stables are three farms down the trail, but it is being renovated, so we are boarding here until the work is done. You?"

"Oh. Yeah, I noticed three new horses. Is she yours?"

Cassie pointed to Shimmer.

"Yep. This is Shimmer," Lexi answered.

"Cinnamon," Cassie said. "We board her here."

Linda and Rand were leading Champ and Pony Girl out of the stables. Lexi pointed to them, telling Cassie that she needed to catch up with her grandparents. Cassie stopped her.

"Lexi, I know we probably won't be friends, but we don't have to be enemies. I think it is so badass what you did to Trey. He deserved it. And I'm sorry."

Lexi looked at her with a slight hint of a smile forming at the corners of her mouth. It might not have been a look of agreement, but it was not a look of disagreement. Cassie smiled back and watched Lexi walk Shimmer out of the stables.

Why Did He Do It?

Lexi and Shimmer caught up with her grandparents on the trail. Without looking back, Rand asked if that was a friend from school. Lexi said that it might be.

The foliage was in full bloom with russet, gold, and brown leaves falling to the ground. The pine needles were shedding also. All three riders were enjoying nature's display. When they reached the meadow, the riders dismounted and let the horses graze. Rand mentioned to Lexi that she was unusually quiet this ride.

"Is there anything about the homecoming that you require my expert opinion on?" Rand asked in jest, knowing that boys and dating were Linda's department.

Lexi looked at her grandfather and said, "Yeah. Why did my boyfriend cheat on me?"

Her question stunned him, or more accurately, the abruptness and directness stunned him. A couple of questions came to his mind. Was she so direct because that was where they were in their relationship, or was she direct because she wanted a direct answer even if the topic was sensitive and uncomfortable? He wondered who would be more uncomfortable, her or him. Was she talking about cheating in a sexual context or in a puppy love context?

He realized the conversation he was having in his mind was taking too long, so he was the uncomfortable one. He looked over at Linda, hoping that doing so would give him clarity or support. Did he even have an answer? Was this going to be a monologue or a dialogue? He was thinking too much, and Lexi was waiting.

"Honey, I think there is only one person in this world who can answer that question, and it might take some time for him to get over being embarrassed before he ever gives you an answer. I'm sorry."

"PopPop, I know you're right, but why did he do it? I want to know what was going on in his boy brain."

"Don't think too much about it, Lexi. Who really knows the reasons why people do what they do? Try to think about all your reasons and experiences that led you to respect yourself enough to turn him down."

Lexi was surprised that her grandfather had figured out what happened. However, for the sake of the conversation, it was not necessary for her to confirm the details.

"Okay, PopPop. I had my reasons, which were well thought out, but it seemed like his actions were just reactions."

"Very true. You are asking an adult question, so I'm going to give you an adult answer."

Lexi nodded. Linda was curious how her sage husband was going to answer.

"Okay. I'm not going to make any judgments, but we were your age once, and we know what it is like. So let's say that when a healthy male gets his engine revved up and he is not allowed to race at the track, he might go to another track."

"Really, PopPop? Another track?"

"Yeah, not my best simile. How about if I just blame it on immaturity?"

Lexi said, "Okay, what about immaturity?"

"Well, science tells us that females mature faster than males, and males don't catch up until around their midtwenties. A sixteen-year-old female typically will be far more emotionally intuitive and big-picture-oriented, even during moments of passion, than her male counterpart, whose judgment and intellect will be less sophisticated and severely clouded by his testosterone."

"So you're telling me that testosterone makes men stupid?"

"Well, let's just say that in my experience of commanding men in the military for thirty years, I know they can do dumb things, make bad decisions, and be completely selfish if opportunities or temptations present themselves. Men can be incredibly strong, but they can also be unbelievably weak. But let us also not forget that men don't cheat by themselves."

"So are you saying that women cheat as much as men?"

"Lex, I don't know if the numbers are the same for dating couples as they are for married couples, but yes, men don't cheat by themselves. However, it seems like men get caught more often."

Lexi thought about her PopPop's thesis. It was too generic. Was he really saying that all people were fallible and prone to cheat? She wasn't buying it.

It was time to head back. Lexi mounted Shimmer and said, "Well, I don't think your thesis is true, at least not as far as my father goes."

Linda instinctively glanced over at Rand, and they exchanged a look. Lexi caught the exchange.

"What was that?" she asked suspiciously.

"What was what, honey?" Linda asked.

"What was the look you two just gave each other? I saw you give PopPop a look. It was like you know something. Is there something you know about my father? What was that look?" Lexi demanded, her voice getting louder with each question.

"What do you know? PopPop? MomMom?"

Rand said in a calm voice, "Lexi, let's just drop it and go home."

She stared at them. Her face became contorted in disbelief and confusion.

Tears began falling down her cheeks, and she cried out, "Oh my god!"

She dug her heels into Shimmer's flanks, causing the mare to bolt into a full sprint down the trail.

Rand flipped Champ's reins against his neck, and the horse ran after Shimmer, with Linda and Pony Girl right behind. They were yelling to Lexi to slow down. She was running Shimmer at a full gallop. When she arrived at the Steadman stables, she halted Shimmer and quickly dismounted. She was leading Shimmer into the stall when Rand and Linda rode in.

"Lexi, stop! Calm down, and we can talk. Let's just get the horses settled, and we can go back to the house. Afterwards, we'll go to Asheville to bring your mom home."

"All this time? All this time?" she yelled at them.

"What, honey? What all this time? What are you asking?"

Lexi was in full crying mode with spit coming from her mouth. They asked her again to calm down. She demanded that they get in the car and take her to Asheville.

Through tears, she yelled, "I want to see my mom now!"

"Lexi! Get ahold of yourself!" her grandmother said as she tried to hug her.

Lexi pulled away and finally caught her breath from bawling.

In a pitiful voice, still trying to catch her breath, she said, "All this time, I blamed and hated my mom because I thought she stopped loving my father. You all knew that he cheated on her? You all knew, and no one told me? You knew, and you let me hate my mom!"

Linda held her granddaughter in her arms. Rand threw his arms around her too.

He whispered to her, "Lexi, let's get you home and get cleaned up. We will tell you everything on the way to Asheville."

Reunited

Three hours later, the car pulled into the Pisgah Wellness Center compound and parked. Before Rand had the engine turned off, Lexi was out of the door, running to the front entrance, searching for her mother.

Cynthia was waiting with Dr. Sylvia in the reception area. Her belongings were packed and ready to go. They heard the front door open and saw Lexi charging toward them. Cynthia stood up barely in time to catch her daughter flinging herself at her. She opened her arms wide and accepted Lexi's embrace. Lexi was crying.

"Honey, what's the matter? I'm here, I'm here. It's okay. I'm coming home, and I won't ever leave you again. Okay?" Cynthia said through her own tears as she held her daughter.

She didn't know what had happened, but she was not going to let go of the first real hug she felt from Lexi since before Tom died. She looked up and spotted Rand and Linda coming through the lobby. She gave them a shrug of surprise but did not let go of Lexi. Rand acknowledged it and returned a look to Cynthia that things would be revealed.

When Lexi finally let go of her mom, she whispered, "I'm so sorry. Can you ever forgive me?"

"Forgive you for what, sweetie?"

"For doubting you, for not understanding, for being such a raving bitch."

"Lexi, what are you talking about? There's nothing to forgive."

"Mom, I know."

"What do you know, Lex?"

"I know that Dad hurt you."

Cynthia shot an angry look toward Rand and Linda.

"What do you mean, Lex?"

"Mom, this is about us, not MomMom and PopPop. I know that you were trying to spare me from sadness and disappointment by keeping it from me. But in the process, you let me hate you even though you were protecting me. I can't imagine how much you suffered when you found out about Dad's betrayal.

"And then you tried to forgive him, but it was too difficult for you to let him back into your heart. And then he was killed, and you had to live with all that guilt combined with the grief of losing your life partner. I made it so much worse for you after that, and you had to live with that too."

Lexi was crying as she begged her mother to forgive her.

Cynthia was too overwhelmed with emotion to say anything. Dr. Morrell was standing by, listening to every word.

Finally, Lexi said, "And you know what? I am disappointed and saddened by what my father did, but it doesn't change how much I love him and miss him with all my heart."

Dr. Morrell waited for right moment and then said, "My prescription for Cynthia to continue her healing at home was to use the cognitive tools we taught her when the stress became too much but most importantly to keep an honest line of communication open with her daughter. I think I can say now with the utmost confidence that she is ready to come home, and home is ready to receive her."

Mother and daughter hugged each other tighter. Cynthia hugged Dr. Morrell goodbye, and Rand carried her suitcase to the car. The drive home through the mountains layered with red-and-yellows ribbons of leaves cascading from the peaks to the valleys was a postcard picture.

Cynthia told Lexi that her father was a good man and that what he did was a one-time lack of judgment.

"He was not a cheater. He was in a place in his life where he needed something. He was going through a life crisis, and he turned the wrong way for an answer. No matter what, I never stopped loving your father. I was stunned and hurt, which made me shut down for too long, but I always loved him."

Lexi listened intently.

"Why didn't you just tell me?"

"You were always Daddy's little girl. You were best buds. I loved that about the two of you. After I found out about the affair, one of my first worries was how it might hurt you if you found out. I was not going to let that happen. You were angry at me, so why would I let you be angry at your father too?"

"Mom, I'm so sorry. I'm sorry you suffered through the cheating, and then you suffered trying to keep your marriage together. Then you suffered through Dad's death, and then you suffered through a daughter who blamed you for everything. I'm so ashamed. I can't stop thinking about how much guilt you must have felt when he died. It was not your fault."

"Lexi, you are all I have left, so I always forgave you. I knew that you were suffering too. You have not lived long enough yet to be able to deal with all that grief all at once, so I gave you a lot of leeway in letting you grieve."

"Mom, I'm so sorry I drove you to the point of giving up."

"Lex, my breaking point had nothing to do with you. None of it was your fault. I was losing myself in my own grief. I needed help finding my way back, and that's why I went away. Dr. Morrell helped me.

"I hoped that the decision to have you live with MomMom and PopPop was the right one for you. We didn't have many choices, but I kind of thought that their gentle nature, the tranquility that comes with working with horses, and the medicinal effects of the pines would help you recover in your own way. Was I right?" Cynthia asked.

"Yeah. I have learned to like it down here pretty good. The horse farm is nice. I love horses, especially Shimmer. My school is okay, and I've made some friends. I had a boyfriend," Lexi said with a little sarcasm.

"I don't want to break a girl code, but your grandmother has been keeping me up to speed on your life at the farm. I've been watching from afar."

"That's okay. Did she tell you about the talks I had with them on our trail rides? I like those rides. I sit in my saddle and just absorb their wisdom as the pine needles crunch under our horses' hooves. It's so peaceful," Lexi said.

Lexi retold her mom about all the events that happened on homecoming weekend and how magical it was for her and her girlfriends. She and her mother talked the whole way home, with Linda popping in and out of the conversation as needed. Rand listened to country music on the radio and focused on the road. He also had one ear in the conversation.

One thing that was settled was that no decisions about the future would be made until after the holidays. Cynthia only asked to meet Shimmer, go on trail rides, and be able to relax beside the hearth of a warm fire, drink hot cocoa while admiring a Christmas tree, and read a good book.

*****

Thanksgiving morning came early as usual with Rand and Lexi heading to the Steadman stables for morning chores. They were in the golf cart when the door opened, and Cynthia came running out.

"Hey, can a daughter/mom get a lift?"

Rand and Lexi both looked at her with surprise.

"We thought you might want to sleep in," Lexi said, smiling.

Cynthia shook her head.

"Nope. I've missed too much of the good stuff. Let's see these horses. I bet Pony Girl remembers me."

The three of them rode down to the Steadman farm.

"Now remind me again why you are renovating your stables, Daddy," Cynthia asked.

"Oh, it just needed it. I can't rent it out in its current condition, and it's big enough to be an apartment, so I figure I might as well make some money off it on RB&B."

"PopPop, you mean Airbnb."

They arrived at Steadman.

"Oh my goodness! She is so beautiful," Cynthia said when seeing Shimmer for the first time.

She carefully approached the young mare and put her hand on Shimmer's neck. Shimmer sniffed the new person. The mare's posture was one of curiosity and easiness. Cynthia smelled like Lexi, so she was no threat. Cynthia left Shimmer and went to see Pony Girl. Pony Girl sniffed her and became excited, moving her head up and down. The threesome cleaned the stalls, fed and watered the horses, and let them out in the paddock for the day. They would come back this afternoon and put them away.

Thanksgiving chores awaited everyone back at the house. Each person was assigned a duty or a dish. Rand was to make his world-famous mac and cheese. Lexi never understood why any dish prepared by PopPop was called world-famous, but when anybody else made a dish, even if it was the best one ever, it was just a dish. He did cook up a rather good brisket on the grill, and his pancakes were the best, but almost everything MomMom made was excellent too.

On balance, she cooked more than he did, but none of her meals was world-famous. Of course, it wasn't lost on Lexi that the one doing most of the award naming was PopPop himself. She catalogued it as one more of those things her mom called the good stuff, something that would stay in her memory forever.

The atmosphere in the house that day was exactly as everyone had hoped it would be. The fall air was cool and filled with the smell of pine. The horse country opening of the hunt season was happening in the morning, and then a football game in the afternoon on TV filled the airwaves with the perfect background noise. The aromas of oak from the fireplace and delicious food from the kitchen filled the house.

Rand was not going to participate in the traditional Sandhills hunt this year, as he had done in the past, but he wanted to watch the start. Right at 10:00 a.m. over ten thousand locals and guests tailgated, awaiting the opening of the hunt season. The master of the hunt, leading thirty eagerly baying hounds, appeared on a hill with one hundred riders decked out in their red jackets and perfectly groomed mounts behind him to kick off the season.

Another one of life's mysteries that Lexi could not figure out was why Grandma always asked Grandpa to carve the turkey and then stand over him, instructing him exactly how to do it. She could just as easily carve the turkey herself, but Lexi remembered this little drama play out every year at Thanksgiving. Sometimes, her mom would do the same thing to her dad. Lexi could almost see her father standing over the turkey while her mother told him exactly how to slice it. The memory lingered in her head. After dinner, Linda announced that Aryana invited them over for dessert and drinks. Lexi missed her dad. But being with her mom, her grandparents, and their dearest friends made this Thanksgiving very special.

December turned out to be much more healing and restorative than anyone could have imagined. Rand and Linda came up with one reason after another why they were too busy to go on trail rides, leaving Lexi and her mother to take the horses out. Lexi reacquainted her mom with saddling Pony Girl, as well as the ins and outs of grooming her and cleaning her stalls. It came back quickly to Cynthia, and she was proficient in no time. Afterward, she would entertain Lexi with stories from her childhood about how Rand taught her how to ride and care for the horses. She had forgotten how relaxing and calming it could be.

The two of them would stay on the trail for as long as time would allow, sharing their truths, their fears, their hopes, and their dreams. Cynthia shared with Lexi how she felt during her time at Pisgah and the kinds of therapy she went through. She talked about how much she struggled, how much she hurt, and how much it helped knowing that her daughter was in safe hands.

Lexi would talk openly and honestly about her loneliness, her anger, her grief about her father, and her talks with her grandparents. She told her mother about Trey, about her friends, about the homecoming weekend, and about the things she had learned about herself. Lexi also told her mother how things could have been so different if only she had known about what her father had done but that she understood why her mother tried to protect her.

The serenity of riding was a therapy that neither one intended but both needed. Cynthia began to clearly see her daughter for the woman she was becoming. Lexi was a mature, self-confident young woman who was beginning to explore her own femininity and find her place in the world. Lexi saw her mother for the wounded woman she was—not the monster who held her back but a mother who loved her daughter with all of her being. She also saw her mother as a woman with faults and blemishes just like herself. She saw her mother in a new light and with so much more love and respect.

Cynthia and Lexi's relationship grew stronger each day. Each woman had learned to respect the other, listen to each other, and let nothing interfere with their love for each other. Cynthia learned these tools at Pisgah. Lexi learned them on the trail.

On Christmas Eve, Lexi, Cynthia, and Rand took the horses out on the trail. It was cold, and each rider was bundled up. Rand stayed quiet in the lead position, listening to the trees bristling in the cold air, hearing the pine needles snapping underfoot. Lexi was in the middle position, pointing out to her mother the critters they saw along the trail. When they arrived at the meadow, they dismounted and let the horses graze for a brief time since the winter solstice had shortened the hours of sunlight.

As they watched the horses graze, Lexi turned to her mother.

"Mom, I love you so much, and I'm truly sorry for how I treated you. Can you ever forgive me?"

Cynthia hugged Lexi to her bosom.

"My darling, there was never anything to forgive. You are my child, and my love for you is unconditional, always. Someday, you will have children, and you will understand."

Lexi hugged her back tightly.

Cynthia then said, "You and I will still have disagreements, but I promise to try very hard to remember that you are becoming an adult, and I must let you make your own decisions and learn from your mistakes. I want you to promise me that you will remember that it is very hard for a mother to let go and that I make mistakes sometimes too, so go easy on me."

Lexi said softly, "I promise."

The end of Lexi's first semester at Union Pines was also a time for reflection and renewal. She became a minor celebrity among her classmates for the way she stood up to Trey. Trey, for all his machismo, lost status among his peers, especially among the females, when his misogyny was exposed. His peeps and bros on the football team still fought for the right to exist in his shadow, but there would always be those kind of sycophants in high school.

Lexi even found a new friend in Cassie. The two of them talked at the stables each time they saw each other. Lexi had learned not to be too quick to judge, which enabled her to learn about Cassie. Over time and with compassion, Lexi learned that Cassie had her own issues but was a good person under an enormous weight of problems at home. Cassie cried out for friendship, and Lexi answered.

Christmas Day was an especially joyous time at the farmhouse. Rand and Linda had worked the previous week, decorating the outside with lights and swags of pine boughs hanging over doors and the porch. Inside, the Christmas tree filled a corner of the family room. It glowed with multicolored lights and glistened with tinsel and ornaments. The base of the tree could not be seen because of the assortment of wrapped presents around it.

The oak logs burning in the fireplace gave off a familiar scent reminiscent of holidays past. The house was also filled with aromas of holiday cooking that Linda and Rand had been preparing for the past several days. Cookies and treats were on trays atop the table in the dining room, and fresh brewing coffee wafted through the house, arousing all occupants still asleep.

Rand was sitting in his chair with his cup of morning brew. He was dressed for the stables when the other women in the house came out in their pajamas.

"Do you all think the horses want to miss Christmas? Let's get to it!" Rand ordered.

Linda, Cynthia, and Lexi understood. Without delay, everyone got dressed for a cold morning at the stables. They took the golf cart down the trail to catch the sun peeking over the treetops. The horses were excited to see the family arrive for morning activities. Lexi and Linda brought carrots and apples. The horses were treated to an extra-special grooming, feeding, cleaning, and early release into the paddock for the day. It was cold, so they wore their turnout blankets, but they appeared to enjoy the pasture.

Rand, Linda, Lexi, and Cynthia stood resting at the fence, watching the horses run loose. Rand gave Cynthia a look of approval.

Cynthia said, "You know, it would not be so bad living here."

They waited for Lexi's response. She was looking over the fence, watching Shimmer play.

"I wouldn't mind that, Mom."

Cynthia asked, "Really, honey?"

Lexi turned toward her mother, focusing seriously on the conversation with great curiosity. Cynthia gave Lexi that look that said she had something to share. She told Lexi that she had been thinking that maybe they could start over right her in Vass. Lexi admitted that she had thought about it too but worried about missing her friends back in Occoquan. However, she worried about Shimmer too. Cynthia said that she would not make any decision without Lexi's approval.

"So what do you think?"

Lexi laid out her thoughts.

"Well, I like the school here. I love being with MomMom and PopPop. I love taking care of Shimmer, Champ, and Pony Girl. And I think back home reminds us too much of sadness. But where would we live?"

Rand cleared his throat.

"Well, it just so happens I have a brand-new two-bedroom apartment above the stables that needs two people to live in it."

Lexi looked at him suspiciously.

"Really, PopPop? Really?"

She walked over and buried her head in his chest under a soft hide winter coat. He wrapped his arms around her. They headed home with hope for a new future.

More Gifts

Back at the house on Christmas morning, Linda decided they would enjoy a warm breakfast before opening their gifts. After breakfast, everyone helped with the cleanup and slowly meandered into the family room.

Lexi appointed herself as the gift disperser. Each adult found their spot to sit and sip hot chocolate while Lexi built small piles of gifts in front of each family member until the last present was doled out. Lexi had the most presents of course, so she declared that she would go first. One by one, they went around the room, opening each gift and declaring it to be exactly what they wanted until there were no more.

The four of them sat for an hour more, enjoying the moment, talking about their gifts, and laughing about past Christmases. Each family member felt Tom's absence, but saying so would only dampen the joy. Later, Linda announced that they were invited to spend the afternoon at an extended Christmas celebration at Aryana's.

Christmas at the Samadanis'

Lexi was excited at the thought of more gift exchanging and food at the Samadanis'. She knew that Aryana and Rashne had their house festively decorated and that the table would be full of food and delicious desserts. Linda made her announcement with enough time for everyone to get dressed for the day. When they were dressed for a holiday celebration, they got in the car and headed to the village.

After they arrived, Lexi rushed in to give a big Christmas hug to Aryana and Rashne. As she turned the corner of the kitchen, Lexi saw that Aryana was in the threshold leading into the dining room, facing a group of people. Lexi stopped in her tracks thinking she was intruding on Aryana's party. She examined the group more closely, and her recognition kicked in.

Wait a minute, she thought. *What are Mr. and Mrs. Johnson doing here?*

Then Lexi said, "Oh my god! Jennifer, what are you doing here?"

She ran over and hugged Jennifer. She didn't even notice Shyanne standing on the other side with her parents. Lexi looked over Jennifer's shoulder and saw Shyanne. She shrieked in Jennifer's ear and hugged Shyanne.

"Oh my god! What are you doing here? I'm so happy to see you both."

Jennifer answered, "Well, my mom and dad loved it so much the last time they were here, they wanted to see it at Christmastime, and my dad is playing golf again. Shyanne's dad plays golf with my dad, so they decided to come too. We are staying at the Carolina Hotel."

"I'm so happy you are here! It's wonderful to see you again, Mr. and Mrs. Johnson. And welcome to Pinehurst, Mr. and Mrs. Williams. Merry Christmas!" Lexi said.

Jennifer said, "We thought that you might be coming to the Samadanis' sometime today, so we called her and wanted to surprise you."

"This is such a wonderful surprise. Thank you so much, Aryana," Lexi said.

After everyone greeted one another and took their coats off, Aryana invited them to come in the dining room and eat. Of course, she had laid out a wonderful table of holiday treats. Even though they were Muslim, Aryana and Rashne had been in the US for so long that they raised their family in both Muslim and Christian faiths, and they celebrated the Christmas holiday with a tree and all the traditions.

The buffet of food and treats could have been on the cover of a Christmas magazine. Everything looked so wonderful, and the aromas were enough to make your mouth water. Lexi took it all in, thinking that Christmas in the pines was enough to warm the coldest soul.

Everyone had eggnog or another festive drink in their hands when Aryana proposed a toast.

"Let's raise a glass to love of family, the bond that may stretch but never break."

Glassed were raised and clinked. Just then, Lexi heard a noise coming from upstairs.

"Ms. Aryana, did you get a dog for Christmas?" Lexi asked.

She caught Jennifer and Shyanne smiling.

"Did she get a dog?" Lexi asked again of her friends.

Both girls shrugged their shoulders. Aryana told Lexi that if she was so curious, she should go up and see. Lexi had it in her mind that she would find a beautiful puppy that Aryana had gotten for Christmas tucked away in a room upstairs. She smiled slyly as she, Jenna, and Shyanne snuck upstairs to peek in on the new furry baby.

She opened the bedroom door slowly. She saw the back of a woman standing in the room, and she apologized for the intrusion. The woman turned around.

"Amy? Oh my god, Amy!" Lexi shrieked once again. "You came down too?"

Lexi hugged Amy and told her how happy she was to see her again. Lexi didn't notice what Amy was doing.

Lexi asked gleefully, "Are we having another sleepover for Christmas break?"

Just then, Aryana arrived in the doorway of the bedroom, and the other adults filled in the hallway behind her.

She said, "You can have a sleepover if you like, but you should ask Amy first."

Lexi didn't understand. Aryana continued.

"After all, this is Amy's bedroom."

Lexi had a look of confusion.

Lexi asked, "What do you mean this is Amy's bedroom? Does Amy live here now?"

Aryana nodded. Lexi ran over to Amy and threw her arms around her. The other girls wrapped their arms around one another. All four girls cried.

Aryana explained that she and Rashne talked about it between themselves and talked it over with her own adult children and agreed that they had enough love in their hearts and enough resources to foster Amy if she wanted them too. They maintained contact with Amy after the homecoming visit and asked her if she would consider letting them be her permanent foster parents. Amy was very thankful for the family who fostered her in Virginia, but after talking it over with them, everyone agreed that the Samadanis would make a wonderful permanent home for Amy.

After hearing Amy's excitement, Rashne and Aryana contacted the Northern Virginia Child Protective Services and applied to be Amy's permanent foster parents. Rashne still had important contacts in Virginia, so they were able to fast-track the paperwork. Being Muslim did not hurt their application either.

Aryana said, "Amy will live with us. She will go to Union Pines High School, and if she wants to go to college, that will happen too. You always have an open invitation, Lexi, so you can come here as much as you want."

After hearing this, the girls all shrieked again. Everyone went downstairs, where they spent the rest of the afternoon and evening eating, laughing, crying tears of joy, and making memories.

Sometime during the night, Cynthia sat alone by the fireplace, enjoying a quiet moment and thinking about all the trials she and Lexi had been through the past year. She was grateful for her parents. Their love, patience, and wisdom got her and Lexi through hell and back. It was a debt that could never be repaid.

She was grateful for her doctors, who helped her get through depression, anguish, guilt, and sadness. She was grateful for friends who stood by Lexi without fail and gave her love and support when she felt unloved and alone. And she missed Tom. She had learned to forgive him for his mistake and forgive herself for her reaction to it. She never stopped loving him.

Lexi was making toasts to friendship with her girls when she saw her mother from across the room. She went over and sat next to her, resting her head on Cynthia's shoulder.

"Penny for your thoughts," Lexi asked.

"I'm wondering if you will be happy here, Boo Bear," Cynthia said.

"Yeah, I think we will be very happy here. There is something special about being among the pines. You'll see. Merry Christmas, Mom. I love you."

"Merry Christmas, honey. I love you too, more than you know."

Acknowledgments

There are very important people in my life without whom this book and my other books would not be possible.

The most important person is my best friend, my support system, my moral compass, my wife of forty years, Liz. She keeps me grounded and does all the things in the background that allow me to have time to write. She is a working RN and still finds time to make a wonderful home for us to live in, and she is my first editor in the process. My writing and I are better because of her.

My two daughters, Jessica Anderson Payne and Jackie Anderson, are my joys, my muses, and my inspiration. Jessica is a brilliant writer and editor who also reviews my work. In between her career and raising three wonderful children, my grandchildren, she edits my work and provides suggestions, which universally improves the clarity, continuity, flow, and realism of my stories. Through her edits too, I am becoming a better writer.

Jackie is a voracious reader and blogger who throws ideas and dialogue at me daily, challenging my knowledge of all manner of topics. We share the joy of tossing out iconic movie lines at random moments in conversation to get a rise out of people. She manages my newsletter and social media, as well as keeping me young at heart.

I owe a huge acknowledgment to my friend and mentor, Lt. Gen. Marvin Covault, retired US Army, and his lovely wife, Debi, for their friendship, editing, and inspiration. Marv and Debi are long-time horse owners. Marv reviewed *Sage among the Pines* for accuracy in equestrian terminology and horse behavior. They own a ten-acre horse farm with a two-story stable and a paddock behind their house.

Marv and Debi ride the trails of a four-thousand-acre equestrian-use-only foundation of pristine pine forest in Southern Pines and Vass, North Carolina. The foundation is available to all riders from the six hundred horse farms in the area connected by equestrian easements. Each year, Olympic-caliber equestrians from all over the world compete at the nearby world-class Five Points Center.

Marv Covault is also a sought-after speaker, op-ed columnist, blogger of *We the People Speaking Can Make a Difference* (Wethepeoplespeaking.com), and author of *Vision to Execution, a Book for Leaders* and *Fix the Systems, Transform America.* In my humble opinion, *Vision to Execution* should be a textbook in all leadership courses.

I want to thank and acknowledge dear friends Mariam and Mohammad Shahvari for thirty years of friendship and for being an inspiration for this book. You know who you are.

I owe thanks to my niece McKenzie Wilson, who is our family's technical support for computers, phones, and iPads but mostly for providing me with the fashion creativity for Lexi's dance outfit.

Cover Design

I wish to thank and recognize Donna Evans and Frank Riggs of Carriage Tours of Pinehurst Village Inc. for allowing their beautiful draft horse mare Shiloh to model for me in the field as I was generating book cover concepts.

The cover concept was created by John "Josh" McIntyre of Philadelphia, Pennsylvania, in collaboration with the author. Thank you, Josh, for your excellent support and hard work. You are a creative force.

About the Author

Mark R. Anderson, along with his wife and his youngest daughter, has been residing in Pinehurst, North Carolina, since 2017. He retired after thirty-five years of distinguished service in the Department of Defense and ten years, concurrently, as an officer in the United States Navy Reserve.

Mark is an alumnus of the University of Maryland and the National Intelligence University (formerly JMIC.) *Sage among the Pines* is his second novel, preceded by *Shadows of Saigon*. He is currently working on a third manuscript. Mark enjoys the challenge and art of conveying subtle yet complex emotions in his literary fiction, especially when he can present the emotions within the context of a historically significant event.

Mark grew up in a military family that relocated to different military bases every few years. He traveled extensively in the US and abroad during his childhood and his career. His lifetime of travel provides a vast and colorful palette of experiences to draw from when his creative spark ignites.

Mark is a member of Pinehurst Country Club, where he golfs several days per week and films his book videos. He also enjoys freshwater bass fishing in the Southeastern US.

Printed in the USA
CPSIA information can be obtained
at www.ICGtesting.com
LVHW042004260624
783940LV00001B/98